the sugar queen

Also by Sarah Addison Allen

Garden Spells

SARAH ADDISON ALLEN

HODDER &
STOUGHTON

First published in Great Britain in 2008 by Hodder & Stoughton
An Hachette Livre UK company
First published in America in 2008 by Bantam,
An imprint of Random House Inc.

1

A CIP catalogue record for this title is
available from the British Library

Trade paperback ISBN 978 0 340 93575 0

Printed and bound by Clays Ltd, St Ives plc

Hodder & Stoughton policy is to use papers that are natural,
renewable and recyclable products and made from wood
grown in sustainable forests. The logging and manufacturing
processes are expected to conform to the environmental
regulations of the country of origin.

Hodder & Stoughton Ltd
338 Euston Road
London NW1 3BH
www.hodder.co.uk

For my dad, with all my love

Acknowledgments

Thanks to my mom for all the sweet tastes of my childhood. Andrea Cirillo, Kelly Harms and everyone at JRA, you're as comforting and refreshing as lemon cookies with frosting. Shauna Summers, Nita Taublib and everyone at Bantam, you're better than hot chocolate with marshmallows. Carolyn Mays and everyone at Hodder, you were the wonderful Tootsie Pop surprise. Daphne Akteson, I owe you more sugar than the world can hold for your time and input just when I needed it. Hershey's Kisses for the loopy Duetters, a chocolate martini for Michelle Pittman and a Sky Bar for Heidi Hensley . . . your enduring friendship sustains me.

1

Everlasting Gobstoppers

When Josey woke up and saw the feathery frost on her windowpane, she smiled. Finally, it was cold enough to wear long coats and tights. It was cold enough for scarves and shirts worn in layers, like camouflage. It was cold enough for her lucky red cardigan, which she swore had a power of its own. She loved this time of year. Summer was tedious with the light dresses she pretended to be comfortable in while secretly sure she looked like a loaf of white bread wearing a belt. The cold was such a *relief*.

She went to the window. A fine sheen of sugary frost covered everything in sight, and white smoke rose from chimneys in the valley below the resort town. Excited, she opened the window, but the sash stuck midway and she had to pound it the rest of the way with the palm of her hand. It finally opened to a rush of sharp early November air that would have the town in a flurry of activity, anticipating the tourists the colder weather always brought to the high mountains of North Carolina.

She stuck her head out and took a deep breath. If she could eat the cold air, she would. She thought cold snaps were like cookies, like gingersnaps. In her mind they were made with white chocolate chunks and had a cool, brittle vanilla frosting. They melted like snow in her mouth, turning creamy and warm.

Just before she ducked her head back inside, she looked down and noticed something strange.

There was a ladder propped against the house, directly underneath her window.

She leaned back in quickly and closed her window. She paused, then she locked it.

She turned and walked to her closet, distracted now. She hadn't heard anything strange last night. The tree trimmers from yesterday must have left the ladder. Yes. That had to be it. They'd probably propped it against the house and then completely forgotten about it.

She opened her closet door and reached up to pull the string that turned on the light.

Then she screamed and backed away, stopping only when she hit her desk and her lamp crashed to the floor.

"Oh for God's sake," the woman sitting on the floor of her closet said, "don't have a cow."

"Josey?" She heard her mother's voice in the hall, then the thud of her cane as she came closer.

"Please don't tell her I'm here," the woman in the closet said, with a strange sort of desperation. Despite the cold outside, she was wearing a cropped white shirt and tight dark blue jeans that sat low, revealing a tattoo of a broken heart on her hip. Her hair was bleached white-blond with about an inch of silver-sprinkled dark roots showing. Her mascara had run and there were black streaks on her cheeks. She looked drip-dried, like she'd been walking in the rain, though there hadn't been rain for days. She smelled like cigarette smoke and river water.

Josey turned her head as her bedroom door began to open. Then, in a small act that changed everything, Josey reached over and pushed the closet door closed as her mother entered the room.

"Josey? What was that noise? Are you all right?" Margaret asked. She'd been a beautiful woman in her day, delicate and trim, blue-eyed and fair-haired. There was a certain power beautiful mothers held over their less beautiful daughters. Even at seventy-four, with a limp from a hip replacement, Margaret could still enter a room and fill it like perfume. Josey could never do that. The closest she ever came was the attention she used to receive when she pitched legendary fits in public when she was young. But that was making people look at her for all the wrong reasons.

"My lamp," Josey said. "It attacked me out of nowhere."

"Oh, well," Margaret said distantly, "leave it for the maid to clean. Hurry up and get dressed. My doctor's appointment is at nine."

"Yes, Mother."

Margaret closed the bedroom door. Josey waited until

the clump of her cane faded away before she rushed to the closet door and opened it again.

Most locals knew who Della Lee was. She waitressed at a greasy spoon called Eat and Run, which was tucked far enough outside the town limits that the ski-crowd tourists didn't see it. She haunted bars at night. She was probably in her late thirties, maybe ten years older than Josey, and she was rough and flashy and did whatever she wanted—no reasonable explanation required.

"Della Lee Baker, what are you doing in my closet?"

"You shouldn't leave your window unlocked. Who knows who could get in?" Della Lee said, single-handedly debunking the long-held belief that if you dotted your windowsills and door thresholds with peppermint oil, no unwanted visitors would ever appear. For years Josey's mother had instructed every maid in their employ to anoint the house's casings with peppermint to keep the undesirables away. Their house now smelled like the winter holidays all year round.

Josey took a step back and pointed. "Get out."

"I can't."

"You most certainly can."

"I need a place to hide."

"I see. And of course this was the first place you thought of."

"Who would look for me here?"

Rough women had rough ways. Was Della Lee trying to tell her that she was in danger? "Okay, I'll bite. Who's looking for you, Della Lee?"

"Maybe no one. Maybe they haven't discovered I'm missing yet." Then, to Josey's surprise, Della Lee reached over to the false wall at the back of the narrow closet and slid it open. "And speaking of discoveries, look what I found."

Revealed now was the large secret space behind the closet. There were stacks of paperback romances, magazines and catalogs on the floor, but most of the secret closet was occupied by shelves piled with food—packaged snacks, rows of sweets, towers of colas.

Josey's entire body suddenly burned with panic. She was supposed to be happy. And most of the time she supposed she was, in an awkward, sleepy kind of way. She'd never be the beauty her mother was, or have the personality of her late father. She was pale and plain and just this side of plump, and she accepted that. But food was a comfort. It filled in the hollow spaces. And it felt good to hide it, because then she could enjoy it alone without worrying about what others thought, or about letting her mother down.

"I need to figure some things out first," Della Lee said, sliding the door back in place, her point made. She was letting Josey know that she knew her secret. *Don't reveal mine and I won't reveal yours.* "Then I'll be moving up north."

"You can't stay here. I'll give you some money. You can stay in a motel." Josey started to turn, to get her wallet, to get Della Lee away from her food. But then she stopped. "Wait. You're leaving Bald Slope?"

"Like you don't dream of leaving this stupid town," Della Lee said, leaning back on her hands.

"Don't be ridiculous. I'm a Cirrini."

"Correct me if I'm wrong, but aren't those travel magazines in your secret closet?"

Josey bristled. She pointed again. "Get *out*."

"It looks like I got here just in time. This is not the closet of a happy woman, Josey."

"At least I'm not hiding in it."

"I bet you do sometimes."

"Get out."

"No."

"That's it. I'm calling the police."

Della Lee laughed. She actually sat there and laughed at Josey. Her front teeth were a little crooked, but it looked good on her, offbeat and sassy. She was the kind of woman who could get away with anything because she had no boundaries. "And what will you say? There's a woman in your closet, come get her out? They might find your stash."

Josey thought about calling Della Lee's bluff. It would serve her right. It might even be worth everyone knowing about the food in her closet. But then her heart began to beat harder. Who was she kidding? It was embarrassing enough being such a sorry excuse for a Southern belle. Her weight, her unfortunate hair, her secret dreams of leaving her mother who needed her, of leaving and never looking back. Respectable daughters took care of their mothers. Respectable daughters did *not* hide enormous amounts of candy in their closets.

"So you stay, you don't tell anyone, is that it?"

"Sure," Della Lee said easily.

"That's blackmail."

"Add it to my list of sins."

"I don't think there's room left on that list," Josey said as she took a dress from its hanger. Then she closed the closet door on Della Lee.

She went to the bathroom down the hall to dress and to pull her very curly, licorice-black hair back into a low ponytail. When she walked back to her bedroom, she stared at her closet door for a moment. It looked completely innocuous. The door and its casing were painted an antique white set against the pale blue of the room. The corner blocks at the top of the casing were hand-carved in a circular bull's-eye pattern. The doorknob was white porcelain, shaped like a mushroom cap.

She took a deep breath and walked to it. Maybe she'd imagined the whole thing.

She opened the door.

"You should wear makeup," Della Lee said.

Josey reached up and grabbed her lucky red cardigan off the high shelf, then closed the door. She put the sweater on and closed her eyes. *Go away, go away, go away.*

She opened the door again.

"No, really. Mascara. Lip gloss. Something."

Josey sighed. The sweater was probably just rusty. It had been sitting there all summer, after all. Della Lee wouldn't be there when she got home. Good things happened when she wore this sweater. She'd had the best haircut she'd ever had while wearing it. When she'd slept in it once, it snowed for three days straight.

And she'd been wearing it the day she first met Adam.

She closed the door, paused with her hand on the knob, then opened it one last time.

"Eyeliner?" Della Lee said.

Josey turned and walked away.

The Cirrinis' new maid spoke very little English.

She was hired earlier in the year to help Margaret bathe after her hip replacement. But Helena could never quite grasp what was required of her. She would sit on the lowered toilet lid, her eyes averted, anxiously wringing her hands while Margaret sat in the tub and played charades to get her to understand *soap*. So Josey ended up doing it.

She was hired to do the grocery shopping. But the first day she was sent off to the market with a grocery list, she spent two hours crying on the front porch, her tears falling into the flower pots where mysterious South American tropical flowers later sprouted without explanation. So Josey ended up doing that too.

Basically, Helena's duties now were light housekeeping, preparing meals and learning English by gossiping with Margaret. Her bedroom was on the first floor, and she anxiously popped her head out of her door every time Josey happened to venture downstairs after bedtime.

When Josey and Margaret arrived home from Margaret's doctor's appointment, Josey heard the vacuum cleaner humming upstairs. That was a good sign. If Helena was still doing housework, that meant she hadn't found Della Lee in the closet.

Josey helped her mother into her favorite chair in the sitting room, then she went upstairs, where Helena was vacuuming the runner in the hallway.

Josey approached Helena and tapped her on the shoulder to get her attention. She got her attention, all right. Helena screamed and ran down the hall without even turning around to see who it was. The vacuum cleaner, still on, fell to the floor and started eating the fringe of the runner.

"Helena, wait!" Josey called, running after her. She caught up with her before she reached the corner at the end of the hall that led to the narrow kitchen staircase. "It's okay! It's just me!"

Helena stopped and turned. "Oldsey?" she said dubiously, like she'd expected someone else.

"Yes. It's me. I didn't mean to scare you. Are you okay?"

Helena put her hand to her heart, breathing heavily. She

nodded and hurried back to the vacuum cleaner. She unplugged it, then knelt to pull the runner's fringe from where it had wrapped around the vacuum's beater bar.

Josey followed, saying, "Helena, did you, um, clean up the broken lamp in my bedroom?"

"I clean." She stood and crossed herself, then she kissed the crucifix on her necklace. "Oldsey's room strange today."

"Strange? Did you see anything . . . unusual?"

"See, no. *Feel*. Cold in Oldsey's room," she said.

Josey sighed in relief. "Oh, I opened my window earlier, that's all." She smiled. "Don't worry about vacuuming up here. Mother is downstairs in the sitting room."

"Oldgret downstairs?"

"Yes. Margaret is downstairs."

That would keep them both occupied and away from Josey's room for a while. Margaret liked to watch Helena clean. And Helena, as far as she was able, liked to spread the latest gossip from the east side of town, which included the Catholic community center, a place Margaret found simply fascinating in a what-can-the-Baptists-do-that's-better kind of way.

As Helena started wrapping the cord around the vacuum, Josey went to her bedroom. For breakfast she'd eaten what her mother always wanted, a modest bowl of rolled oats and blackberries. Her stomach growled as she stared at her closet. Her food was there. All her lovely food.

The secret closet was the closet in the adjoining room. That bedroom had a huge armoire in it, a ridiculously heavy old Cirrini heirloom. It took up most of one wall and hid that closet. She'd found the door between the two closets by accident, when she would sit in her closet and eat candy she hid in her pockets when she was young. Back then she used to hide from her mother in the secret space just to worry her, but now she stocked it with magazines, paperback romances and sweets. Lots and lots of sweets. Moonpies and pecan rolls, Chick-O-Sticks and Cow Tales, Caramel Creams and Squirrel Nut Zippers, Red Hots and Bit-O-Honey, boxes upon boxes of Little Debbie snack cakes. The space had a comforting smell to it, like Halloween, like sugar and chocolate and crisp plastic wrappers.

Josey took off her coat and put it and her purse on the chaise, then went to the closet. She pulled her lucky cardigan tightly around her, made a wish, then opened the door.

"Did I just hear your maid call you and your mother Oldsey and Oldgret?" Della Lee asked, laughing.

Of course Della Lee found that funny. Some people liked to call Josey and her mother the Cirrini Sisters. Margaret had Josey late in life. Josey was only twenty-seven, so they were essentially calling her an old woman, but they were comparing her to Margaret, who was once the belle of Bald Slope, the woman married to the late, great Marco Cirrini. There were worse things to be called. Margaret didn't like the nickname and discouraged it whenever possible. Margaret was small, fair and ethereal. Josey looked like a thick dark blob next to her. *Sisters?* Margaret would say. *We look nothing alike.*

Josey's shoulders dropped. "It's a wonder she didn't see you. You're going to get caught."

"It's just for a little while."

"Define 'a little while.'"

"However long it takes, I guess. Days? Weeks?"

"I hear the closets at the Holiday Inn are fabulous. You should try them."

"Ah, but they don't come with a built-in snack machine like this one," Della Lee said, and Josey had to accept that Della Lee, cocky, mascara-stained and stubborn, was going to stay in her closet until *she* decided to leave. "You're not going to argue?" Della Lee asked.

"Would it do any good?"

"It might make you feel better."

"There's only one thing that makes me feel better. Excuse me," Josey said as she leaned in and slid back the false wall.

Della Lee scooted quickly to a corner, more dramatically than Josey thought was necessary, as if afraid Josey might decide to touch her. Josey grabbed a red tin of Moravian cookies and a packet of Mallo Cups, then she went to her desk and sat. She opened the tin of cookies and started eating slowly, savoring each thin spice-and-molasses bite.

Della Lee watched her for a while, then she turned and sprawled out on the floor of the closet, staring up at Josey's clothes. She lifted one jeans-clad leg in the air to brush the clothes, and for the first time Josey noticed that Della Lee was wearing only one shoe. "So this is the life of Josey Cirrini," Della Lee finally said.

Josey focused on her cookie. "If you don't like it, you can leave."

"Is this really what you do all day? Don't you have friends?" Della Lee asked, shaking her head. "I didn't know your life was like this. I used to envy you when you were a kid. I thought you had everything."

Josey didn't know what to say to that. She couldn't imagine someone as beautiful as Della Lee envying her. Josey didn't have everything. She had only money. And she would give that away, that and everything else she had, every grain of sugar, for the one thing she wanted most in the world but would never have.

Suddenly her head tilted to one side.

Like magic, she felt him getting nearer, felt it like a pull in the pit of her stomach. It felt like hunger but deeper, heavier. Like the best kind of expectation. Ice cream expectation. Chocolate expectation. Soft nougat pulling from a candy bar.

So the red sweater *did* still have some luck left in it.

"What's the matter?" Della Lee asked as Josey pushed back her chair and went to her window.

He was coming up the sidewalk. He was early today.

The Cirrini house was located in one of the oldest neighborhoods in town. When Marco Cirrini made his fortune with the Bald Slope Ski Resort, he bought a house in the neighborhood he'd always dreamed about living in, then promptly tore the house down. He built a large bright blue Victorian lady in its place. He said he wanted a house that would stand out even among the standouts. He wanted everyone who passed by the house to say, "Marco Cirrini lives there." All the houses in the neighborhood were recessed except the Cirrini house, which was front and center, the eager look-at-me house built by the son of poor Italian immigrants.

Adam would be at the door in no time.

Josey hurried out of the room.

Helena and Margaret were talking in the sitting room when Josey came down the stairs, slowing her pace to a walk. "The mail is here," she called to them.

Margaret and Helena didn't stop their conversation, which sounded something like this:

"Naomi O'Toole?"

"Yes, Oldgret."

"*She* was there?"

"Yes, Oldgret."

Josey opened the front door with its crazy colorful stained-glass panels, then she pushed open the screen, her eyes on the front porch steps, not wanting to miss a moment of him. The screen door abruptly stuck, hitting something soft. She realized, to her horror, she'd hit Adam Boswell with the door as he was putting the mail in the black-flapped mailbox hanging to the right.

"Whoa," Adam said, smiling, "what's your hurry, Josey?"

He was dressed in his cooler-weather uniform, the pants covering the scars on his right leg, the leg he favored. He was a good-looking, athletic man. His round face was always tan, golden, in fact, like something warm and bright was glowing inside of him. He had curly dark-blond hair he sometimes pushed back with a bandana tied around his head. He was in his thirties, and he had a secret. She didn't know what it was, but she could tell.

Adam wasn't from here, Josey knew that much. Three years ago he'd shown up on her doorstep, mail in hand, and her dreams had never been the same. Adventurous types flocked to Bald Slope and its famous steep ski runs. She'd always wondered if the slopes had brought him here, and if that was the reason he stayed. Though her mother sold the resort shortly after Marco died, it made Josey feel happy to think that she had something, however tenuous, to do with Adam being here.

He popped one of the ear buds from his iPod out of his ear when she just stood there and stared at him. "Josey, are you okay?"

She immediately felt herself blush. He was the only person in the world she was tongue-tied around, and yet the only person she really wanted to talk to. "I'm sorry," she said. "I didn't know you were already here. You're early today."

"The mail was light. This is all I have for you," he said, handing her the catalog he'd been about to put in the mailbox before she pummeled him with the screen door.

"Thank you."

He looked at her for a moment. "You have something"—he pointed to her lips, then touched the corner of his own mouth—"right here."

She immediately put her fingertips to her lips and felt the cookie crumbs there. She brushed them away, embarrassed. Oh yes, she was witty *and* clean.

"Beautiful day, isn't it?" he said, taking a deep breath. The cool noon air was flavored with the mulchy scent of fallen leaves and the last of the hardiest flowers curling away for the winter. "I love fall."

Josey's fingers froze on her lips, completely enchanted by him. "Me *too*."

"It makes you want to do something, doesn't it?" he said, grinning. "Like get out and . . . play in trees."

That made Josey laugh. Adam watched her as she laughed, and she didn't know why. It was like she'd surprised him.

Adam finally said, "Well, I'll see you later."

"Right," she said. "Bye, Adam."

She held her breath, her own superstition, until he walked down the steps and crossed the street. As soon as he reached the other side, disappearing from her world, she went back in the house.

She walked into the sitting room, where Helena had set up the ironing board to press some of Margaret's dresses.

"Only a catalog in the mail today," Josey said. "I'm going to take it to my room, okay?"

"Wait," Margaret said, squinty-eyed as she looked Josey over. "Were you wearing that sweater at the doctor's office?"

Oh no. She meant to take it off when she came in. "Yes," she said, then added quickly, "but I had my coat on over it."

"Josey, I asked you to get rid of that sweater last year. It's been washed so many times that it's far too small for you."

Josey tried to smile. "But I like it."

"I'm just saying you need to find something that fits. I know you love your catalogs. Find something in a larger size. And red isn't a good color on you. I could wear red when I was your age. But that's because I was blond. Try white. Or black."

"Yes, Mother."

Josey turned and walked back out of the sitting room. She went up the stairs to her room, where she sat at her desk and stared at the wall. She tugged on the sweater self-consciously.

"So who is he?" Della Lee asked from the closet.

"Excuse me?"

"The man you ran out of here to see."

Josey immediately sat up straighter. She put the catalog on the desk and opened it, startled. *How on earth did she know that?* "I don't know what you mean."

Della Lee was silent for a while as Josey ate cookies and pretended to look at the catalog. "It feels like he's taken your heart, doesn't it?" Della Lee finally said. "Like he's reached in and pulled it from you. And I bet he smiles like he doesn't know, like he doesn't know he's holding your heart in his hand and you're *dying* from him."

It was the truest, purest, saddest thing she had ever heard spoken. It was like hearing gospel for the first time, how it shocked you, how it made you afraid because you thought no one could see inside you. Josey leerily turned to look at Della Lee.

"You're wondering how I know. Girls like us, when we love, it takes everything we have. Who is he?"

"Like I would tell you."

Della Lee leaned forward. "I *swear* I won't tell anyone," she said seductively.

"Yes, and we both know how honest you are."

"Fine. Tell me when you're ready. I can help you, you know. Yes, that's what I'm going to do. I'm going to help you." Della Lee leaned back. Josey caught a whiff of tobacco and mud.

"You're in no shape to help anyone. What happened to you, Della Lee? You still look like you're wet."

Della Lee looked down at her clothes, then she touched her hair, which was heavy and flat. "Oh, I forgot," she said. "I took a little dip in the river."

"You swam in the river at this time of year?" Josey asked incredulously.

"Seemed like a good idea at the time. The last stupid thing I did before I went up north." Della Lee shrugged. "Like redemption, you know?"

"Redemption for what?"

"More than you could ever imagine. Listen, I want you to go to a sandwich shop on the first-floor rotunda of the courthouse. It's across from the elevators. A woman named Chloe Finley owns the place, and you'll love her. She makes a grilled tomato and three-cheese sandwich that will make your head spin it's so good. Get me one, will you?"

Josey, stuck on the image of Della Lee in the cold Green Cove River, dunking herself in her own version of a baptism, was caught off guard by the sudden change of subject. "You want me to get you a sandwich right now?"

"Why not?"

"Because I have to eat lunch with my mother at twelve-thirty. Then I have to sit with her when our financial advisor comes by this afternoon. Then I have to get her into the bathtub this evening, then get her settled in bed."

Unfazed, Della Lee said, "Tomorrow, then."

"I take my mother for her manicure and pedicure tomorrow."

"Thursday?"

"I have to take my mother to her ladies' club meeting Thursday."

"No wonder you have so many travel magazines. If you ever manage to get off this gerbil wheel, I bet you'll take off."

"*I will not,*" Josey said, indignant, because respectable daughters stayed. Never mind that she dreamed of leaving every single day. "What if I like living like this? Did you ever think of that?"

Della Lee snorted.

Josey put the lid back on the cookie tin and stood. She took it and the uneaten packet of Mallo Cups back to the closet. "You can eat anything you want back here. I'm not getting you a sandwich."

"No, thanks. I'll wait."

"You're going to be waiting a long time."

She laughed. "Honey, I've got nothing but time."

2

SweeTarts

For nearly a century, the town of Bald Slope barely sustained itself as a High Country summer getaway for the hot, wilted wealthy from North Carolina's Piedmont. The town slept like a winter beast during the cold months, summer houses and most downtown shops boarded up. Locals got by on vegetables they'd canned and money they'd made in the summer. By the time the last snow melted, they were weak and hungry and couldn't wait for the summer residents to return.

Marco Cirrini had been skiing on the north face of Bald Slope Mountain since he was a boy, using the old skis his father brought with him from Italy. The Cirrinis had shown up out of nowhere, walking into town in the middle of winter, their hair shining like black coal in the snow. They never really fit in. Marco tried, though. He tried by leading groups of local boys up the mountain in the winter, showing them how to make their own skis and how to use them. He charged them pennies and jars of bean chutney and spiced red cabbage they would sneak out of their mothers' sparse pantries. When he was nineteen, he decided he could take this one step further. He could make great things happen in the winter in Bald Slope. Cocky, not afraid of hard work and handsome in that mysterious Mediterranean way that excluded him from mountain society, he gathered investors from as far away as Asheville and Charlotte to buy the land. He started construction on the lodge himself while the residents of the town scoffed. They were the sweet cream and potatoes and long-forgotten ballads of their English and Irish and Scottish ancestors, who settled the southern Appalachians. To their way of thinking, the way it had been was the way it should always be. They didn't want change. It took fifteen years, but the Bald Slope Ski Resort was finally completed and, much to everyone's surprise, it was an immediate success.

Change was good!

Stores didn't shut down for the winter anymore. Bed-and-breakfasts and sports shops and restaurants sprouted up. Instead of closing up their houses for the winter, summer residents began to rent them out to skiers. Some summer residents even decided to move to Bald Slope permanently, moving into their vacation homes with their sleeping porches and shade trees, thus forming the high society in Bald Slope that existed today. Marco himself was welcomed into this year-round society. He was essentially responsible for its formation in the first place, after all. Finally it didn't matter where he came from. What mattered was that he'd saved Bald Slope by giving it a winter economy, and he could do no wrong.

This town was finally his.

Josey stopped in front of a small yellow bungalow and compared the number on the mailbox to the address she'd copied out of the phone book that morning. This was it. She leaned into the steering wheel and peered out the windshield. The paint looked fresh, and the windows were clean. But Della Lee obviously hadn't tended to her small yard since summer. Garden gnomes and plastic flowers still lined the walkway to the porch, and there was a long plastic chair for sunbathing still in the yard, now covered with small red-black leaves that had fallen from the dogwood by the house.

She put the large gold Cadillac—her mother's idea—in park and cut the engine.

This blue-collar neighborhood was one Josey was faintly familiar with because her father would pass through it on their Sunday drives when Josey was a child. Josey lived for those drives. It was the only time in her entire childhood she ever felt calm. The rest of the time, she was locked in a constant power struggle with her mother, a struggle Josey couldn't even explain today. She had no idea why she'd been so mean as a child. She had no idea why she'd pitched such fits. Her mother certainly deserved better. But during those drives, Josey would relax while Marco talked. He knew everything about Bald Slope. He knew every neighborhood by heart. He was in his late sixties when Josey was born, and by that time he was an established figure in town, rich, silver-haired and swaggering. His father was a chimney sweep, and Marco dropped out of school in sixth grade to work with him. He used to tell Josey that he'd stand on rooftops when he was a boy and look at the houses and dream of owning the tallest house in the best neighborhood, where no one could look down on his roof, let alone look down on him.

Marco died when Josey was nine, and it felt like someone waking her up with a hard pinch. All she had left was her mother, and she'd been so terrible to her. That's when she decided, even if it took forever, she was going to make up to her mother every horrible thing she'd done. The day her father died was the first day Josey bit her tongue, the first day she took criticism and didn't fight back, and the day she began to realize how hard it was going to be to change the way people saw her as a child. Almost twenty years later, she was still trying.

Taking a deep breath, Josey got out of the car.

She'd caught a lucky break that day after taking her mother to the salon. Josey usually sat and waited for her, chatting with the older ladies, making sympathetic noises when they told her all about their sciatica and arthritis. But her mother reminded her that she had to pick up the peppermint oil Margaret had specially made by Nova Berry, the strange woman whose family ran the organic market. They were running low. And obviously not enough was being sprinkled on the thresholds of their house. That would certainly explain how Della Lee had managed to get in.

Josey went to pick up the oil, but Nova didn't have it ready yet. She said to come back in a few days, then she told

Josey once again that red was a magic color for her, which Josey always liked to hear even though Nova probably only said it to get her to buy one of her red crocheted scarves or hats. After leaving the market, Josey only meant to drive by Della Lee's house. She didn't have time for this. Still . . . Della Lee had been in Josey's closet for two days now, and Josey was still no closer to figuring out why she was there, or how exactly to get her out without revealing Josey's secret stash to the world. Maybe Della Lee's house would give Josey something to bargain with. Maybe there was something in there Della Lee was hiding.

Nothing like a little breaking and entering to liven up a day.

The dogwood leaves crunched underfoot as Josey picked her way across the yard, trying not to look like she was sneaking around. When she reached the porch, she was surprised to find the door open, even on this cool day. Did Della Lee have roommates?

She raised her hand to knock, then hesitated. Holding her fist in the air with indecision, she finally knocked once on the screen door.

No answer.

"Hello?" she called. Even from outside, she could smell the tight, hot, closed-in scent of the interior, like old linens left in a dryer for too long. The furnace was running on high.

Still no answer. It occurred to her that Della Lee might have left in a hurry, that she might have left the door open. Curiouser and curiouser.

She looked over her shoulder to see if anyone might be watching her, then she opened the screen door and entered.

The place was a mess. There were beer cans everywhere. There was a broken coffee mug on the floor and a stain of coffee on the far wall, as if the mug had been thrown. A chair was overturned.

She had taken only a few steps in, kicking a beer can and what looked to be the ripped-off sleeve of a woman's denim shirt, when she stopped short, her scalp tightening and her heart jumping against her rib cage like a startled cat.

There was a man sleeping on the couch.

She stood there for a few moments, paralyzed, afraid that she might have made enough noise to wake him.

He was, very clearly, not the kind of man you wanted to wake.

He didn't have a shirt on and his jeans were unzipped, one hand tucked halfway inside his fly. He had a smug smile on his lips like he knew, even in his sleep, that women all around him were dying from love because he'd taken their hearts and hidden them where they'd never find them.

His muscles indicated he spent a lot of time in a gym. His cheekbones were high and his hair was long and straight and dark. He smelled of alcohol and of something else, like if you took a match to a rosebush. It smelled good, but dark and smoky, and it made Josey feel heady, like she was losing herself in it somehow.

All at once she understood.

This was the reason Della Lee left.

She'd come here to get something on Della Lee, and look what she found. She took a step back, profoundly ashamed of herself. She should just get out of there. Pretend she didn't know.

But then something on an elemental level stopped her. She felt a connection to Della Lee at that moment, one she couldn't explain. She *felt* her here, felt her genuine, profound unhappiness, like it was her own. It felt so familiar, that belief that nothing was ever going to change so why try anymore.

Okay, so maybe letting Della Lee know that she knew might help. It might keep Della Lee from coming back to this . . . this *violence*.

She turned her head slightly, and she could see down a short hallway.

She took a few more slow steps backward, keeping her eyes on the man's face, watching for movement. She then turned and walked on the balls of her feet down the hallway, bypassing small piles of his dirty clothes. There were crooked photos on the wall of Della Lee as a child, with dark hair and eyes. Josey wondered when she started dyeing her hair blond. In one photo she was standing on top of a jungle gym. In another she was diving into the public pool from the high dive. She looked like she was daring the world to hurt her.

Della Lee's bedroom at the end of the hall looked like something out of Josey's teenage dreams. Back then Josey had politely asked her mother if she could hang a poster or two, if she could have some colorful curtains or a bedspread with hearts on it. Her mother had responded with disappointment. Why would Josey ask for something else, as if what she had wasn't good enough? The heavy oak bed, the antique desk and the sueded chaise in Josey's room were all Very Nice Things. Josey obviously did not appreciate Very Nice Things.

The walls in Della Lee's room were painted purple and there were sheer lavender curtains on the single window. A poster of a white Himalayan cat was taped on one wall, along with some pages torn out of fashion magazines. There was a white mirrored dresser that had makeup tubes and bottles littered across the surface. Some tote bags with names of cosmetic companies, like department store gifts with purchase, were stashed in the corner near the dresser.

Josey grabbed a few bags and slowly slid open the drawers until she found socks and panties and bras. She stuffed one bag full, then she put the makeup in another bag.

Her heart beating thickly, she went to the closet and took clothes off the hangers as quietly as possible. She knelt to get a few pairs of shoes. There were two very different sets of shoes: grease- and food-stained sneakers that she obviously wore to work, and leather boots and strappy heels she probably wore out at night. Josey took two from each category. She was just about to stand when she noticed the cardboard box in the corner of the closet. It had sweaters stacked on top of it and PRIVATE written on the side in green marker.

She crawled to the box and slid the sweaters off. Inside the box were dozens of old spiral notebooks, bundles of letters and photographs. And a couple of old pieces of jewelry, sentimental but not expensive, were wrapped in yellowy tissue paper. There was a yearbook from Bald Slope High with Della Lee's name embossed on it. Her birth certificate was folded inside.

She suddenly heard some movement coming from the living room. She turned her head, brushing a coat that was hanging above her. One shoulder of the coat slipped off the hanger and it swayed precariously, a breath away from falling off altogether. She heard the man sigh and then the squeak of the springs on the old couch.

He was coming down the hall.

Her body felt tight, and her ears actually felt like they turned as she strained to hear what he was doing. It took a moment to realize that he was using the bathroom, which shared a wall with the closet.

The wire hanger was still swinging above her, squeaking slightly. If the coat slipped off, the hanger would hit the wall and he would hear. She watched it desperately, saying all sorts of prayers.

The commode flushed and he shuffled out into the hall. His steps were slow, sleepy.

The squeak of the couch springs again.

Silence.

Josey waited until her muscles were quivering with tension from keeping the same awkward position for so long, then she scooted out of the closet with the box. She stood stiffly and grabbed the tote bags. She went to the bedroom doorway and peered out before slowly walking down the hallway. She stopped just before the turn into the living room.

She could hear him breathing.

But was his breath shallow enough to indicate he was asleep again?

She screwed up her courage and took that final step into the living room.

Then she almost dropped everything she was carrying.

He was sitting up on the couch.

But then she saw that his head was resting back against the cushions. He'd fallen asleep sitting up. There was a cigarette almost burned down to the filter in an ashtray on the coffee table in front of him. Next to the ashtray there was a scuffed leather pocketbook with a shiny purple wallet sticking out of it with the initial *D* on it in white.

Della Lee would need her ID.

Josey was trembling as she took those few steps to the pocketbook. She had to lean down, box and tote bags and all, to get the wallet and slide it out.

Josey then backed quietly to the door, pushing open the screen with her butt, her eyes not leaving him until the last possible moment when she had to turn.

She tried to catch the screen door with her elbow so it wouldn't slap shut, but she was too late. It hit the casing with a bang.

She took off down the steps. It had been so hot inside the house that running in the chilly air outside felt like falling into water. The damp hair at the base of her neck instantly turned cold and gave her goosebumps. She stopped on the sidewalk and dropped Della Lee's things by the car. She fished her keys out of her coat pocket and electronically opened the trunk with the device on her key chain, at exactly the same time the screen door to the bungalow slapped shut again and the beautiful long-haired man walked out onto the porch.

"Hello? What are you doing?" the man called out to her. His voice was melodic, and the air carried it to her like a present. She actually stopped for a moment and turned to him. Seduction was his sixth sense, and he knew he'd caught her.

"You," the man said, smiling with an edge as he walked down the steps toward her. With a beautiful swing of his head, he tossed his long dark hair over his shoulder. "Were you just in my house?"

She heard the caw of a crow nearby, a portent of danger, and she gave a start. Snapping out of his spell, she quickly threw the things into the trunk, then slammed the lid closed.

Josey hurried to the driver's side and got in. As she drove away in the largest, goldest Cadillac in the entire Southeast, the man stood on the sidewalk and watched.

He was still there, his stare as dark as a gypsy curse, as she made the turn at the stop sign and sped off.

After getting her mother settled in bed that night, the lotion that smelled like lemon tarts rubbed on her small, pretty feet, her sleeping pill and water beside her on the nightstand, Josey crept down the stairs and outside to the car. She was barefooted and her toes curled against the frosty pavement of the driveway, but it was quieter this way.

Regardless, Helena stuck her head out of her bedroom doorway when Josey came back in with Della Lee's things.

"It's okay, Helena. Go back to bed."

She ducked her head back in.

Josey took the things up to her room, then she opened her closet door and set the box and bags in front of Della Lee.

"What is this?" Della Lee asked, surprised. She set aside one of Josey's well-thumbed travel magazines. She had washed her face since Josey had last seen her earlier that day, so the mascara streaks were gone. How she'd managed to do that without anyone noticing was a mystery. There weren't any washcloths smeared with makeup left behind, no sounds of water running hollowly through the pipes from upstairs while Josey and her mother and Helena sat in the sitting room downstairs and watched television.

Josey smiled. She'd barely been able to contain herself all day, waiting for her mother to finally go to bed. "A surprise! I went to your house today."

"You did *what*?"

Josey went to her knees and opened one of the bags. "Look. I picked up some of your things. Here are some clothes and makeup and here's your wallet. And this box. It looked like the kind of thing you wouldn't want to leave behind."

Della Lee was shaking her head, slowly at first, then

more and more quickly. "I wanted you to get me a sandwich, not go to my house!"

"I did this so you wouldn't have to go back. Say thank you, you closet thief."

"Of course I'm not going back there!" she said. She scooted away from the things, farther into the shadows of the closet. "Josey, get rid of this stuff. Now! People can't know you have this."

"Shh! My mother will hear you," Josey said. "And I don't have it. It's yours. No one knows."

Della Lee's eyes went from Josey, to the box and bags, then back to Josey. "Was Julian still there?"

"The man with long hair? He was asleep on the couch with his hand halfway down his pants. Does he sleep like that all the time? If he had a nightmare, I bet he could really hurt himself."

"But you saw him," Della Lee said, seeing past Josey's too-casual assessment of him.

"I saw him."

"Then you understand."

Josey swallowed. "Yes."

"Bastard. I hate that he's still in my house. That was my mother's house. I wonder what's going to happen to it."

"Well," Josey said, "if you're really leaving, you can sell it."

Della Lee smiled, like there was a secret joke in there somewhere. "Sell it. Yes. That's what I'll do."

"I can help you."

Della Lee's smile faded. "You have to promise me not to do anything else like this, Josey. Don't go back there to him. Don't contact realtors. And don't tell anyone about me. *Promise!*"

"Okay, okay. I promise."

"I can't believe you would do this for me." Della Lee reached out tentatively to touch the box, like she wasn't sure it was real. When her fingers touched the cardboard, she gave a surprised laugh.

"When you go up north, you're going to need your things."

Della scooted the box toward her. It made a loud scraping noise against the hardwood floor. "Oh, I get it," she said as she lifted the lid. "You're trying to get rid of me because I know about your sweets."

"Well, there is that," Josey said.

"Josey!" she heard her mother call from down the hall. Josey swung her head around.

"No one's ever done anything like this for me. You know, maybe I *can* keep this stuff." Della Lee suddenly grabbed the bags and brought them toward her, hugging them. "*My* stuff," she said, laughing. "My stuff, my stuff, my stuff. I never thought I'd see it again. Could I have a little privacy here?"

Josey hesitated at first, then got to her feet.

"Close the door, will you? And don't forget to go see Chloe at the courthouse and get my sandwich," Della Lee said as she brought a shirt out of one of the bags and put it to her face, inhaling. She frowned, then smelled the shirt again. "That's strange. This doesn't smell like I remembered."

When Josey closed the door, Della Lee was taking out another shirt.

Josey shook her head, thinking, if Della Lee were a candy, she would be a SweeTart. Not the hard kind that broke your teeth, the chewy kind, the kind you had to work on and mull over, your eyes watering and your lips turning up into a smile you didn't want to give.

"Josey!" Margaret called again.

Josey turned quickly and went to check on her mother.

Margaret liked to look at one particular photo after she took her sleeping pill, because sometimes it made her dream of him. She was thirty-one in the photo, but she looked much younger. She always had, until recently. When she looked in the mirror these days, she saw someone she didn't recognize. She didn't see the beautiful woman in the photo. She saw an old woman trying to be beautiful, her skin dry and her wrinkles like cracks. She looked like a very well-dressed winter apple.

Long ago, when she was a young woman, younger even than in the photo, she thought she would be happier here in Bald Slope than she was in Asheville. It meant she would be away from her family and their demands of her. She was only twenty-three when she married Marco, a match made by her father. Marco was almost twenty-four years her senior, but he was rich and charismatic and he had no interest in having children, so it could have been much, much worse. She got what she wanted, a life away from her family and no younger siblings to look after anymore, while her family got what they wanted, money. But Margaret didn't realize how lonely she would be in this strange cool place with the Gothic arches of its downtown buildings and an entire culture devoted to bringing visitors to their town in order to survive. And it didn't take long to understand that Marco only wanted a beautiful wife and the cachet of her old Southern family name. He didn't want *her*. But when she was thirty-one, for one brief wonderful year, she wasn't lonely. She was happy, for the first and only time she could ever remember.

The photo had been taken at a picnic social, and he wasn't supposed to be in the picture. He was caught by accident so close to her. She'd cut the photo in half years ago, when she thought cutting him out of her life was the right thing to do. But she could still see his hand in the photo, a young man's hand, just barely touching hers. The hand wasn't her husband's.

She could hear Josey moving around in her room. Josey was talking to herself, which was a new development, one Margaret wondered if she should be concerned about. Today Josey had taken entirely too long to fetch the peppermint oil, especially considering Nova Berry didn't even have it ready yet. Josey had been doing something else. The thought of Josey making a wider circle, one outside this house, made Margaret feel uneasy. Margaret had given up everything for this life, for this house, for this money. Josey would too.

She heard some scuffling, like something being dragged across the floor in Josey's room.

"Josey!" she called, putting the photo under her pillow.

A minute passed with no response.

"Josey!" she called again.

Soon Josey tapped on Margaret's bedroom door and entered. Margaret knew she wasn't a good mother. But somehow, all the horrible things Josey did when she was young, all the treasures she broke, all the tantrums she threw, all the scratches and bruises she gave, would have been a little easier to forgive if she just didn't look so much like Marco. Marco, who would swoop in once a week to take Josey on a drive because Margaret forced him to. Where was he the rest of the time, when Josey was screaming or breaking the good china? The first nine years of Josey's life, Margaret could only stare at her daughter, at what an unattractive, spoiled child she was, and wonder if she was punishment. She'd had Josey out of desperation and spite. So maybe Margaret got what she deserved. But Marco could do what he wanted, married or not, and he had no consequences to face. Men were thieves.

"Is something wrong, Mother? Do you need something?"

"What are you doing in your room? I heard a scraping sound."

"I was sitting at my desk," Josey said. "I pulled back the chair. I'll go to bed now. I won't make any more noise."

"All right," Margaret said. Josey started to turn. "Josey?"

"Yes, Mother?"

"Did you get rid of that sweater like I asked?"

"Yes, Mother."

"I wasn't trying to be mean the other day. It just doesn't look good on you."

"Yes, Mother," Josey said.

The truth was, that sweater, that color, looked good on her daughter. And every time she wore it, it hinted at something that scared Margaret.

Josey was growing into her beauty.

Margaret watched Josey leave.

She used to be a beautiful woman, the most beautiful woman around.

She brought out the photo again.

But that was forever ago.

3

Rock Candy

Across town, early the next morning, Chloe Finley stared at the door of her apartment.

Her boyfriend Jake was on the other side of the door, outside in the hall.

She couldn't believe this was happening. She'd just kicked Jake out after he'd admitted he'd cheated on her.

Dazed, she turned around . . . and tripped over a book on the floor.

She looked down at it and sighed. She'd half expected

this. Whether she liked it or not, books always appeared when she needed them. She'd stopped reading as much once she met Jake. And over the past five years, ever since moving in with him, books had come to her less and less frequently. When they did show up, she ignored them. After all, how did you explain such a thing? Books appearing all of a sudden? She was always afraid Jake would think she was crazy.

She could remember very clearly the first time it happened to her. Being an only child raised by her great-grandparents on a farm miles from town, she was bored a lot. When she ran out of books to read, it only got worse. She was walking by the creek along the wood line at the end of the property one day when she was twelve, feeling mopey and frustrated, when she saw a book propped up against a willow tree.

She walked over and picked it up. It was so new the spine creaked and popped when she opened it. It was a book on card tricks, full of fun things she could do with the deck of cards her great-grandmother kept in a drawer in the kitchen for her weekly canasta game.

She called out, asking if anyone was there. No one answered. She didn't see any harm in looking through the book, so she sat under the tree by the creek and read as much as she could before it got dark. She wanted to take it with her when her great-grandmother called her home, but she knew she couldn't. The owner of the book would surely want it back. So she reluctantly left it by the tree and ran home, trying to commit to memory everything she'd read.

After dinner, Chloe took the deck of cards out of the kitchen drawer and went to her bedroom to try some of the tricks. She tried for a while, but she couldn't get them right without following the pictures in the book. She sighed and gathered the cards she'd spread out on the floor. She stood, and that's when she saw the book, the same book she'd left by the creek, on her nightstand.

For a while after that, she thought her great-grandparents were surprising her with books. She'd find them on her bed, in her closet, in her favorite hideouts around the property. And they were always books she needed. Books on games or novels of adventure when she was bored. Books about growing up as she got older. But when her great-grandparents confronted her about all the books she had and where did she get the money to buy them, she realized they weren't the ones doing it.

The next day, under her pillow, she found a book on clever storage solutions. It was exactly what she needed, something to show her how to hide her books.

She accepted it from then on. Books liked her. Books wanted to look after her.

She slowly picked the book up from the apartment floor. It was titled *Finding Forgiveness*.

She stared at it a long time, a feeling bubbling inside her. It took a few moments for her to realize it was anger. Books were good for a story or to teach a card trick or two, but what were they really? Just paper and string and glue. They evoked emotions and that was why people felt a connection with them. But they had no emotions themselves. They didn't know betrayal. They didn't know hurt.

What in the hell did they know about forgiveness?

She went to the kitchen, put the book in the refrigerator and shut the door. She slid her back down the door and sat on the floor. Jake had woken her up that morning by kissing his way down her stomach. She could feel her lower abdominal muscles clench at the memory, even though she was furious with him now, *livid*. But she could never seem to help her physical reaction when it came to Jake. She was sometimes frightened by how much she felt for him, frightened by his intensity, by the way he never closed his eyes when they made love. He pulled her to him the way wind pulled leaves, like she had no control. She'd never loved anyone as much, or felt such passion. To this day she could make tap water boil just by kissing him. And she thought Jake was just as consumed by her. The day they met at the courthouse, on his first day of work out of law school, he forgot where he was going and sat at her shop staring at her until the district attorney herself came to look for him.

As he had moved over her that morning, she'd met his eyes and felt that rush of overwhelming feeling, her body panicking with it. It was almost too much, yet she could never imagine being without it.

"I would die before I could ever be with anyone else," she'd said, reaching up to touch his face. His eyes bored into hers, just as his body did.

I would die before I was a game they played. One of those things couples did. An inside joke. If they were in a restaurant, one of them might say, *I would die before I would ever eat that much again*. And the other would say, *I would die before I let you*. Or if they were out walking through the park, one of them might laugh and say, *I would die before I would ever make a dog of mine wear a bandana*. And the other would say, *I would die before I let you*. But it was always serious in bed. *I would die before I would leave you. I would die before I could ever get enough of this*.

Jake had suddenly closed his eyes, which he never did when they made love.

He stopped and fell away from her.

And that's when he told her.

There was only her. *There's only you, Chloe.*

He made a mistake. He hadn't meant for it to happen.

It was just one time, he'd said. Three months ago. The office had been celebrating after winning the Beasley murder case. Everyone had committed so much time to it and there had been all this stress, all these emotions needing a release, and before he knew it he'd done it.

He loved Chloe, not the other woman.

He begged her forgiveness, telling her he'd do anything to make this right. Anything, it seemed, but tell her the name of the woman he'd slept with.

Chloe sat on the floor in front of the refrigerator and stared into space until the phone rang. The voice that came over the machine was Hank's, one of the security guards at the courthouse, wondering where she was.

She got up, got dressed and went to the door. The book was sitting on the console by the door. She frowned at it as she left.

It was on the passenger seat of her car when she got in.

It was lying on the counter by the cash register when she lifted the security gate to the shop.

Downtown was busy that afternoon. Josey had forgotten that preparations had begun for the three-day Bald Is Beautiful festival, which was held every year to kick off the ski season. There was always live music and beer to attract college kids, and a famous bald-head contest the first night that received a lot of media attention. The festival had been Marco's idea. Josey used to go to the festival with him when she was young, but it had been almost twenty years since she'd last attended. After Marco died, the town invited Margaret and Josey to the festival as guests of honor, but Margaret always refused, and the invitations eventually stopped. They were poor substitutes for the charismatic man who had once ruled the mountain, anyway.

Because of the preparations, it took Josey longer than she thought it would to get to the courthouse downtown and find a place to park. She finally found a parking space big enough for Lola the Large Cadillac, then, when she entered the courthouse, she set off the metal detector twice. When the security guards finally waved her on, she walked across the cavernous pink marble rotunda that smelled of grease from the old elevators and went to the small shop Della Lee had told her about. It looked like a newsstand from a distance, with shelves of magazines and newspapers and paperback books, but as she got closer she noticed there was a sandwich counter and two small café tables.

There wasn't anyone there when she approached.

She looked around and checked her watch anxiously.

Suddenly she heard from the back room behind the counter, "Would you please go away? I don't need you!"

"Excuse me?" Josey said, surprised.

A young woman with the most beautiful hair Josey had ever seen popped her head out of the doorway. "Oh, I'm sorry," she said as she walked all the way out of the room. "I didn't know anyone was out here. Can I help you?"

Her color was high and her brown eyes were shining. Her gorgeous red hair was a thick mass of curls that fell down her back. She looked like a painting, fragile, caught in a moment she couldn't get out of. "Are you all right?" Josey automatically asked.

The woman's smile didn't quite meet her eyes. "I'm fine, thanks. What can I get for you?"

"A grilled tomato and cheese sandwich to go, please."

"Coming up," the woman said, and turned around to the grill.

Josey sat at one of the small café tables. She kept checking her watch. She had just sneaked out of her mother's ladies' club meeting. She had about twenty minutes by her estimation, twenty minutes to get back to Mrs. Herzog's drawing room before the meeting ended. Josey wasn't a member of the group, and she always stood off to the side with the nurses and paid companions of some of the older ladies. Not even they paid any attention when she slipped out. The only person who seemed to notice was Rawley Pelham, the older man who owned the local cab company. Some mysterious part of the Pelham family tree forbade them from breaking promises. Once a Pelham gave you his word, he had to keep it. If Rawley promised he'd pick you up at ten o'clock, he was always there at ten o'clock. Annabelle Drake hired him to take her to these meetings, and he always waited outside and stared at the house as if the gathering of women inside was a mystery he was trying to solve. He smiled at Josey as he leaned against his cab, his collar up against the cold wind. She knew he wouldn't say anything. For some reason, he went out of his way to avoid speaking to her mother.

Sneaking out was another risk, yes. But someone had to take care of Della Lee. As far as Josey knew, she hadn't eaten anything since she'd shown up three days ago, stubbornly holding out for a grilled tomato and cheese sandwich.

Josey checked her watch again, then she suddenly felt a pull in the center of her body. She put a hand to her stomach automatically, thinking it was hunger. The smell of peppery warm cheese and thick, yeasty grilled bread was beginning to fill the air. She would give the sandwich to Della Lee when she got home, and while Della Lee ate the sandwich Josey would eat oatmeal pies and candy corn and packets of salty pumpkin seeds from her closet. She daydreamed about that for a moment.

She heard the metal detector go off and turned.

That's when she realized it wasn't hunger she felt.

It was Adam.

He was emptying his pockets before walking through the metal detector again. He was still in his work uniform, but he wasn't carrying his bag. He had on a well-worn blue fleece hoodie, and a bandana was pushing his hair back.

Her lips parted when he began to walk across the rotunda toward her.

But he didn't even look at her as he went straight to the counter.

"Chloe?"

The woman turned from the grill, saw who it was, then turned back around without a word.

"Come on, Clo. Talk to me. I just got home from work and found him on my front step."

"I don't care," Chloe said.

Adam stared at Chloe's back, at her beautiful hair. "He never meant to hurt you."

That made Chloe turn again, spatula in hand. "*You knew about it?*"

Adam hesitated. Whatever it was, he knew.

Chloe turned back around. "Just go."

"Do you want me to tell him anything?"

"I'm not talking to him, and I'm not talking to him

through you." She looked over her shoulder. "Unless, of course, you want to tell me who it was."

"I don't know who it was," Adam said. "Listen, he asked me to go over to your place and get some of his things because he knows you don't want him there right now. But I'll wait until you're there to do that, okay? I'll call you tonight before I come by. Jake will be staying with me for a while. You know the number." He waited for her to say something, but when she didn't he finally turned and walked away. He glanced at Josey as he passed her. He'd taken a few steps before he stopped. "Josey," he said, as if the glimmer of recognition finally penetrated. "What a surprise."

"Hi, Adam," she said breathlessly.

"What are you doing here?"

"I'm waiting on a sandwich." She quickly added, "It's not for me." *It's not for me?* Brilliant.

"Oh, right. Of course." He studied her for a moment. Her hand went covertly to her mouth to feel for crumbs. "Are you okay?"

"You ask me that a lot."

"Do I? I'm sorry. You just seem a little sad."

She shook her head. "I'm fine," she lied.

He looked over to Chloe, then turned back to Josey. "Well, I'll see you later."

She watched him go. "Bye."

"Here's your sandwich," Chloe said, putting a white paper bag on the counter.

Josey stood and approached the counter as Chloe punched some buttons on the cash register. "So, you know Adam?" Josey asked as casually as possible.

"He's my boyfriend . . . my *ex*-boyfriend's . . ." Chloe

shook her head and looked frustrated that she couldn't articulate just what Adam was to her, which made Josey's heart sink even lower in her chest. They had history. They had a relationship. "He's my boyfriend's best friend," she finally said. "It's four dollars even."

"Oh." Josey dug around in her purse a little too long, working up enough courage to ask, "Do you mean you and Adam aren't a couple?"

"No," Chloe said, as if surprised Josey would think that. "How do you know him?"

Josey finally brought out the money and handed it to Chloe. "He delivers my mail."

Chloe took the money, now staring at Josey. "Do I know you from somewhere?"

"I don't think so."

Chloe suddenly smiled. "Oh, I know! You're Cirrini, Josey Cirrini. There's a portrait of you and your father in the lobby of the ski lodge. I see it every time I go there."

Josey hadn't thought about that portrait in a long time. Her mother had insisted on having it commissioned, and had been vehement about it hanging in the lobby for everyone to see. It had immortalized her as a fat child, but Josey had loved sitting on her father's lap for hours while having it done. "I'd almost forgotten about that. I didn't know it still hung there."

"You know, now that I think about it, Adam did once mention he delivered the Cirrinis' mail."

"He did?"

"But he never said he knew you."

Embarrassed, Josey picked up the warm white bag. "He doesn't," she said, and turned to leave. She knocked a book she didn't know was there off the counter. She picked it up and looked at the cover. *Finding Forgiveness.* "I'm sorry. Is this your book?"

"Unfortunately." Chloe took the book. As Josey walked away, Chloe went to the back room, saying, "I said, *go away.*"

"And then Adam walked in! I couldn't believe it! Apparently Chloe's boyfriend is his best friend and he's staying with him now. I think she and her boyfriend lived together and she kicked him out."

Josey was sitting on the floor in front of the closet, talking with animation. The white bag with the sandwich in it, long since cool because Josey had to leave it in the trunk of the car until she could sneak out and get it without her mother seeing, was sitting on her lap.

While Josey was out, Della Lee had obviously occupied herself by playing with the things Josey had brought from her house. She was wearing a child-sized tiara and all the old necklaces from the box, and had put a rhinestone-studded denim shirt over her T-shirt. She'd gone slaphappy with her makeup—her lips were bright glossy pink and her fingernails were each painted a different color.

"Who is Adam?" Della Lee asked, blowing on her fingernails.

"He's my mailman."

"Aha!" Della Lee looked up with a triumphant smile. "*He* was the reason you ran out of here so quickly the other day."

Josey felt like she'd been caught with a mouth full of jelly beans.

But Della Lee didn't seem to feel like making her squirm that day. "I always worried about Chloe being so wrapped up in Jake. She never got to know herself. You and me and Chloe," Della Lee said, flopping onto her back on the sleeping bag and pillow Josey had given her. She held her hands above her face to admire her fingernails. "We can't hold on to our hearts to save our lives. *You* even let yours go off in some man's mailbag."

"You know these people?" Josey asked.

"Not personally." Della Lee dropped her hands and stared up at Josey's clothes. "But I know Chloe is a good kid. She's . . . twenty-five, I think. I remember I was ten when you were born and twelve when she was born."

Josey looked at her oddly. "You remember when I was born?"

"Of course. I bet most people in town do. You were Marco Cirrini's *beloved only child*."

"Oh." Della Lee hadn't made a move for the bag, so Josey proudly put it on the floor in front of her. "Long story short, here's your sandwich!"

Della Lee turned her head to look at the bag. "I ate some things from your closet while you were out." She lifted a corner of the sleeping bag to reveal some empty candy wrappers. "I didn't think you'd really do it. Oh, I mean, I appreciate it. You're being very nice to me in my time of need. But I already ate. That's what you wanted, right? *You* eat the sandwich. You know you want to. Get me another one tomorrow."

Josey eyed the bag. That would be selfish, wouldn't it? She admitted that she wanted the sandwich, but she'd gotten it for Della Lee. That wasn't the same as getting it for herself. She couldn't eat it. Could she? "Are you sure?"

"Positive," Della Lee said with a devilish smile. "Go on, eat. And tell me about seeing *Adam*. Tell me what everyone said. The more I know, the better I can help you."

Josey sighed and opened the bag.

When Chloe heard the knock that evening, she muted the television with the remote and took the book that had appeared beside her and stuffed it under the couch cushions.

When she stood, *Finding Forgiveness* had appeared on the couch again.

She stuffed it under the cushions, more firmly this time. Books usually gave up after a while when she didn't want to read them. But not this one. "Behave," she told it.

She walked across the open living-room/dining-room area. The kitchen at the other end was separated only by an island counter. It was all very clean, masculine. No clutter. Just the way Jake liked it. She lost herself in him, in this. She *let* it happen.

She took a deep breath before she opened the door. She knew who it was. Adam had called earlier and said he was coming by. She waved him in. "His suitcases are under the bed."

Adam entered the apartment and waited while she closed the door. "How are you doing, Clo?" he asked as he unzipped his jacket.

"I'm great. Let's go to the bedroom and get this over with."

"I can't tell you how many women have said that to me."

Chloe had to smile. Everything about Adam made him seem carefree—his sense of humor, his naturally tan skin, his curly blond hair. He looked part surfer and part ski bum. And it was true, if there was an extreme outdoor sport, Adam had done it at least once. Up until three years ago, that is. After his accident, he said it was time to settle down. No more risks, no more travel, for him.

But Chloe always sensed he wasn't really happy here.

She followed him and watched from the bedroom doorway while he took the suitcases out and began to put Jake's clothes in them. She wished he could pack Jake's smell. She wished there was a way to put it in a bottle and stopper it. It was in the mattress, in the wallpaper, in the couch cushions. It was like a feral mark. This was his space. These were his things. It didn't feel like security as it once had, when she first moved in with him. It felt like gloating now. Like Jake saying, *Look at all I have. You need this. You need me.*

"Josey Cirrini asked about you, after you left the shop today," Chloe said, because that was neutral territory. "She thought you and I were a couple. She seemed relieved that we weren't."

Adam stopped packing, giving Chloe the strangest look.

"I take it this is a surprise to you?"

"She's a nice woman and I deliver her mail, that's all."

"She *is* nice. And I didn't realize she was so young," Chloe said. "Come on, I know you've noticed more than her mail."

"She smells like peppermint," he said, after giving it some thought.

"You *have* noticed."

But he didn't say anything else. It wasn't like their usual banter, when she would tease him about dating more. He disappeared into the attached bathroom and she crossed her arms over her chest and looked down at her feet.

"I'm going to lose you, aren't I?" she said when he came out of the bathroom with Jake's toiletries.

She liked Adam, but he was friends with Jake first. Jake had met him at the gym. Adam hadn't been in Bald Slope for very long at the time; it had only been a few months since his accident on Bald Slope Mountain, and Jake invited him to have drinks with him and Chloe. Everything around her had been Jake's first. The apartment was Jake's, a stylish red-brick place in the historic renovated firehouse downtown. It had been a gift to him from his parents when he graduated from law school. She had some furniture left from her great-grandparents' house, along with hundreds of boxes of books that had appeared over the years, in a small storage rental. She'd never asked to put her things here. She didn't know why now. She guessed she didn't think they would fit. And she had wanted to fit in Jake's life, wanted it so much she got lost in it.

Adam walked over to her and put his hands on her arms. He had to bend a little to make sure he met her eyes. "You're not losing anyone, least of all me. It was a one-time thing, three months ago. He was stupid. People do stupid things. I mean, you don't do stupid things. Asking him to leave wasn't stupid. I'm not saying that . . ."

She smiled at him again. "Adam?"

"Yes?"

"You're really bad at this."

He seemed relieved that she'd called him on it. "I know." He dropped his hands from her arms. "I guess I should be going." He went back to the bed and zipped up the suitcases, then he noticed a book on the nightstand. "Is this your book?" he asked as he picked it up.

She looked over at it, expecting it to be that damn book that had been following her all day.

But no.

This was a new book. *Old Love, New Direction*.

"This is good, Clo." He held the book in the palm of his hand like a scale, as if the words had weight. "It's good that you have this."

Confused, Chloe leaned out of the room and looked over to *Finding Forgiveness*, back on top of the couch cushions in the living room.

Good Lord, it had called in reinforcements.

"I should go," Adam said, putting the book down. He slid the suitcases off the bed and she followed him to the front door. "Do you want me to tell Jake anything?"

She opened the door for him. "That I look happy?"

"Clo . . ."

"No, I don't want you to tell him anything. Good night, Adam," she said, and closed the door behind him.

She whirled around. *Old Love, New Direction* had joined *Finding Forgiveness* on the couch, like they were waiting to have a talk with her. Great. She was being stalked by self-help books.

She stomped to the bathroom to take a shower. Books never appeared in the bathroom. Like cats, they hated water. She stood under the spray until the water turned cold. Just when she thought she had washed all thoughts of Jake out of her mind, at least enough to sleep, she opened the bathroom door and found the books, stacked neatly one on top of the other, on the floor in front of her.

"If I see you again tonight, I'm putting you both in the toilet," she said as she stepped over them and went to the bed to set her alarm.

When she turned around again, they were gone.

4

Sno Caps

The next day at work, Chloe spent her downtime reading magazines from the periodical inventory that had come in that morning. She wanted distractions, any distractions. She wanted to forget about how quiet the apartment was last night, how out of place she felt in it alone. Unfortunately, *Finding Forgiveness* kept appearing by her on the counter, nudging her, reminding her. At least *Old Love, New Direction* had decided to stay home, though it had poured out of her box of cereal that morning, clanging onto the bowl and causing Cheerios to fly everywhere. She had just knocked *Finding Forgiveness* off the counter again when she saw someone crossing the rotunda toward her.

She straightened as the woman approached. "It's you!" Chloe said, unreasonably glad to see her again.

Josey Cirrini stopped and turned around to see who Chloe was talking to. When she saw no one was there, she said, "Me?"

"Yes, you," Chloe said, laughing. "Another grilled tomato and cheese to go?"

Josey walked up to the counter. "You remembered."

"I remember what everyone orders. I get that from my great-grandad." Chloe turned and put on a pair of disposable clear plastic gloves, then she started to assemble the sandwich. "He used to run this shop. He left it to me. I don't get too many orders for grilled tomato and cheese. There was this one woman who always ordered it, but I haven't seen her in a while."

"Oh?" she heard Josey say, as if that interested her.

Chloe shrugged and said, "A pretty woman, older, a little rough. Blond hair and lots of makeup. Every time I saw her, she was coming from court. Domestic disturbance. Every time. Except that one time she was here on solicitation." Chloe stopped and looked over her shoulder at Josey. "I'm not talking trash. She told me. She told Hank too." Chloe nudged her shoulder toward Hank at the security gate in front of the main doors. "She wasn't ashamed. That's just the way some people live."

As soon as the bread turned golden and the cheddar and Colby and Jack began to melt and sizzle onto the grill, Chloe scooped the sandwich up with a spatula and wrapped it in wax paper. When she turned, Josey had the money ready.

She was dressed that day in a long gray coat, its cloth-covered buttons secured all the way to the top, where a red cardigan peeked out from under the collar. It was something easy to overlook, but she was really very pretty. She had beautiful pale skin, which was a stark contrast to her dark eyes and hair, like black marble and snow. It was very dramatic, like she would be cool to the touch. But she smelled sweet, like candy. No, that wasn't it, Chloe thought. She smelled like *Christmas*. "Adam's right," Chloe said as she set the bag on the counter in front of Josey. "You smell like peppermint."

"Adam said I smelled like peppermint?" Josey said, her voice pitching slightly.

"Uh-huh. Last night when I talked to him."

"Is that good or bad?"

"I'd say it was good," Chloe said, trying not to smile at how nervous that seemed to make Josey. It was sweet. She and Jake had never had that fluttery infatuation, that nervous *Does he like me?* feeling. From the beginning it had been like a cannonball, all that passion. There had never been time for a traditional courtship.

She took the money from Josey and rang up the purchase just as the elevator farthest from them opened and a wave of suits poured out. Court had recessed.

Chloe looked up and found him right away. It was as if thoughts of him had made him appear.

Jake's shoe was untied and he hadn't noticed. He had papers sticking out of his briefcase, which someone had just pointed out to him. He looked embarrassed. He didn't know how to handle this any better than she did, which was a strange thing to take comfort in.

Jake began to walk toward her shop. He had dark hair

that, compared to Josey's black hair, was warm chocolate-cake brown. His eyes were light green, a striking shade she could make out even from across the rotunda. He was so intense. Did the other woman see that in him too? Had he focused on her like he was focusing on Chloe right now? Had she been helpless to resist? A single hard impulse hit her and she wanted to go to him. She wanted to leave Josey and the shop and everything else behind and run into his arms. He'd hug her and they would kiss and the water in the coffeemaker would start to boil and everything would go back to the way it was. Everything would fit in the too-tight way it did before, but that would be all right. Wasn't that better than her life falling off of her altogether?

But she stopped herself. That wouldn't make it right. You didn't forgive because it was the only choice you thought you had. That didn't make it forgiveness, that made it desperation. She'd always been too desperate about Jake. *Always*.

And how could she forgive him when he wouldn't even tell her who he'd slept with?

"Excuse me," she said to Josey, starting to turn, to hide in the small storeroom.

"Are you okay?"

Chloe looked at him again. He was getting closer. "I'm just trying to avoid someone."

Josey turned to see who it was. "Jake Yardley?"

"You know him?"

"Sort of," Josey said, turning back around. Chloe wasn't surprised. As prosecutor, Jake had been on the local television news almost every night for the duration of the Beasley murder trial in Bald Slope this past summer. Murder in a small town is pervasive, growing like kudzu until it envelops everyone in its sensationalism. People would still come up to Jake on the street to talk about the case, wanting to know what went on behind the scenes at the trial, wanting assurances that Wade Beasley was behind bars for good.

"He cheated on me," she said, and it was the first time she'd said it out loud.

"Oh," Josey said.

Chloe hurried into the storeroom. After she'd dropped out of college when her great-grandparents fell ill, she'd had to sell the farmhouse and put them in a nursing home. She'd had nowhere to live, so she'd secretly moved into this storeroom and lived in it for almost six months. Every bit of money she'd made during that time went toward her great-grandparents' care. Hank was the only one to find out, and he let her get away with it. Her great-grandparents died within months of each other. Just weeks after her great-grandmother's death, she met Jake, and she clung to him. She'd lost almost everything, and there he was, offering her so much.

"Clo, please come out here," she heard him call.

"I don't think she wants to." Chloe cocked her head. That was Josey's voice.

"Chloe, if you don't come here, I'm coming back there." He was ignoring Josey.

She steeled herself for his presence. He could make her forget that it was desperation. He could make her forget everything. And this small room couldn't contain what they had when they were together. The temperature would rise. Ice would melt. Eggs would fry in their cartons. After it had happened a few times when they first met, she had insisted he stay away from her at work because she lost inventory when he was around.

A few moments passed.

"All right, here I come," he said.

"No," Josey said. "You're not going back there."

"Who *are* you?" Jake demanded in his lawyer voice, which made Chloe feel anxious for Josey. Josey was no match for him in lawyer mode.

But to Chloe's surprise, she heard Josey say with some exasperation, "I'm Josey Cirrini, Jake. I stole your piece of chocolate cake at your grandmother's Christmas party when I was six and made you cry."

"Josey!" Jake said, as if his memory had suddenly kicked in. "Where is your mother? What are you doing here?"

"I'm helping out a friend."

"I know all of Clo's friends."

"Maybe you only thought you did," Josey said. A few moments of silence passed before Chloe heard, "He's gone."

She walked out sheepishly. She should be handling this better. "Thank you," Chloe said.

"I hope I didn't . . ." Josey waved an arm in the direction Jake had obviously left. The movement revealed the watch on her wrist. When she looked at it, she said, "Oh no. I have to go."

"I'll walk you out," Chloe said, falling into step with Josey as she grabbed the sandwich bag and hurried into the rotunda. They reached the doors and walked out into the cool afternoon. The park in front of the courthouse was a flurry of last-minute activity before the kickoff to the Bald Is Beautiful festival that night. Leaves skittered across the grass on the breeze created as the canopies went up. The clouds were low in the sky, bright gray and full of sparkles. "Wait," Chloe said once they reached the courthouse steps, a little out of breath. Josey could really move. "Are you going to the festival tonight?"

Josey looked out over the park warily. "No. Are you?"

"I usually do. I mean, I always went with Jake. I'll go if you go." She met Josey's eyes. They were about the same height, and their eyes were the same shade of dark brown.

"Surely there are other people you'd rather go with?"

"They'd all grill me about Jake. I get the feeling you wouldn't."

"It's none of my business."

"See? You're perfect."

Josey gave a small laugh and shook her head. "I haven't been since I was little," she said. She looked down, confusion coming to her face. She bent and picked up a book that was lying on the steps. "Isn't this your book?"

Chloe sighed. "Oh, thanks."

"Didn't you just leave it on the counter?"

"Yes. I think I will go tonight. I didn't do anything without him. That's going to change. I'm going to do this."

Josey's eyes went from the book to Chloe's face. "Do you think you'll forgive him?"

"I don't know what I'm going to do yet." She took a few steps over to a large green trash receptacle and threw *Finding Forgiveness* away. "Listen, I'll be at the stage around eight o'clock if you change your mind and want to come tonight."

"Here, eat this, quick," Josey said as she opened her closet door. She put the bag in front of Della Lee, who was sitting on the floor on the sleeping bag. She was still wearing the tiara and all the necklaces, but today she was wearing several of her shirts layered over her T-shirt, and it looked like she'd put a pair of jeans on over the pair she was already wearing. Josey wasn't quite sure what Della Lee was doing.

Maybe she was bored. Maybe she thought the only way she could take her things with her was if she was wearing *everything.*

Not that she was making any noise about leaving. And considering what she had to go back to, that was probably a good thing. In fact, Della Lee seemed perfectly at home here, with no desire to even stand or walk around, at least during the day when Josey could see her. Josey, of all people, understood the appeal of living in there. If Della Lee wasn't in the closet, Josey would crawl in there right now. She would eat raspberry caramels and chocolate-covered cherries and read a romance novel.

Josey took off her long gray coat, then slipped out of her lucky red sweater. Was today really lucky? She didn't know how to feel exactly. Things were changing, in tiny ways, but enough to throw her off her normal course. First there was Della Lee. Then Chloe. And then Adam said she smelled like peppermint.

He'd *smelled* her.

"Why eat it quick?" Della Lee asked.

Josey walked over to the blue tufted chaise lounge and set her purse, sweater and coat on it. "I wanted you to eat it warm, so I put it in my purse when I brought in the groceries. But I think my mother smelled it on me." She turned around, trying to smooth the sides of her windblown hair.

"So what?" Della Lee said.

"So, I don't want her to find it here. I was late coming home. She was worried. And if on top of that she thinks I'm sneaking food in here . . . well, it would embarrass her. And I think I've embarrassed her enough as it is."

The truth was, she sneaked food in all the time, there was just never anyone else involved. She bought a lot of things at the grocery store every week, extra things on her own debit card so her mother wouldn't find out. There were coconut drops, Pixy Stix and several pretty bottles of orangeade in the trunk right now. She kept the things in the car trunk until her mother went to sleep at night, then she'd sneak them in. Helena knew about Josey going out to the car at night, but she seemed to think it was normal behavior and after a while she stopped offering to help her carry the things in. She only stuck her head out of her bedroom to make sure it was Josey and not some ghostly midnight mover.

"What have you done to embarrass her?" Della Lee asked. "It seems to me that you've given up all semblance of a normal life just for her."

Josey shook her head. "I was a terrible child."

"So what?" Della Lee said again.

"So, I owe her this. And she's my family, my only family."

Della Lee laughed. "That you know of."

"What is that supposed to mean?"

"Joke. It was a joke." She shook her head. "You need to stop this hero worship of your mother. She's not *that* great. And she doesn't give a flying fig about you. You did the same thing with your father."

"How do you know that?"

"The whole town knows that. You adored your father."

"Imagine that. I loved my father. I probably need therapy."

"Thank you for the sandwich, but I already ate. Here," Della Lee set the bag outside the closet, "you eat it."

Josey stared at the bag. Eating that sandwich would make her feel better. And it would make her feel worse. It was a familiar dilemma. She'd never experienced anything that was simply and entirely good for her. She wondered if such a thing even existed.

She sighed and walked over to Della Lee. She sat on the floor in front of the closet and opened the bag. "I talked with Chloe today. She remembered you, not by name, but that you always ordered this." She unwrapped the sandwich. "She said you were always coming from court. Domestic disturbance and solicitation." She took a bite, not looking at Della Lee. It was always easier after that first bite. No turning back. She had to eat the whole thing now.

"And I'm sure that rankled your prim sensibilities."

"I don't have prim sensibilities." She finally looked up from the sandwich. "Were you really a prostitute?"

"I did it to make Julian jealous. Well, sometimes I would do it for the money too. At one point it was even easy. You'd be surprised how easy some things can be, things you never thought you'd do, when you take self-respect out of the equation." Della Lee smiled and waved her hand dismissively when she saw the look on Josey's face. "Never mind. So, Chloe remembered me? That's nice. I wasn't sure she would."

"She asked me to go to the Bald Is Beautiful festival tonight."

"That's great! I knew the two of you would hit it off."

Josey shook her head and took another bite of the sandwich. "I can't go."

"Why not? Wear that sweater you like so much, the one you just took off. It looks good on you. Go and see what happens."

Josey lowered the sandwich. "You think the sweater looks good on me?"

"You know you want to go," she said seductively, leaning forward so that her hair fell over her shoulder, stirring the air with the scent of river water. "Go, then come tell me everything. I'm forming a plan for you."

"Della Lee, you're living in my closet, you're blackmailing me over candy, and you are currently wearing sixteen articles of clothing. It's amazing to me that you think *I* have problems. You need to form a plan for yourself."

Della Lee shook her head. "I gave up on me a long time ago. There's still some hope for you, though."

Josey approached the stage. She was too late for the bald-head contest, and a band was now setting up. There were lots of college-aged kids milling around in groups, laughing, holding plastic cups of beer, waiting for the music. She spotted Chloe by her hair, a blaze of red shining in the stage lights, like spun cinnamon sugar. She stood near the Bald Slope Ski Resort booth to the right of the stage. The people in the booth were handing out free lift tickets, free CD cases and free skullcaps with the resort's logo on them.

Josey made a beeline for her. She knew people weren't really looking at her. It only felt that way because Della Lee had insisted she wear her hair down, and she was wearing some of Della Lee's makeup.

Makeup. She couldn't believe it.

She used to experiment in her room with tubes of lipstick and bottles of rosewater blush she'd sneak out of her mother's vanity when she was a child, trying to imitate her mother's beauty. But she'd never worn makeup in public before. Her mother always said that, with Josey's coloring, it would only make her look cheap. And Cirrinis were in no way cheap.

That's why Josey had decided not to tell her mother she was going out tonight. It's why she'd waited until her mother had taken her pill and was fast asleep. It wasn't really such a big deal. Her mother might not have even minded Josey going. But more than likely it would have involved a lot of guilt and a lot of criticism, and Josey just didn't want to deal with it.

She was twenty-seven years old. There was something profoundly wrong with sneaking out of the house at her age.

Yet, here she was.

When Josey finally walked up to Chloe's side, Chloe looked relieved to see her. "Josey! I was about to give up on you." She stepped back. "You look great. Wow."

With her gloved hand, Josey touched her cheek self-consciously. "I don't usually wear makeup."

"You should. The hair, the makeup. It looks like you."

Josey hesitated, then pushed her curly hair behind her ears, feeling better. "So, what do we do?" she asked.

"Want to get a beer?"

"A beer." Josey smiled slightly. "Okay."

"Why are you smiling?" Chloe asked.

"I know someone who is going to love when I tell her this."

Once they got their cups, Chloe said, "Want to get something to eat?"

Josey didn't answer, because that wasn't something she normally admitted in public, but Chloe was already heading to the food booths, so she followed. The area was encompassed in a bubble of warm, fragrant steam from the funnel cake deep-fryers. It smelled like sweet vanilla cake batter you licked off a spoon.

She never went to the food booths when she was young. She would sit at the judges' table with her father during the bald-head contest, then the chauffeur would take her home. Margaret always met her at the door with questions. Did he introduce her to anyone? Did everyone see them together? She was obsessed with Marco showing pride in his only child, even though it was something Margaret herself could not do.

Chloe and Josey ate caramel apples and pecan sandies made by tiny old women from madly competitive church groups. Slowly, she began to relax. No one was watching. She was eating in public and it didn't feel bad. It felt good, in fact. *Wonderful*. Maybe it was the food itself. Maybe it was the normalcy of it all.

As she became more bold in looking around, she saw some people she recognized, but no one seemed to recognize her. Chloe was the exact opposite. People constantly stopped her to talk. There was Brittany, a girl she'd gone to high school with. June, whom she used to babysit. And then a woman named Flippa invited them both to a Tupperware party. Being here felt strangely empowering, like she now had a secret identity, a super power. She could go out looking like this, and no one knew her as Josey Cirrini. She was now just Josey, Chloe's friend. She could eat and no one would say anything about it, look at her like it was wrong.

She bought a plume of blue cotton candy before they left the food booths, and she picked at it while they headed down the row of booths occupied by residents of Bald Slope who had spent all summer making walnut salad bowls and jars of pickled watermelon rind to sell at the festival. Snow flurries began to fall and they swirled around people's legs like house cats. It was magical, this snowglobe world.

They were at the end of the craft booths, ready to turn toward the stage because Chloe wanted to listen to the band, when they suddenly turned at the sound of someone calling Chloe's name.

Jake Yardley was standing under the colorful lights strung above the walkway formed by the booths. People were walking around him, giving him curious glances. He was a mesmerizing man, intense and smart, with those strange green eyes all Yardley men had. People used to say that Yardley eyes could see right through you. The Cirrinis knew the Yardleys socially, both families having money and large real estate holdings in town. But Jake was a few years older than Josey, and he'd gone to boarding schools and Josey had been home-schooled by a long string of tutors, so they'd rarely crossed paths as children. When they had, at the odd social function or holiday party, Josey had been absolutely fascinated by him, by his eyes, by how polite he was, how quick he was to obey his parents. She'd never seen anything like it. She'd never socialized much with kids her own age, so she'd thought it was perfectly acceptable to pinch him to get his attention, to make him look at her. When he was younger, he would cry. As he got older he began to look at her with such sincere pity that it made her run away.

"Clo, *please*," he called, his voice desperate, a little slurred.

"Crap. I didn't think he'd be here. And I think he's been drinking," Chloe said tightly as she led Josey away, looking over her shoulder as they walked. "Oh, good, at least Adam is with him."

Like a hypnotist's command, that made Josey stop and

turn, as if not of her own will. Adam was trying to talk to Jake, standing in front of him and pushing him back. Jake gestured in Chloe's direction and Adam turned his head. He froze, his mouth open as if in mid-sentence. His eyes had fallen on Josey. Did he recognize her? What was that look? Men didn't look at her that way. *He'd* never looked at her that way. Long looks from head to toe were for women like Della Lee and Chloe, not Josey. She looked down at herself to try to see what he saw. She saw her red sweater, but most of her seemed to be completely obliterated by the huge cloud of cotton candy she was holding. She quickly hid the cotton candy behind her back. But it was too late. Adam had already turned away and was pulling Jake with him.

"How long?" Chloe asked.

Josey turned to find Chloe looking at her thoughtfully. "Excuse me?"

"How long have you been in love with Adam?"

She brought the cotton candy from behind her back. "Is it written on my forehead?"

Chloe smiled.

"Since the moment I saw him," Josey said quietly.

"I don't think he knows, Josey."

"Oh, I know he doesn't."

Chloe looked again to where Adam and Jake had disappeared, then she locked her arm in Josey's. "Come on."

As they made their way to the stage, Josey threw the stupid cotton candy away. What adult eats cotton candy, anyway? It was a stupid thing to buy.

It was crowded in front of the stage as Josey followed Chloe into the warm and frantic hive of people. It was like nothing she'd ever experienced before, the movement and cohesion. It was like being enveloped by a warm wave of humanity. She felt anxious at first, like she was going to lose Chloe, or suffocate. But then she let herself move with the flow, like water.

And she *loved* it.

The band's heavy bass boomed so loud she could feel it vibrate from the ground through her boots. For years Josey would lie in bed and hear the music from the festival, but she never dreamed she'd actually be here like this.

About an hour later, Josey suddenly stopped moving with the crowd. She knew he was there before he spoke.

"Chloe?"

Chloe turned her head slightly. "Adam," she said, looking back at the stage.

"I took him home." Adam leaned forward, talking loudly in order to be heard. "To my home. He was a little sauced. He's trying to give you space, he really is. He feels horrible about what happened."

"Good."

Adam's eyes fell on Josey, curious. "Well, hello, Josey."

"Hi, Adam."

He straightened and she turned back to the stage, but she was acutely aware of his presence. She knew when he moved slightly, jostled by the crowd. He was now standing behind her, directly behind her.

She could feel the hair on her arms stand on end. It was like static. If she leaned back just slightly, she would actually touch him. She closed her eyes, wondering what it would feel like if he actually put his arms around her from behind. She felt an anxious pull, a longing she usually filled with food. She wanted the cotton candy back.

She could feel him move a little closer. Was it her imagination, or was he leaning down, his nose close to her hair?

She opened her eyes.

He was *smelling* her.

Oh, God, she thought. Her life had become so weird since Della Lee had shown up in her closet. Was this really real? Or was she making it up? What if she was going crazy?

The fear was so real that she turned around quickly, just to make sure.

And she bumped right into Adam's chest.

His hands went out to steady her and she looked up at him. His blue eyes had seen too much sun. Papery snow flurries were sticking to his curly blond hair. If his hair got too wet, the curls would tighten. She knew that from years of watching him walk up to her porch in the rain. He always seemed to like when it rained, and out here in the snow, he was in his element.

She immediately turned back around and his hands slid off her arms.

"I should be going," she leaned over and said to Chloe.

Chloe looked from Josey to Adam, then back again. "Are you okay?"

"Yes, I'm fine. I just have to go."

"Okay. Adam, will you walk Josey to her car?"

"No!" Josey said frantically. Then she tried to smile. They were both looking at her like she'd lost her marbles. "No, I'm fine. Really. To walk. To my car. Thank you. I'll see you soon."

Stupid, stupid, stupid, she said to herself as she walked away.

Adam and Chloe watched Josey disappear into the crowd.

"You know what that was all about, don't you?" Chloe said.

Adam shook his head. "That's just Josey."

"She's in love with you."

He paused. "Excuse me?"

"Josey Cirrini is in love with you," she said in a louder voice, as if he hadn't heard her over the band the first time. Oh, he'd heard her. He just didn't believe her.

"That's ridiculous."

"She told me. She said she's been in love with you since the first day she saw you. Open your eyes for once, Adam. That mountain didn't kill your libido. Don't mess this up. Why do men have to mess things up?" Chloe turned and left him there.

He watched her go, stunned.

He'd always liked the way Josey smelled. He thought about how she was wearing her curly black hair down that night, how she was in that tight sweater he'd seen her in so many times, the red so striking against her pale skin. And he wasn't the only man here who had noticed.

And damn if she wasn't wearing makeup.

Was it for him?

He suddenly felt uneasy, the way he felt about anything that involved chance.

Oh, hell.

His leg was hurting.

It was time to go home.

The next morning, Adam got up and went to the kitchen of his small home, which was around the corner from the high school. It had taken him months of searching to find just the right place, with just the right view. He wanted a place that would let him see Bald Slope Mountain, like he had to keep an eye on it.

His brother Brett, thankful that Adam had at least stopped risking his life for sport, called him every week and said the same thing. "Why Bald Slope? You always have a place here. Get the hell out of that town and come home."

He groggily made coffee, strong, bitter coffee for a morning like this when his leg burned like a red-hot poker. He'd grown up in the California Sierras. He'd been a competitive skier in high school. He loved the cold and he especially loved the snow, but he was paying now for standing out in it last night. Enjoying snow was yet another thing the mountain had taken from him. Every day, he woke up humbled by that mountain, his aching leg a constant reminder of what you got when you teased fate to the point of payback. That was it for him. No more taking chances. He'd settled down in the place that had broken him. He was safe here. As long as he was here, he was away from all the temptation out there in the world, the cliffs to jump from, the oceans to swim.

He knew he couldn't go back to practicing law. His brother was ten years older than Adam and had an established law firm, so the job was waiting for Adam when he graduated. But he'd hated it. It had only been a way to make the kind of money he needed to do what he wanted on vacations.

Now he didn't know what else to do, so he just stayed still. Nothing could happen to him if he stayed still, right?

He turned, startled, when he heard Jake stumble down the hall. It was hard to get used to having someone else in the house. But he liked Jake, ironic considering Jake's profession. It was hard not to like him, and Adam had tried for a while.

He didn't want friends, he didn't want any sort of connection after his accident. He just wanted to be alone. But he found that Jake and Chloe actually made staying here bearable.

When Jake appeared in the kitchen doorway, Adam said, "You look like hell."

"That's a relief. It's not all in my head. Give it to me straight. How big of an ass did I make of myself last night?"

"You don't remember the motorcycle gang? Doing the striptease in front of them at the bar? The iguana? Good God, man. Tell me you remember the iguana!"

"Funny. You're a funny guy. I remember seeing her. I was following her. Was she running from me?"

"Walking."

"Who was she with?"

Adam turned to get a bottle of Tylenol from the cabinet. "A woman named Josey Cirrini."

"Oh, yeah. She never said she knew her." Adam waited, his back to him, for Jake to say more about Josey. But he didn't. "So I didn't talk to Chloe? I didn't say anything stupid to her?"

"No." Adam downed three pills and turned back around.

"I need to tell her I'm sorry."

"I went back to the festival last night. I explained it to her."

"Thanks, man."

Adam leaned against the counter. "I have a question for you, Jake."

"Don't make it a hard one." Jake went to the coffeemaker and poured a cup. "My head might explode."

"Why in the hell did you tell her? It happened three months ago. She never even suspected."

"You sound like my father." Jake took a gulp of the coffee and made a face. He set the cup down and then scratched his palms over the stubble on his cheeks. "I told her *because* she never suspected," he finally said. "She trusted me, and I let her down. And I was just walking around like it didn't happen. Like I got away with it. Then that morning she looked at me with those eyes and told me that she could never be with another man. She's too good for me."

Adam crossed his arms over his chest. "Let me get this straight, you told her to punish yourself? Like there was no other way to do that except by hurting her?"

"I'm not saying it was the smart thing to do. I love Chloe. I can't believe I did this to her. I wish to God I could take it back. I wish I could take everything back. I wish none of this had ever happened."

Adam shook his head. If it had been up to Adam, he never would have told his brother about his accident. But he'd been touch and go there for a while, and the hospital had contacted Brett, his next of kin. Now he would never live it down. Sometimes you weren't supposed to share pain. Sometimes it was best just to deal with it alone. "Stupid, man. Stupid."

"I know."

The mail was heavy Monday. It usually was at the first of the week. It meant Adam was later getting to the Cirrinis' neighborhood. Until now, he'd never paid much attention to the fact that he saw Josey almost every day, that she always seemed to know when he was coming up her walk. He looked up at the immaculate Victorian as he approached, thinking once again that it stuck out among the other houses like a big blue toe. No curtains moved. What did she do in that house all day?

The front door opened as he walked up the steps, and she appeared like a spirit in a black dress. She didn't have on the red sweater. That, at least, was a relief. But the scent of peppermint swirled around her and reached out to him as he got nearer. Damn, she smelled good. She always made him smile and remember things he hadn't thought of in ages—Christmases, hot chocolate with his family, schnapps at lodge bars. He made it to the top step and stopped.

"Hi, Adam," she said as she walked up to him.

"Josey," he said cautiously, handing her the mail.

"Thank you."

"You're welcome." He wondered if he'd done something to lead her on. A smile could be interpreted the wrong way. His smile faded. Then he didn't know what else to do but turn and walk away.

She looked confused as he left. She watched him cross the street before going back into her house.

He walked into the Fergusons' yard, feeling like a prick. Hell, he didn't want to hurt her. But he didn't want what she wanted . . . whatever that was. What *did* she want?

Mrs. Ferguson, a stout woman of about sixty, was hand-trimming the grass bordering her driveway with a pair of cuticle scissors. She was bundled in a fuzzy wool cardigan buttoned to her neck, and she wore a pair of pink gloves with the fingers cut out. Mrs. Ferguson was a nitpicker. Her husband spent a lot of time at his club, which was really a cigar shop downtown, to get away from her. It had taken Adam nearly a year to get her mail delivery exactly how she liked it. Flats together, folded and secured with a rubber band. Letters always separate. The two things placed in the mailbox side by side, never stacked.

"Hello, Mrs. Ferguson," he said as he opened her box and put the mail in.

"Nice to see you, Adam," she said. "That happens every day, you know."

He stopped and reached into his bag for the mail for the next couple of houses. "I'm sorry, what?" he asked absently.

"Josey. She watches you walk across the street every day."

Adam looked up.

"She's a nice girl." Mrs. Ferguson lifted herself to her feet with a grunt. "It's too bad no one sees it."

"What do you mean?"

"You aren't from here. You don't know the reputation Josey earned when she was a child."

"What sort of reputation?"

"That girl was the meanest, rudest, most unhappy child I've ever known. She could pitch the loudest fits when she didn't get what she wanted, so loud I could hear her from inside my house. I think she broke just about everything her mother ever owned. And she threw tantrums in public just as often. Ask anyone if you don't believe me. Every store owner in town has a story, and a bill. She used to steal candy. Her father was the only one who could control her, but he was hardly ever around. Her mother had her hands full. That's why Margaret never sent Josey to school. She hired tutors to teach her at home."

"*Josey*?" Adam said incredulously.

"I know. If I hadn't seen it for myself on many occasions, I'd find it hard to believe too. She grew up to be so pleasant.

But she looks sad, don't you think? She reminds me of Rapunzel. You know, like in the fairy tale. The only time she leaves that house is to take her mother to her few social activities, or to run errands for her."

No, Adam thought. That's not the only time she leaves.

He turned to look at her house, more curious than he wanted to be.

Rapunzel had been sneaking out of the castle.

5

Lemon Drops

After leaving the letters with her mother, Josey hurried up to her bedroom and went to her window. Adam was still in the Fergusons' yard. With a gasp, she took a step back when he suddenly turned to look at her house.

Adam was acting strangely and she had a bad feeling this had something to do with Friday night. They had a system, a routine, every day very much the same. She'd obviously startled him by stepping outside of that. While there was a part of her that relished the thought of Adam seeing her in a different way, she was mostly terrified of losing what she already had with him. She went to her closet and opened the door.

"Don't give me any more advice," she said.

Della Lee was reading through one of the old notebooks from her box. She was still dressed in most, if not all, of her clothing. Her hair was in a bun today, precariously held in place by her tiara. She looked up and said, "What?"

"I said, don't give me any more advice. Stop trying to help me. I don't particularly like the way your plan is working out."

"Why?"

"Because Adam is acting funny," she said. "If you hadn't encouraged me to go out Friday night, I never would have seen him at the festival and . . . and freaked him out."

"Did you touch him inappropriately? I never told you to do that."

"Of course I didn't touch him inappropriately!"

Della Lee closed the notebook she was reading, then she scratched her forehead. She was getting a little more pale every day, her skin becoming this glowing sort of white transparency. Maybe she'd gotten sick from swimming in the river at this time of year. Well, it served her right. Who goes swimming in the Green Cove River in November? "Then how exactly did you freak him out?"

"By showing up outside of this," Josey waved her arm, indicating her room, "in makeup and my hair down."

"Oh my God, you mean he found out you're a woman? What if this gets out? What will you do when people start treating you like an adult instead of a ten-year-old?"

Josey snorted. "Like that's going to happen."

"Right," Della Lee said. "You'll actually have to stop acting like a ten-year-old first."

Josey frowned, then reached over to the false wall in the closet and slid it back. She took out a bag of white chocolate and peanut butter popcorn and a packet of Little Debbie Swiss Cake Rolls.

Della Lee leaned away while she did this, then sat back up. "This is what I'm talking about. This closet took a lot of planning. It looks like years went into it. This closet is the fantasy of every shy, chubby kid in America."

Josey went to her desk and sat. "Every shy, chubby kid in America fantasizes about having a middle-aged woman living in her closet? I didn't know that."

"I am *not* middle-aged," Della Lee said. "I'm just saying if you spent half the time that went into this closet fixing what's outside of it, maybe your mailman wouldn't look at you like an alien every time he sees you in public."

"You're pointing things out to me like I don't know what's wrong," Josey said, ripping open the popcorn bag. "I know what's wrong, so stop assuming that I want to change. I'm fine with the way things are."

"You're dying with the way things are," Della Lee said harshly, causing Josey to lower the handful of popcorn she was about to put in her mouth. "You're going to lose yourself in this, Josey. It's going to happen if you don't change. I know. I lost myself trying to find happiness in things that didn't love me back."

Josey hesitated, looking at the popcorn in her hand, before giving in and eating it. It was always easier after that. She chewed and swallowed. There. "I hate to break this to you, but I don't think you're the best person to be giving advice on relationships," she said, feeling better. "I'm not listening to you anymore."

"Oh, but I *am* the best person," she insisted. "You have to understand the wrong way to have a relationship to be able to do it right. I'm a bona fide expert in the wrong way."

Josey turned in her seat to face the closet. "Okay, you can give me one last piece of advice. One. Then you give this a rest. Make it good."

"One last piece of advice. Oh, the pressure." Della Lee thought about it a moment, then she said, "Julian and I met at a bar. I was there with some girls from the Eat and Run. I was sort of seeing someone, one of my customers from the diner, so I wasn't really looking. No, that's not true. I always looked. That was wrong thing number one. When I saw Julian, my breath literally left my body. He walked over to me and I felt like I was going to die, sort of shivery and lightheaded. But when he finally reached me, everything was fine. I let him take my heart before we even left the bar. Wrong thing number two. And, Jesus, we had the best sex of my life that night! He moved in two days later. Wrong thing number three." She smiled ruefully. "Julian is in his element in a bar. He moves so slowly, you don't realize how good he is. He's like a spider. You don't know you're trapped until it's too late. But that's why we were so good together, or so bad. Julian had never met another spider until he met me."

Josey waited for something more, but Della Lee had that satisfied look of someone who had made her point. "Let me get this straight," Josey said. "The one thing you want to leave me with, your last significant piece of advice to me is, basically, don't fall in love with Julian."

Della Lee shrugged. "Well, I wish someone had said it to *me*."

Chloe remembered the story Jake had told her about his first year away at school when he was a boy. He fell in love with a skinny stray cat that would skulk around the dining hall during meals. Every day, Jake would offer it sausage or egg from breakfast and pepperoni or hamburger from lunch. Every day, it ran away from him. But Jake didn't give up. Even when he had the stomach flu, he snuck out of the infirmary to try to feed it. He was not going to let it down. He would watch it from classroom windows. He even made up a poem about it that he sent home to his mother in a letter. Three months later, the little cat was finally hungry enough to trust him. It never occurred to Jake that the cat wouldn't eventually come to him. Look at what he offered, after all.

All weekend, alone in the apartment, Chloe would catch herself almost calling for Jake when something funny was on the television, or when she was doing a crossword puzzle and had a question. It finally occurred to her Sunday evening that this was probably what Jake intended. *He knows you want your space,* Adam had said. Space enough for her to see how much she needed him. She was that cat, just sitting there getting hungrier and hungrier. She was doing exactly what he wanted her to do, confident that she was going to come to him eventually.

Look at what he offered, after all.

Chloe knew some people from Jake's office went for after-work drinks at Jiggery's, the pub on the square across from the courthouse. Jake wouldn't be there Monday because it was his dinner night at his parents' house, so she made plans to be at the pub that night. She wanted Jake's coworkers to see her. She wanted it to get back to Jake that she was happily out on her own, thank you very much. And maybe, just maybe, she could get some information from his coworkers. She desperately wanted to know about the woman who had caused all this trouble. *Who was at the office party three months ago,* she would say casually, *you know, the Beasley case celebration?*

After work on Monday, she went home and changed clothes and carefully applied her makeup. She wanted to look good, but she didn't want to look like she was trying too hard. It took a while to find the balance. A few hours later she walked into Jiggery's, feeling excited and proactive. She stood just inside the door and looked around . . . and slowly realized she didn't see anyone she knew. She'd spent so much time getting ready that she'd gotten there too late. Her shoulders dropped as she went to the bar and ordered a lemon drop.

She was aware of his stare before she was aware of him. It was like feeling rain in the air before it falls. She found him on the other side of the bar, staring at her. He was beautiful, like he'd been carefully drawn with a charcoal pencil, every line perfect, every smudge deliberate. She was a little startled when he moved, to see that he was real. He picked up his drink and walked toward her.

She watched him, feeling breathless, and she wasn't sure why. "I don't want to bother you," he said when he reached her, his voice the melody to all her favorite songs, "and I swear I'm not trying to pick you up, but would you mind if I sit here? I'm meeting some friends and I can see the door better from this side."

She was finally able to take a deep breath. What was

the matter with her? Why was she panicking? It wasn't like she'd never been hit on before. She just wished someone Jake knew was here to see it. "Be my guest."

He took the stool beside her. "Are you okay?"

"I'm fine," she said, because she didn't want to say that she felt like she'd lost her left arm. She didn't want to say she was afraid that she couldn't function on her own. So she stuck with *I'm fine*. That's what she told Hank at the security gate, and everyone who called that weekend, and Jake's father, who'd come to see her at the shop today. But he looked so much like Jake, with those strange, lovely light green eyes, that she had to stand so far away from him she was practically in the storeroom. "Why do you ask?"

"The look on your face, for one. This book, for another." He gestured toward the bar without taking his eyes off her.

She finally looked away from him and found, next to her drink, a book titled *A Girl's Guide to Keeping Her Guy*. It looked new, as all books that came to her did, but this one was dated. On the cover was a young woman circa the 1950s, wearing crinoline, high heels and a creaseless half-apron. She was serving coffee to a young man who was reading a newspaper in a living room by a fire. "Oh, that," she said, as if taking a self-help book to a bar was the sanest thing in the world to do. She quickly turned the book over, hiding its cover.

"Are you worried about keeping your guy?" he asked gently. "If you don't mind my asking."

"It's just . . ." *Crap*. Books had gone crazy. That was all there was to it. She wouldn't be admitting this to a perfect stranger if it weren't for them. "I found out last week that my boyfriend cheated on me."

"Damn," he said. He looked away and lifted his beer mug to his lips. "Looks like we're in the same boat. Last week my girlfriend took off without a word."

"Damn."

He smiled at that. "If you're here, you must not be taking this book too seriously."

"If you're here, you must not think your girlfriend is coming back."

"Hearts break. There's nothing you can do except wait for them to heal. Alcohol helps. So does talking to someone about it."

That was all the prompting she needed. "I want to know who it was," she confided, moving in closer to him. It was almost like a pull, like the way a man might pull a woman into an embrace, but he didn't even have to touch her. "I want to know who he slept with. I can't stop thinking about it. All I know is that she was at an office party three months ago and that's when it happened. Some people from his workplace come here. I was going to ask around, but I got here too late."

He was nodding as she spoke, encouraging her. "The courthouse crowd?"

"The DA's office."

"How about this: I'll keep my ear to the bar for you. See what I can find out."

His offer startled her, but at the same time she accepted it without question. He made her feel heady, like her thoughts weren't straight, but it was almost a relief. "I've never seen you here before."

"And I've never seen you. I'm here most weekend nights. I just happened to be here tonight to meet some friends." His eyes drifted over her shoulder. He grabbed his beer and slid off the stool. "And they just walked in. If you ever want to talk again, you know where to find me."

She turned on her stool as he moved past her. She'd known his hair was pulled back into a tail, but she didn't realize how long it was until he turned his back on her. It was beautiful. She wanted to touch it. "Wait, what's your name?"

He smiled at her over his shoulder. He didn't wink. He didn't make it cheesy. "Julian."

Jake's cell phone rang just as his mother served cocktails in the living room. It had been a long time since he'd had to have dinner at his parents' house alone. Sitting there without Chloe, he felt like an exposed wound his mother wanted to bandage but his father kept poking. Jake was the only son of Kyle and Faith Yardley. His mother softened him like clay. She'd fought Jake's father over sending Jake to boarding school, but Kyle Yardley wanted his son to have character and independence, and staying here with a mother who spoiled him mercilessly was not going to achieve that. Kyle Yardley withheld his approval because it was the way generations of green-eyed Yardley men had always shown love for their sons. *You can do better. You're capable of more.*

"Jake, you know I don't like you to answer calls while you're here. We don't get to see you enough as it is," his mother said in a mock scold.

He set his drink down and took his cell out of his pocket. "It might be work." In fact, he hoped it would be work. His parents knew that he and Chloe were having problems. Jake would feel a hell of a lot better if he didn't have to discuss it with them to the clinking rhythm of silverware on their best china. It would be such a *dignified* thing, making his heart an acceptable dinner topic by turning it into polite conversation.

He took the phone out to the porch. The night was blue-black and brittle, a perfect late-fall evening. His mother had already decorated for Thanksgiving with swags of leaves, artful displays of gourds and a wreath on the door she made every year from the bittersweet growing beside the guesthouse in back.

He flipped open his phone and said, "Hello?"

"Jake, it's Brandon."

Thank God. It *was* work. Brandon was a fellow ADA. "What's up, Bran?"

"I'll get straight to the point," Brandon said, which Jake didn't find alarming. Brandon began every conversation this way. If he was going to lunch, he'd say, *I'll get straight to the point. I'm going to McDonald's.* "I went to Jiggery's after work, and then came home and realized I'd left my wallet there. Long story short, I went back and Chloe was there."

Jake, pacing the porch to keep warm, suddenly stopped. "Chloe was at Jiggery's? Alone?"

"No, that's just it. She was talking with someone. His name is Julian something. I can't remember his last name. I've seen him in court a few times. Petty stuff, but he's a hitter. I know you and Chloe are having some problems, but I thought you needed to know this."

His body felt coiled, ready to spring. He was not going to let Chloe get hurt again, by anyone. Not that he thought she would actually go off with another man. She said she would die first. She wouldn't really . . . no, of course not. Chloe wouldn't do that. But, God, just the *thought* of it. He couldn't imagine what she must be going through knowing,

knowing he'd been with someone else. "Thanks, Bran. I'll go now."

Jake closed his phone and put it back in his jacket pocket. He turned to go inside, to get his coat and make his excuses, only to find his father at the front door, leaning in the doorway with his drink in his hand. "Trouble?" Kyle asked, almost leisurely.

"I have to go, Dad. I'm sorry."

"No, you don't."

"It's work . . ."

"I heard the whole thing. It's Chloe. I told you this when she kicked you out, son. Give her some space, some time. You're not doing yourself any favors by having people keep tabs on her, then showing up wherever she is. You shouldn't have told her in the first place." Though everyone in the DA's office that night had agreed not to say anything because it would jeopardize all the work that had gone into winning the Beasley murder case, word had somehow leaked out to the courthouse about Jake-the-wonderboy's indiscretion with an unnamed woman. It had eventually reached his father, who just happened to be the mayor of Bald Slope. Kyle had managed to stop the rumor like a tourniquet, not letting it bleed outside the building. But even he didn't know whom Jake had slept with. That at least stayed in the office, though it killed Kyle not to know, and Jake wasn't telling.

"I'm not trying to keep tabs on her," Jake said.

"I went to see Chloe today, at her shop."

Jake's hands fisted at his sides. His father told him not to see Chloe, yet he went to see her himself. "I appreciate that you're concerned, but I can handle this on my own."

"No, you can't. She could barely stand to have *me* near

her. The balance of power was never equal between the two of you. You stand back. You let her realize that she needs you. If you push too hard, she's going to walk. And don't think I'm saying this for your benefit. It's her I'm worried about. Chloe is good for you. I want her in this family. You messed up once, don't do it again, because if you do it again, you'll lose her for good and she'll be left with nothing and nowhere to go. Do you want that?"

"Of course not."

Kyle pushed himself away from the doorway. "Then come inside and compliment your mother on her dress and assure her that everything is going to be all right."

"I don't suppose you ever did anything like this," Jake said as he watched his father disappear inside.

"If I did, you can be damn sure I never told your mother about it," Kyle called out into the darkness.

Tuesday afternoon, after a long day of nothing new, of trying not to watch for Jake or think of the mystery that was Julian, of pushing a slightly scorched *Finding Forgiveness* off the counter for the eighty-second time, Chloe was about to clean the grill and reluctantly go home. But then she saw Josey walk across the rotunda toward her and her day suddenly got a little brighter.

"Josey!" she said. "I'm so glad you came by. You rushed away so quickly at the festival. I didn't have any way to contact you to find out if you were all right."

"I know. I came by to tell you I'm sorry," Josey said as she approached the counter. "I'm just a little . . . ten years old sometimes." She made a face, as if it pained her to say that. "I have a cell phone. I'll start checking messages if you want to call me. Do you have something to write on? I'll give you the number."

Chloe took one of her business cards from the little stand by the register and handed it and a pen to her. Josey turned the business card over and wrote a number on the blank side.

"So, what can I get you today?" Chloe asked. "Grilled tomato and cheese?"

"No, thanks," Josey said, capping the pen and putting it beside the card after she'd finished writing.

"Oh, come on," Chloe said. "I make a great fried egg sandwich. Want to try it?"

Chloe stared at her with an encouraging smile until Josey finally laughed and nodded. "Okay."

"Great!" Chloe put on a pair of disposable gloves, then she took butter and two eggs from the under-the-counter fridge. "Go ahead and take a business card. You can call me here if you want. And the bottom number is my cell." She plopped a pat of butter onto the grill. When the butter melted, she cracked the eggs into it, close enough for their whites to merge. While they sizzled, she buttered two slices of sourdough bread and put them on the grill.

"I didn't know this place was called Red's," Josey said, reading the card.

Chloe smiled when she thought of her great-grandfather. "Another family tradition. My great-grandfather had red hair. So did my mother." Chloe sprinkled the eggs with salt and pepper and a pinch of dill, then turned them over with her spatula. She flipped the quickly toasting bread too. She'd spent her childhood watching her great-grandfather do this, and here at the shop was the only time she felt him near anymore. "Do you want this for here or to go?"

"To go."

Chloe sprinkled a little more salt and pepper on the eggs, made sure the yolks had firmed ever so slightly, then topped them with cheese. She let the cheese melt before scooping the eggs up and putting them on the buttered sourdough. She wrapped the sandwich and bagged it, then turned around to Josey. "On the house," she said, waving away Josey's attempt to pay her. "Why don't you stick around for a minute while I clean up? We can leave together."

Josey leaned against the counter as Chloe turned around to scrape the grill. "I see you fished the book out of the trash," Josey said.

Chloe looked over her shoulder. *Finding Forgiveness* was back on the counter, close to Josey. Josey was stroking the cover, making sympathetic noises when she noticed the scorched places from where it had appeared on the grill in front of Chloe that morning. Chloe could almost hear it purr from the attention. Shameless book. "Um, yeah."

"Where do you get your books? The library? The bookstore?"

Chloe hesitated. She finished with the grill, then wiped down the counters. She'd always wanted to reveal her relationship with books, about how they came to her. She wanted to be told it was all right, that strange things happened to other people too. But she could never bring herself to do it. The fear that she alone was odd, that no one would understand, was too strong. "I collect them," she finally said, going to the sink. "I have hundreds of boxes of them in storage."

"Wow."

"Do you read a lot?" Chloe shut the water off after washing a few things.

"I have favorites I read over and over. Every once in a while I'll pick one up at the grocery store."

"You can borrow any of mine," she said, wiping her hands. "In fact, let's go to the storage rental now!"

Josey looked surprised. "Now?"

"I just need to cash out, then I'm finished here. Do you mind?"

"No," Josey said. "But you don't have to do this just for me."

"It's for me too. I haven't been to the storage rental in a while. I have some of my great-grandparents' things there. Maybe it's time I decorate the apartment with some of my stuff." Chloe cashed out and put the money bag in the safe in the back room. After she locked the security gate, they walked outside. The days were getting shorter and the sun was already low in the sky. "I walked to work today. My apartment is about two blocks away, if you want to take my car."

"That's okay. I'm parked right there." Josey pointed to the far corner of the park, where there were two spaces, one occupied by a blue Land Rover and the other by a sparkling metallic gold Cadillac that looked like a large Las Vegas dancer.

They walked down the steps and crossed the park. Chloe stopped at the SUV, but Josey continued on to the enormous gold Cadillac. "Oh, I thought . . ." Chloe shook her head and walked ahead. "Well, this is a nice car."

Josey laughed as she electronically unlocked the doors with the device on her key chain. "It's on loan from Elvis."

When they got in, Chloe told her the name of the storage rental. Josey knew where it was and headed toward the highway. For the first few minutes, Chloe surreptitiously looked around the car. Cars were very personal and they usually said a lot about their drivers. This car was a couple of years old, but it still smelled new. Everything inside was very neat, very clean, and she was afraid to touch anything. There was nothing personal, or even the slightest bit messy, about it. It wasn't Josey at all.

When she finally looked up from her perusal and saw where they were, she suddenly said, "Oh, wait! Stop right here!"

Josey came to a sudden stop in the street. "What? What's wrong?"

She had cut through a neighborhood just south of downtown. They were on a street called Summertime Road, so named because it was the route the old summertime residents used to take when they first entered the town for their summer stays. The Bald Slope natives always watched this road, waiting for them. Little kids perched in trees to better see the caravan of carriages, then, later, automobiles. Small boxy houses lined the street, looking like old wooden children's blocks left outside, light pink and yellow and green.

"Right here," Chloe said. "This house. What do you think of it?"

Josey looked at Chloe curiously, then leaned forward and stared at the buttercup-yellow house with white trim. There was a realtor's sign in the neat front yard. "Same owners for over thirty years. A neighborhood that's being revitalized, lots of young families moving in." Josey sat back in her seat, shaking her head. "But they're asking entirely too much for it. It's been on the market for over a year and they haven't budged on the price. They're too emotionally attached."

Chloe laughed. "How do you know all that?"

"It was brought to us as an investment opportunity. We were interested, but not at that price."

"Oh." Chloe turned back to the house. Money had never meant a great deal to her, but at that moment she envied Josey's wealth. Josey didn't want to buy the house, but she *could*. "They've had a couple of open houses over the past year. It has the most wonderful library, to the right, just off the entrance. That window there. See? In a small house, you don't expect something like that. When I first walked in and saw it, I remember thinking, *This is it*." Chloe sighed. "I love this house. I pass by it all the time. Even if where I'm going is in the other direction. Jake thinks it's funny."

"He doesn't like it?"

"He likes it. He likes it because I like it. But at the price they're asking, we'd never be able to afford it without asking Jake's parents for money. Jake has big issues with that. They gave him the apartment we live in, and he feels awkward enough about that as it is."

"So, you don't own the apartment together?"

"No, just him."

Josey looked worried. "Is he going to give it to you? I mean if the two of you don't get back together?"

"I don't know." The car was quiet for a moment. Life without Jake. She felt panic ballooning in her stomach, but she feigned a smile. She was *not* going to have an anxiety attack in front of Josey. "That's it. I just wanted to show it to you."

"It's a beautiful house," Josey said.

As they drove away, Chloe couldn't help but look behind her, watching it disappear. "Yes, it is."

The sun had almost set by the time they reached the

storage rental place—a large sprawling maze of low-slung buildings on an inky black tarmac. The security lights lit up the area like noon. The rent she shelled out for this place would pay for a small apartment. Each rental was temperature controlled and had overhead fluorescent lights.

When Chloe lifted the bay door to her unit and turned on the lights, Josey walked in and said, "Wow, look at all this stuff."

Chloe followed her. She had forgotten how much this place smelled like the farmhouse—long since gone—of furniture polish and Borax detergent. She felt calmer all of a sudden. Why hadn't she come here sooner? When she sold her great-grandparents' land to a developing company, they'd let her keep the things in the house for months after closing. She sold some of the furniture during that time. Then, when she met Jake, the rest went directly into storage. Jake never suggested that she move her things into the apartment, and she knew she was partially to blame for that. She was so excited to be with him, to move in with him and into his life, it never occurred to her to bring any of herself with her.

Chloe walked to a long bank of boxes, stacked chest high, a lifetime of books that had come to her. "So, what do you like to read?" She put a hand on one of the marked boxes. "I have mysteries. I have romance. I have history. Self-help. Classics."

"Romance," Josey said.

"I have the most of those, ironically," Chloe said, walking over to the boxes on the far end. Josey followed. "I read these just before I met Jake. Tons of them. As soon as I finished one, there was another."

"How magical," Josey said.

Chloe shifted uncomfortably. "Books aren't always

right. But maybe they weren't meant for me. Maybe they were meant for you. For you and Adam." Chloe lifted the lid of one box and said, "Help yourself."

Josey paused with her mouth open for a moment, as if Chloe had literally shocked the words right out of her. "Um, listen, about Adam. Would you mind not saying anything about me to him? He seems distracted lately, anyway."

"Uh-oh," Chloe said.

"Uh-oh?"

"I sort of already told him."

"Told him what?"

"That you've been interested in him for a while." Chloe laughed at Josey's expression, then reached out and took her hands. "It's a good thing, Josey! Adam isn't seeing anyone. He moved here, so I know he wants to be here, but he's just had some problems adapting. He needs to get out more. You could ask him out. There's nothing wrong with that. Are you all right?"

Instantly, Josey smiled and nodded. "Oh, yes. Yes, I'm fine."

"Are you sure?"

"Of course! What could be wrong? I have my choice of romance novels. I'm in heaven."

Josey began to go through the books, so Chloe walked around, touching things, smiling. There was the headboard of her old childhood bed, the same bed her mother slept in as a child. The pie safe. The jelly cabinet. These things weren't meant to just take up space in order to make a point. They'd been waiting all this time for her to *use* them. Furniture was a lot more patient than books. Furniture waited for space in your life instead of just showing up and demanding attention.

About a half hour later, Josey had a respectable pile of

books on the floor. "I'll get these back to you as soon as possible," she called.

Chloe wove her way around ladder-back chairs and braided rugs rolled up and set on end. "Don't bother. Take all the time you need. They'll make their way back to me eventually," she said as she reached Josey. She found an empty box and together they loaded the books into it. "What are you doing this weekend?"

Josey shrugged. "Taking my mother to tea on Saturday. That's about it."

"Do you want to go out? I don't think I could stand another weekend in that apartment alone."

"I don't know. Maybe," Josey said doubtfully. She put the lid on the box and picked it up. "So, what did you decide to take with you?"

Chloe turned and looked around the storage bay. "Nothing."

"No?" Josey said, surprised.

"No." Chloe took a deep breath, and the decision was there before she was even fully aware of it. She needed these things. She'd tucked too much of herself away as it was. But she also needed a place to put them. This wasn't exactly the happy ending books had led her to believe. But what did she expect from paper and string and glue? She shouldn't have trusted them in the first place. "I think I need to move out of Jake's apartment."

Late that night, Josey was finally able to get the box of books out of her car and bring it up to her room. She stopped by the kitchen to get the fried egg sandwich from the refrigerator's crisper drawer, where she'd hidden it earlier for

Della Lee. She knew now that Della Lee did eat, at night when everyone was asleep. She probably washed then too. Maybe even did laundry. For days Helena had been complaining about things moving around the house overnight, and about faucets being left on and the refrigerator door being left slightly ajar, causing the milk carton and jam jars to sweat.

As she headed up the stairs, she didn't have to see Helena to know she'd popped her head out of her bedroom. "It's okay, Helena. Go back to sleep," she said, then heard Helena's door click shut in the darkness.

She got to her room and went to her closet. "I found out the real reason Adam is acting funny," she said when she opened the door.

Della Lee didn't look up from reading one of her notebooks. "Why?"

"Chloe told him I was in love with him," she said morosely as she sat down with the box and sandwich bag.

This was obviously worthy of her undivided attention, so Della Lee finally looked up. "How did she know?"

"I told her." Josey still couldn't believe it. Adam was more secret than chocolate, yet she had *told* Chloe. What was the matter with her?

Della Lee rolled her eyes. "I can't believe you blamed me."

"Well, it never would have happened if it weren't for you."

"You're welcome." Della Lee indicated the box. "What do you have there? Oh my God, you didn't go to my house again, did you?"

"No. Chloe loaned me some books." Josey took the sandwich bag off the box and put it in front of Della Lee. "Here. It's a cold fried egg sandwich."

"No, thanks. I'm not hungry. You have it," Della Lee

said, and Josey didn't need to be told twice. After today, pride seemed stupid. "What kind of books did she loan you?"

"Romance novels," Josey said as she took the sandwich out of the bag.

Della Lee held her arms out on both sides, as if to take up as much space as possible in the closet. "Don't you dare put them in here."

Josey took a bite of the sandwich and looked at Della Lee curiously. "But that's where the rest of my books are."

"Don't you get it yet? You find out your mailman knows you love him and what do you do? You bring back romance novels to read in your closet."

"Well, obviously I can't read them in my closet. You're there."

Della Lee made a frustrated sound. "Adam knows how you feel about him. Why don't you do something about it? Ask him out. *Something.*"

"You sound like Chloe. He doesn't want to be asked out. He found out I was interested in him, and he backed off. Way off. He's wondering what he's done to encourage me, how he could have prevented it from happening. I'm not going to make either of us feel more uncomfortable than we already do. Soon this will all blow over and we'll get back to the way things were."

"When are you ever going to get fed up enough to do something about this life of yours?"

Josey snapped her fingers in an aha! moment. "I know, I'll start with kicking you out."

There was a knock at the door, which made Josey jump. She hurriedly wrapped her sandwich and wiped her mouth. "Scoot over," Josey whispered, trying to push the box into the closet.

"No way. You are not putting that in here."

"Della Lee . . ."

Another knock.

"Just a minute," Josey called, turning to push the box under her bed, then stuffing the rest of the egg sandwich into the bag. She threw it under the bed too. She quickly closed the closet door on Della Lee, then stood and said, "Come in."

The door opened. It was Helena. She was wearing a long robe and her hair was in paper rollers, covered with the silk scarf Josey had given her for her birthday in the summer. She stood in the doorway and looked around Josey's bedroom leerily. "Oldsey," she said, bringing a small peanut butter jar out of her deep robe pocket, "I bring this."

Josey walked over to Helena in the doorway. "Peanut butter?"

Helena unscrewed the lid and showed her. "Dirt."

"Oh," Josey said, nodding though she had no idea what Helena was talking about. "Right. Dirt."

"Look. Look what I do." Josey watched as Helena sprinkled dirt in a thin line on the floor at the threshold. Then she handed the jar to Josey. "You do at that door." She pointed to the closet across the room.

"You want me to sprinkle dirt at my closet door?"

"Yes. Dirt from my home. My sister send." Helena indicated the jar. "It keep bad thing away. No more downstairs."

"Oh, I see." Helena knew something was going on, and she knew it had something to do with Josey's closet. Great.

Josey went to the closet and sprinkled dirt at the door to make Helena feel better. Every so often Josey would find that Helena had sewn small crosses into the hems of Josey's dresses for luck, and she always knocked on door casings three times before entering a room that had been empty for more than a couple of hours, to chase ghosts away. Helena didn't speak often of where she came from, but she held fast to beliefs that were obviously deeply rooted.

She brought the jar back to Helena, who was nodding now. "There. Oldsey sleep. No bad thing."

"Thank you, Helena."

"Oldsey a good girl," Helena said, and walked away.

Josey closed the door, then went directly to her bed.

"You live in a crazy house," Della Lee called from the closet.

"You can always leave," Josey said, going to her knees and crawling under the bed to get her sandwich bag.

"And miss all this fun? I don't think so."

Sour Patch

Saturday afternoon Margaret changed her shoes three times, her purse twice, and snapped at Josey for no other reason than because she was standing there, waiting patiently to take Margaret to tea.

Margaret *hated* having tea with Livia Lynley-White. She second-guessed everything she wore and actually practiced answers to possible questions Livia might ask. Margaret knew she should be past the point of feeling intimidated by this woman. Livia was ninety-one years old now. No one that old should still have so much power.

But she did have power. She was the only person in town, besides Marco, who knew about Margaret's affair. It had happened over forty years ago, but Livia would not let it go. Every month, like a queen, Livia commanded Margaret to join her for tea, and every month Margaret had no choice but to go. They met in a private, sectioned-off area of the tearoom in what used to be Livia's old family home, the oldest home in Bald Slope. Thirty years ago, at Marco's encouraging, Livia had donated the house to the preservation society and it was turned into a museum with a tearoom. Livia thought Marco could do no wrong. She'd even consulted him on the perfect place to build her new home on the mountain. She lived there now with her nurse, her maid and a cowed granddaughter. Though it had been three decades since she'd actually lived in the historic home, Livia still thought it her right to come and go as she pleased, entertaining and sometimes offending tour groups and walking into the kitchen and criticizing the pastry chef like she was still the mistress.

Josey finally drove Margaret to the Lynley-White Historical Home, though Margaret still wasn't happy with her choice of shoes. But it would be even worse if she was late, so she made do. Once there, Josey walked with Margaret into the private room. Margaret always insisted on this. She wanted Livia to see that her daughter was attentive. But also, since her hip replacement, Margaret wasn't very steady on her feet without her cane, and she wanted Josey there to lean on to keep from stumbling. She never walked with her cane around Livia. She didn't want to give her that satisfaction. Livia had never needed a cane. She was as tall and bony and straight as a calcified tree.

Livia was already seated in the tiny room. She checked her watch pointedly, though Margaret knew she was on time. When they reached the table, Livia said, "Josey, wait outside with Amelia."

"Yes, Mrs. Lynley-White," Josey said, then left.

"Margaret, what are you waiting for? Sit down."

"Yes, Livia." Margaret pulled out the chair and sat, with considerable effort going into doing it gracefully and not wincing.

"Your daughter looks different," Livia said, her long knobby fingers toying with the pearls at her neck. "What's different?"

Margaret put her napkin in her lap. "I don't think anything is different."

"She was never a pretty child, was she?"

"No, Livia."

"We're ready!" Livia yelled, and Margaret closed her eyes briefly. The curator, always the curator, slid back the partition that separated the small space from the rest of the tearoom and rolled in the cart with the tea service. All the other employees refused to do it. "It's still such a surprise, you being a beauty. It's hard to believe she's your child. In fact, knowing your ways, I would've even doubted she was Marco's child if she didn't have his eyes," Livia continued as the curator poured the tea into fine china cups. "But my Amelia isn't pretty, either. They need to stay that way, to stay at home and take care of us. The uglier the girl, the more helpful she is, that's been my experience. Pretty girls aren't very trustworthy."

"Josey is going to stay at home," Margaret said as the curator set small bowls of sugar cubes and lemon wedges on the table, then a three-tiered server laden with cucumber finger sandwiches, flaky raspberry jam puffs and thin slices of rum-and-butter cake. She made haste and left without a word. Lucky woman.

"Hmm, you hope." Livia stirred two sugars into her tea. "So tell me about your month. I heard you went to the ladies' club meeting."

"Yes. It was very nice."

"And that you had a manicure and pedicure the day before you went."

Margaret smiled and nodded, annoyed that Livia asked questions she already knew the answers to. She was just testing Margaret. Livia had an endless network of acquaintances who kept tabs on things for her. Margaret was always aware that, every public place she went, there was someone who would, inadvertently or not, be Livia's telescope into her life. "That's my routine."

"Rawley Pelham still takes Annabelle Drake to the ladies' club meeting in his cab, doesn't he?"

"I believe he does, yes," Margaret said.

"He might be sweet on her, I heard."

Margaret reached for the sugar tongs. "Oh?"

"Interested, Margaret?" Livia said slyly.

Margaret wondered at the power of her own heart. All these years of doing what she was supposed to, of sacrificing happiness for her place here in Bald Slope, and it still hurt. Her damn old heart still hurt for him. Three sugars later, Margaret managed to say, "No, Livia."

"It was a long time ago. Surely you don't still have feelings for him. I'm disappointed in you. I've tried very hard over the years to give you guidance, direction."

"And I'm very appreciative."

"Bald Slope is a different place from your Asheville. We have different rules here. Rules that can't be forgotten. I'd always hoped you would take up where I leave off, making sure things are done right here, when I die."

Margaret took a sip of tea instead of commenting on the improbability of Livia ever dying.

"Everyone said you knew the rules. Pretty little Margaret from Asheville. *She doesn't do anything wrong.* Oh, how everyone used to envy you. But I knew you weren't good enough for Marco. It's a shame he's not around to see how much I've helped you."

"A shame," Margaret said tightly.

Livia had been in love with Marco. Margaret knew it from the moment she met her. And Livia had watched and watched for some misstep, anything that would dishonor Margaret, make her not worthy of the great Marco Cirrini. And Livia found it, all right. She had to have known about all of Marco's affairs, but that was acceptable in Livia's eyes. Perhaps she'd even hoped that one day he would have an affair with *her*.

But for Margaret to have a little happiness?

That would never do.

Out in the main tearoom, Josey sat with Livia's granddaughter Amelia at a table near the windows. They were served tea, but Amelia just stared out into the side yard, watching the leaves whip around.

Amelia was a short, earnest woman who bit her fingernails and wore her blond hair in a bowl cut. She'd been bred for this. When Amelia was born, Livia took one look at her with her red splotchy face, her crusty cradle cap and her calm, almost morose disposition, and said, "This one will take care of me." So Amelia's mother, eager to keep her trust fund, had told Amelia all her life what she was going to do. Right after high school graduation, Amelia had moved in with Livia and had been her personal servant ever since.

Josey produced a bag of caramels and chocolates from her purse, knowing from years of these teas that, when allowed a dessert, Amelia always chose the chocolate caramel torte. "Here, Amelia, I brought you this," she said. She always brought Amelia candy, even though it was like trying to make friends with a stuffed doll.

Amelia's eyes slid toward the partition separating them from Livia and Margaret. "I really shouldn't."

"I know."

Amelia took the bag miserably. "You're a bad influence on me. Ma'am-mother always says, 'Don't eat so much! You'll end up like Josey Cirrini.' "

Josey smiled ruefully. "Yes, I'm a warning to all children."

"She doesn't like your mother. I don't know why she invites her to tea."

"And I don't know why my mother accepts. I guess ours is not to reason why. Do you want to walk around outside?"

"No, Ma'am-mother might need me." Amelia opened the bag Josey had given her and pulled out a chocolate. She stared out the window vacantly as she put the chocolate in her mouth.

"Did you ever have plans of your own, Amelia?" Josey suddenly asked. Amelia was in her early forties, and sometimes Josey would look at her and wonder if this was what was going to become of her. It wasn't a cheery thought. "Or do you still? I mean to do something more, something else?"

"It's my job to take care of Ma'am-mother. My father passed away last year, so my mother will probably move in with Ma'am-mother soon, and I'll take care of her too."

Josey hesitated before asking, "Have you ever thought of leaving?"

"Ma'am-mother doesn't like to travel."

"No, I mean just you."

Amelia looked aghast. "Alone?"

That answered that question. "Have you ever been in love?"

Amelia blushed. "No."

"Do you like to read?"

"Not much."

"Ever want to go on vacation? See the ocean?"

Amelia pushed the bag across the table, giving it back to Josey. "You're a bad influence on me."

"Then I really hope a rough, disreputable woman never shows up in your closet," Josey said. "I don't think you'd be able to handle it."

"There's something wrong with you, Josey," Amelia said. "I'm going to go sit over there."

After tea, when they all walked outside, the wind hit them with surprising force. It was getting colder. Crickets were taking up residence in fireplaces. Woolly worms had more black on them than brown. And every persimmon sold at the market turned out to have seeds in the shape of a spoon. Everyone knew what that meant. Natives of Bald Slope were hardwired to recognize the signs that snow was coming. Josey hoped it would be a big snow, even though that seemed too much to ask of November. The big snows came in late winter, even early spring, in western North Carolina.

Livia and Margaret said their goodbyes, their dark coats flapping around them like blackbirds. Livia turned and walked to her car, and Amelia trailed behind her like a stray thought.

Josey and Margaret watched them go, similar expressions on their faces.

Margaret sighed. "Well, that's over."

"Yes," Josey said.

"Until next month."

"Is it just me, or do you imagine it's always going to be a more pleasant experience than it actually ends up being?"

Margaret shook her head. "I stopped believing that a long time ago. Hope is for fools, Josey. Let's go home."

While Josey and Margaret were suffering through tea, Chloe was across town going over apartment rental listings in the newspaper. Jake was doing it again this weekend, not contacting her. He was just waiting. Waiting for her to come to her senses. *Where else would she go?* he was probably saying to himself, not with arrogance, because Jake wasn't arrogant. But he saw some things as simply inevitable. That every Monday night he had to have dinner at his parents' house. That people would always like him. That he and Chloe would always be together. Did he think about that while he was sleeping with the other woman? Was he thinking, *This doesn't matter. This doesn't count. Chloe will always be with me?*

She angrily circled another listing in the paper. She didn't have to depend on Jake for her social life, for the roof over her head, for her sense of security. She was going to take steps to forget all about him. Soon she would forget about his voice, how good it felt to have him around, how amazing his body was, the things he could do to her in bed. And she would stop imagining him making the other woman feel the same way.

She set her pen down on the newspaper. Julian had been in the back of her mind all week, lingering, not pushing. He said he was at Jiggery's most weekends. She could go there tonight and maybe talk to him some more about their shared misery. He understood what it was like to be hurt by someone you love. It was a step, and that's what her life was all about now. Taking steps, random steps, in any direction that took her away from the center of the hurt.

She spent a lot of time with her hair and makeup again. She even used her shimmery eyeshadow. She wore her heeled boots and her short wool plaid skirt and her favorite soft cabled sweater. When she looked at herself in the mirror, she liked what she saw. What she looked like couldn't be the reason he slept with someone else, could it?

She guessed that depended on what the other woman looked like.

When she got to Jiggery's, she spotted Julian right away. He was more handsome than Jake. Or rather, more beautiful. Jake was good-looking in a prosperous kind of way. You could tell he came from money. You could tell he'd worn crisp school uniforms with crests on the blazers. You could tell he knew how to play polo and golf and squash, though, in fact, he didn't anymore. He didn't want his parents' lifestyle. They'd had high hopes for him when he went to law school, but they were sorely disappointed when he went to work at the DA's office. Now, even they could see that he was so good at what he did that he was going to go far.

Julian's confidence was different, mercurial. He could be whatever you wanted him to be. He was seated at the bar, surrounded by women, women who existed only at night, thin sheets of steel, all sharp edges and shine, undulating and unsteady. He was something different to each of them, and that made them swoon and think the other women were no competition at all, because each thought she had the true Julian.

When Julian saw her, he immediately left them to come see her, which felt nice. "Hello there," he said. "I didn't get your name last time."

"It's Chloe."

"Would you like a drink, Chloe? Let's sit." He led her to the end of the bar, past the shiny, undulating women who would simply wait there for him to come back to them. He and Chloe sat and he ordered their drinks, remembering that she'd been drinking a lemon drop last time. "I see you didn't bring a book with you. How are you?"

She nodded. "Fine. Better."

"I'm glad you came. I've been wanting to talk to you. I even showed up here a couple of nights during the week last week to see if you'd be here. Your boyfriend, would his name happen to be Jake Yardley?"

She felt a slight pinch of apprehension. "How did you know that?"

"I've been asking around, and I might have some leads." She looked at him, confused. "You said you wanted to find out who the other woman was," he clarified. "The woman he cheated on you with."

Her heart started to race. "You know who it is?"

"Not yet. But I'm close. There's only been one soap opera in the DA's office in the last three months, and I was told it had to do with a golden boy named Jake Yardley. No one has wanted to give up the details yet."

"I can't believe you'd do something like that for me. You don't even know me." She put her hand to her chest. His eyes followed the movement to her breasts. He didn't look long, but long enough.

"I know hurt when I see it. I guess my next question is, do you want to know her name? There's no going back once you know."

"I want to know," Chloe said without hesitation.

"Then I'll find out for you. I have some connections at the courthouse."

Their drinks arrived and Chloe took a sip of hers, trying not to stare at him outright, but she couldn't help it. "You don't work at the courthouse, do you? I've never seen you there."

"No, but I've had plenty of legal matters settled there, enough to become friendly with people who can help me out if I need it."

"What can I do for you, then? I'd like to be able to help you."

"You can start by taking off your jacket and staying a while." He got off his stool and stood behind her. He slowly slid her jacket off, touching her neck ever so slightly as he did so.

He put her jacket on the bar, then sat beside her again. She felt light-headed. She blinked a few times, trying to corral her thoughts. "So, um, have you heard from your girlfriend?"

"No."

"This must be so hard for you. Did she leave you a note, anything?"

"No." He put both his hands around his beer mug and stared down into it. "We've been fighting a lot lately. After our last fight, she got in her car and left. She'd been acting strangely for a while, depressed and prickly, like she knew she was going to leave and she was just waiting for the next big fight for the excuse. But she didn't take her clothes or purse or anything. Then, a couple of days after she disappeared, a woman came into the house while I was sleeping and took some of her clothes and her wallet. So I know she's still around. She just doesn't want to come back, or see me."

"So, is it over between the two of you?"

"Probably." He met her eyes. "What about you and Jake?"

"I don't know."

He smiled slightly. "You still love him."

She looked away. After a few moments she said, "I can't seem to help it."

"Your Jake, is he tall with blond curly hair?"

She turned back to him curiously. "No."

"Then is he medium height with dark hair and light eerie eyes?"

He was beginning to scare her. "I wouldn't say they were eerie, but yes. Why?"

"Because a big blond and a shorter guy with those eyes just walked in and zeroed in on us. And they look none too pleased." He smiled like it meant nothing, like it actually amused him.

She looked over to the door and locked eyes with Jake. The force of it nearly knocked her over. As much as Julian could do, as much as he wanted to do, he could not affect her the way Jake could. It was the difference between a tickle and a punch.

Jake walked toward her, Adam on his heels. They got caught in the group of shiny women on their way. Walking through that group was like walking into a sudden dust devil. They emerged on the other side looking rumpled and windblown.

By the time they reached her, Julian had disappeared.

She looked around, confused that he could slip away without her even being aware. He was nowhere to be seen.

"Clo, what are you doing?" Jake said. His eyes were all over her, drinking her in like sweet tea with lemonade. He *missed* her. She felt it as clearly as she felt her own sense of loss.

She got off her stool and grabbed her jacket. "It's none of your business."

"You don't know that guy. He's bad news."

"Oh, really?" she snapped. "Let me tell you something, Jake. You lost the right to have any say in my life the moment you slept with another woman."

"I didn't sleep with her."

"You're splitting hairs?" she said incredulously.

"When it's this important, you're damn right I'm splitting hairs. I had sex with her. That was all it was. It didn't mean anything. Everyone was tired, everyone was high on winning, and there were all these emotions looking for release. I didn't make a conscious decision . . ."

"Will you listen to what you're saying?" Chloe's voice was rising and people were starting to stare, but she didn't care. "You're blaming cheating on me on *a murder case*. There was a decision, a decision whether or not to do it, and you made that decision. The case didn't. *You* did. Who was she?"

He paused, and for one brilliant moment she thought he was going to tell her. But then he said, "She was no one."

"Get out of my way." She tried to push him, but he didn't budge.

He took her by the arms. "Chloe, please, just promise me you'll stay away from him."

"I never *ever* told you to stay away from other women! I trusted you."

"I trust you," Jake said. "I don't trust him. He has a record."

She sucked in air so quickly she almost choked. "How do you know that? Have you been spying on me? You don't think I can handle myself. You don't think I can do anything without you. You don't even think I can handle knowing who you slept with. I'll show you, Jake." She barreled past him this time. "I'll show you."

Jake went after her, but she ran to her car in the side lot by the bar and raced out without another word. He watched her car disappear. At least she was heading in the direction of their apartment.

He went back in and found Adam at the bar. He'd already ordered beers.

"Did you know she was going to be here?" Adam asked as Jake took a seat. "Is that why you wanted to come?"

"Someone from work said they'd seen her here earlier in the week, talking to that scumbag. I just wanted to tell her what he was."

"I feel so used."

Jake tried to smile at that. He didn't think it was possible to miss a single living human being this much. When he'd seen her across the bar, his heart had nearly beaten out of his chest. He missed her passionate earthiness, her easy laugh, her warmth. He missed the smell of her skin. He wanted to touch her again. But when she'd seen him, she had looked so profoundly unhappy that his hands had fisted at his sides with frustration. He didn't know how to fix this. And it looked like he'd made things even worse tonight. For the first time, he began to wonder if things were truly going to be all right.

He'd just picked up his beer when he looked across the bar to where Chloe had been seated. Her drink, probably a lemon drop because that was her favorite, was still there. And next to it was a book. He knew it was hers. When he first met her, she was never without a book. And she had more books in storage than he had ever seen one person own. It had always fascinated him that she'd consumed so many words, that her head was full of stories, told a thousand different ways. She'd always seemed a little embarrassed by her books, so he'd never pushed the subject. But this book could be the key to seeing her again. He could return it to her and say he was sorry, start some sort of dialogue. To hell with what his father said.

He put his beer down and began to walk around the bar, keeping his eye on the book. He got caught again in that group of drunk, touchy-feely women along the way. He heard Adam call to him, "Don't panic! They can smell your fear."

Eventually he managed to untangle himself from them.

By the time he reached the other end of the bar, her drink was still there.

But the book was gone.

Chloe woke up feeling parched and headachy.

"Jake," she said automatically, reaching for the other side of the bed. He always made her feel better when she was ill. But when her hand touched his flat, empty side of the bed, she remembered. He wasn't here. He wasn't here and she was. In bed. In her clothes. She sat up slowly, squinting through the pain in her head.

She moved her legs to the side of the bed and sat on the edge, putting her head in her hands. She'd spent hours crying when she got home, crying in a ball on the floor, crying so hard her chest felt like it was going to cave in. It physically hurt to cry that hard. A hard cry could draw walls in, it could bend metal, it could turn a full moon into a sliver.

She began to shiver, so she grabbed her jacket from the bottom of the bed. It smelled like cigarette smoke from the bar. She slowly got up and headed to the kitchen for some water, ignoring *Old Love, New Direction*, which had perched itself on one of the blades of the slow-moving ceiling fan above the couch. *A Girl's Guide to Keeping Her Guy* was sitting primly on the coffee table.

Paper, string and glue.

As she walked she stuffed her hands into the pockets of the jacket. She felt something in the left pocket and pulled it out.

She stopped and stared at it. It was a cocktail napkin, and on it was written a phone number and a name.

Julian.

7

Sugar Daddy

Monday afternoon, on her way to the organic grocery store to pick up the peppermint oil that was finally ready for her mother, Josey stopped by the courthouse to see Chloe. The moment she caught sight of her, even from halfway across the rotunda, she knew something was wrong. Chloe was sitting at one of the two café tables in front of the counter, a cup of coffee in front of her, staring into space.

"Chloe?"

She immediately looked up. When she saw who it was,

she smiled. "Oh, hi, Josey." She didn't have on any makeup, although there was some leftover glitter dotting her brow bone, and her red hair was pulled up into a tangled ponytail. There was sadness under her skin, giving her a fragile, matte pallor.

"What's wrong?"

Chloe stood and picked up her cup. "Nothing, I'm fine," she said as she walked around to the sink and poured out the coffee.

Josey went to the counter. "No, you're not."

Chloe shrugged, her movements uncomfortable. "I guess I was in shock for a while—Jake telling me he'd slept with another woman, then kicking him out. This weekend I think it finally hit me. Bam!"

Josey suddenly felt ashamed of herself for getting so worked up over Della Lee. Chloe had real problems. Josey just had a woman living in her closet. "What can I do?"

"Nothing. I wish there was something you could do, you know, to make this move faster. I just want to hurry and get to the part where it's over and I feel better."

Josey tried to think of something comforting to say, maybe about the slowness of some parts of life, or how quickly things can change, or how, when all else fails, it helps to eat chocolate.

But then Chloe shook her head. "I'm sorry, I didn't mean to put that on you. Would you like a sandwich? Grilled tomato and cheese? Fried egg?"

Chloe seemed to like the distraction that food preparation gave her, so Josey said, "What's your favorite?"

"My favorite?" Chloe said, as if no one had asked her that before. "I guess I like plain turkey on jalapeño cheese bread the best."

"Okay, I'll try that."

"To go?"

"Yes. I have to go to the organic grocery for peppermint oil. I just wanted to stop by to say hello, and to thank you for the books again. How goes the house hunting?"

"I've been going over rental listings and making appointments," she said as she assembled the cold sandwich. She bagged it and handed it over to Josey. "Peppermint oil? Is that why you always smell like Christmas?"

Josey laughed at that. "My mother insists that peppermint oil be used on the casings of our house. It's supposed to keep unexpected guests from arriving on the doorstep. I'm pretty sure the old herbalist at the organic grocery propagates these superstitions for profit. She claims that she can whip up love potions, elixirs for pleasant dreams, charms that will give you more hours in a day. All made from natural ingredients found in the mountains. Nova Berry, she's quite a character."

"I've never heard of her."

Josey gave her the money for the sandwich even though Chloe tried to wave it away. "Not many people have. She works with referrals only."

As Chloe put the money in the cash register, she said thoughtfully, "Do you think you could refer me?"

"Well, sure. What do you need?"

"I don't know," Chloe said. "Maybe she can tell me."

Nova Berry looked like a hickory switch—tall, thin and knobby. She could trace her family line back hundreds of years in the Appalachian Mountains. These days people treated what she did as a novelty, but there was a time when the Berry women were known far and wide for their natural remedies. Slippery elm for digestive problems. Red clover for skin conditions. Pot marigold for certain monthly female ailments. Nova had been forced to spice things up a bit now that there were things like Maalox and Midol on the market, so easily acquired. So she made it known that her cure for heartburn also mended a broken heart, and her cure for cramps also made you more fertile, or less, if that's what you wanted. Half the time it really worked, because if it was one thing generations of Berry women knew, it was that confidence was the primary ingredient in every potion.

Nova's children ran the market, and Nova had her own workroom in the back. Josey led Chloe there, pushing back the curtain that separated it from the rest of the store. Nova was sitting at her workbench, crushing lavender with a mortar and pestle, listening to Patsy Cline on the CD player her grandchildren had given her.

She looked up when they entered. "Josey! I have your mother's peppermint oil right here. Please tell her I'm sorry it took so long. There was a sudden outbreak of constipation that kept me busy." She got to her feet and gave Josey a small glass vial. Josey discreetly gave her the cash for it. Nova stuffed it in her bra. "Now, can I interest you in a scarf this time?" She gestured to the corner of the room, which was an explosion of yarn, in baskets, on shelves. She knitted two or three scarves a week, and they were hanging everywhere, even alongside bundles of dried herbs. "Red is your magic color, Josey. Try red."

"No, thank you." Josey gestured for Chloe, who was standing by the curtained door, to come forward. She did, but leerily. Josey took her hand and pulled her the rest of the way. "Nova, this is Chloe Finley."

Nova looked her up and down. "The Finleys who grew corn?"

Chloe cleared her throat. "Yes, my great-grandparents used to."

"I knew your great-great-grandmother when I was a small child. She traded my mother bushels of white corn for a horse chestnut remedy for her varicose veins. Is that what you're here for?"

"Varicose veins?" Chloe said, surprised. "No."

"Then what?" Nova said. When Chloe hesitated, Nova turned to Josey and said, "Go and try on my scarves in front of that mirror. Red, Josey. Red will get you what you want. Go." When Josey walked over there, she saw Nova take Chloe by the arm and lead her even farther away. But Josey could still hear when she said, "Now, what can Nova do for you?"

"I want to forgive someone," Chloe said, "or I want to move on. Do you have anything that would help?"

Nova thought about it a moment. "You need a tisane of stinging nettle." She went to her workbench and opened one of the dozens of clear glass jars. "You use this like tea leaves, to drink." Nova scooped some of the dried plant into a small paper envelope.

"Stinging nettle," Chloe said, trying to laugh, but she sounded nervous. "That sounds painful."

"Love sometimes hurts. This is painless, though. It tells your heart what to do. Your heart, child, remember. When you have a decision to make, listen to your heart."

"Thank you," Chloe said, taking the envelope. "How much do I owe you?"

"Josey's paying for it," Nova said. "That's what she gets for eavesdropping."

Josey dropped Chloe off at the courthouse, then went home. As soon as she walked through the door with the peppermint oil, Margaret admonished her for taking too long, then grabbed the oil and went in search of Helena. The oil had to be put on the casings immediately, she said, because Thanksgiving and Christmas were almost upon them and people didn't think twice about dropping in during the holidays. Margaret wanted to nip that in the bud.

Josey went upstairs to get out of her mother's warpath. Margaret hated the holidays. She went to all the holiday social functions because it was expected of her, but there was something about Christmas that always set her off. Josey had learned years ago to try to stay out of her way when she got like this.

Josey unbuttoned her coat as she walked into her room. She went straight to her closet, because that's what she always did. It used to be just for the candy. Now it was also to see Della Lee, to talk and to argue. She was actually starting to *look forward* to it.

Which meant that Della Lee had finally succeeded in driving her insane.

When she opened the closet door, Della Lee was sitting where she always sat, on the sleeping bag, but she was no longer poring over those old notebooks. She was still wearing all her clothes, but she'd taken off her makeup and she was holding the small tiara in her lap, looking at it wistfully.

"Della Lee?"

She looked up and smiled. She looked younger without makeup, her skin even more translucent, like that of a child.

"I won this in the Little Miss Bald Slope pageant when I was six years old."

Josey went to her knees. Her long coat spread around her on the floor. "You must have been a pretty child."

"I was." She put the tiara on the floor and pushed it toward Josey. "Here, you can have it. Put it on."

Josey shook her head. "My hair wasn't made for wearing a crown. It would get lost."

"Please?"

With a sigh, she put it on her head, then she spread her arms, inviting snide comments.

But Della Lee said, "Very nice. And nice scarf, by the way."

Josey looked down at it, then immediately took it off. Thank God it had been under her coat. "Thank you for reminding me. Nova Berry insisted I buy it, but my mother hates me in red. I bought you some nonperishables while I was at the market, things you can keep up here to eat, but they're still in the car. I'll get them when Mother goes to sleep. You have to stop moving things downstairs. You're driving Helena crazy. She can't figure out what's going on. Oh, and I also got you a sandwich at Chloe's but I ate it on the way home."

"Josey, there's something important I have to tell you," Della Lee said seriously. "I've been debating whether or not it really has anything to do with me being here, but I think it does, so I think you should know."

"Let me guess, you're a serial closet squatter and I'm not your first victim."

"No." Della Lee reached into a corner of the closet and brought out the box Josey had taken from her house. She set it in front of her, then she pushed it halfway between her and Josey. "Look inside."

Josey scooted the box the rest of the way toward her and lifted the lid.

"See those notebooks?" Della Lee said. "Those were my mother's. Go ahead. You can look in them."

Josey lifted the first one out. It was a regular spiral notebook, the kind kids carried to school in backpacks. The paper was thin and graying but the ink was still dark and feathery, like that from a felt-tip pen. "Are these diaries?"

"More like logbooks. My mother liked to follow Marco Cirrini and write down what he did. She did it for almost twenty years. When I was a child she would drag me around town in our car, driving wherever he drove. I remember sitting outside homes and office buildings and the ski lodge for hours while he went inside. Mama would talk to herself the whole time, cursing him while scribbling in those books. Sometimes, when he would park his car, she would get out and break his windshield wipers or scratch his doors, then she'd run back to our car and laugh about it. She was obsessed with knowing what he was doing, and who he was with."

Josey looked over a few pages, feeling uncomfortable. Most of it was written like this entry, dated March 30, twenty-three years ago:

Marco drove down Highland Street.

Marco parked in the seventh parking space from the corner.

Marco used two dimes in the parking meter.

Marco was wearing his gray suit with a red tie.
They stood on the sidewalk and talked.
Marco laughed three times.
She touched his sleeve.
License plate numbers of cars in the street: ZXL-33, GGP-40, DIW-07, FNE-82, HUN-61, CMC-75, DFB-93.

Josey closed the notebook, shutting out the frantic energy emanating from the pages. "I don't understand. Why would your mother do this?" Marco Cirrini had been a very public figure, but as far as Josey knew, he'd never had any real enemies. She was ashamed to admit that she knew very little about her father, just how great everyone said he was, and the snippets he'd sometimes shared with her on their Sunday drives. He'd had his own apartment at the lodge, so he'd rarely even slept at the house.

Della Lee ran her tongue over her crooked front teeth, thinking about her answer. "My mother was a troubled person," she finally said. "And she was too beautiful for her state of mind. She always looked like she knew more than she did. She left home when she was sixteen because her stepfather was molesting her. She dropped out of high school and got a job as a checkout girl at the Winn-Dixie. When she met my father, she thought he was going to be her savior. She loved to tell me the story of how she was sitting on a bench downtown one Saturday, drinking a bottle of Pepsi-Cola with a straw, when he walked up to her and said, 'You are the most beautiful creature I've ever seen. Can I buy you dinner?' It was like something out of a movie. I came along nine months later. She was eighteen."

Josey thought about it, and she vaguely remembered Della Lee's mother, small and pretty and rough like Della Lee, but with big green doll eyes. "Your mother was Greenie Baker, right?"

"Yes."

"I remember seeing her around."

"I'm not surprised. Following you and your father on your Sunday drives was one of her favorite things to do."

"She followed him when I was with him?"

Della Lee nodded.

Time lines, like strings of thread, were weaving together, forming connections. "Were you with her?"

"Sometimes. But as soon as I was old enough to stay home alone, I did. I hated following you. Hated it. But then I would always hear about it when she got home, where he took you, how you used to laugh when you were with him. Sometimes I would put my fingers in my ears so I wouldn't hear it. I didn't want to hear about him acting like a good father with you."

"What happened to *your* father?"

"He died when I was nineteen."

"And he let your mother do this?"

"I don't know if he actually knew. I didn't even know who he was until I was nine. He paid off my mother when I was born. Bought her the house. Bought her a car. Bought her silence."

"Why would he do that?" Josey asked, absolutely transfixed by this time.

"Probably so his wife wouldn't know. But my mother, God bless her, went to his wife when I was nine. 'This is your husband's daughter,' I remember her saying. 'Look at her. His own flesh and blood and he won't even see her.' "

"That must have been horrible for you."

"Actually, that was the day everything made sense," Della Lee said. "That was the day I realized why my mother was following Marco Cirrini around town."

"Why?"

Della Lee's eyes went past Josey's shoulder. She looked around the bedroom. "I've been in your house once before. That day when I was nine years old. I stood in your living room. Well, you weren't born yet, so I guess it wasn't your living room at the time. I couldn't believe how beautiful this place was. It *smelled* rich."

Josey started coming back to herself, pulling away from the story. No, no. She didn't want to hear the ending.

"Your mother gave my mother more money. Bought her silence again. That Margaret is one smart cookie," Della Lee said, shaking her head. "Marco may have had a child, but she was the only one who could give him a *legitimate* child. It was well known that Margaret and Marco didn't want children, but a year after Margaret found out about me, suddenly there was Josey, their late-in-life baby! The baby that would bind Margaret to Marco's fortune, no matter what."

Josey stood and backed away from the closet, half tripping over her long coat and ripping the tiara out of her hair. She stood across the room and stared at Della Lee in horror.

"Hi, sis," Della Lee said.

Jawbreakers

It seemed like hours passed.

They just stared at each other. Della Lee was sitting cross-legged with her hands placidly on her knees. Josey was breathing heavily with anger and indignation.

"That's it!" Josey said. "I've had enough!"

"Finally," Della Lee said.

"I mean I've had enough of you! I will not tolerate anyone saying such things about my father. Everyone knows he was a great man. He loved my mother and my mother loved him. He saved Bald Slope." She pointed to her bedroom door, her hand trembling. "Get out!"

Della Lee rolled her eyes. "Oh, grow up, Josey."

She couldn't believe it. Was there no way at all to intimidate this woman? "*This* is the real reason you decided to come to my closet. It had nothing to do with running from Julian. Are the two of you in this together?"

"Julian and I are in nothing together anymore. And I didn't run from him. He's a bastard, but I was running from myself," Della Lee said as she scooted the box back toward her and put the lid on it. She seemed a little sad, or disappointed. Well, what did she expect? That she could just say that Marco Cirrini was her father and have Josey embrace her?

"If you needed money, why didn't you just say so? I'll give you money. You didn't have to go through this whole production of pretending you wanted to help me." Josey went to her purse on the chaise lounge and took out her checkbook. She opened it and poised her pen. "How much?"

"I don't want your money," Della Lee said, moving her box back into the closet.

Josey dropped her arms. "Then what are you doing here? Why are you doing this? Why are you saying these things?"

"Because they're true. And I do want to help you. That's why I'm here."

Josey snorted, because being angry helped hide the completely ridiculous hurt she felt. She should have known. She should have known Della Lee had something like this up her sleeve. "Nothing you say is true."

"You love your mailman. Is that not true? You feel stuck here. Is that not true? You're trying to make up to your mother for something you did as a child, something she's never going to let you live down. Is that not true? You want to leave this place. You want to wear red. You want to take your candy out of your goddamn closet and eat it in front of everyone!"

"My father did not have a child with another woman," Josey said, and the words fell out of her mouth with a clatter.

"You don't believe me? Ask your mother," Della Lee said.

"No!" Her mother would have a conniption if she got wind of Della Lee's allegations. She turned and stuffed her checkbook back into her purse. "And don't you dare say anything about this to her. Don't say it to anyone. Just tell me what you want."

"Okay, I want you to ask Samuel Lamar."

Josey turned back to her. "My father's old lawyer?"

"Yes."

"Why ask him?" she said leerily.

"Who do you think set up the money, house and car transfers? The confidentiality agreement?"

Josey stared at her, not saying anything. She couldn't believe this was happening. How had she let things get to this point? She should have kicked Della Lee out that first day. "Fine," she finally said. "I'll write him right now." She went to her desk and pulled out a sheet of paper. She didn't know Mr. Lamar's address by heart, but it was in the address book downstairs. She sent him a Christmas card every year. He'd moved to Massachusetts some time ago, to live with his daughter's family. "But I want you to agree, right now, to leave when I get his answer. When he writes and says my father never had any other children, you will leave this house and never bother me again. Understood?"

"Sure," Della Lee said. "But calling would be faster."

"I don't have his number. I just have his daughter's address in Massachusetts."

"Ever heard of dialing information?"

"I don't know his daughter's married name."

"You could find that out from anyone in town."

"I'm writing him."

"If you really wanted to know the truth, you'd call."

"I already know the truth, Della Lee. I don't need proof." Josey closed her eyes and rubbed her forehead. "Did it ever occur to you that I was doing this to give you time to leave? Time to make plans?"

"No. That never crossed my mind."

"A week, maybe two, and I'll get a response," Josey said, putting pen to paper. "That should give you enough time."

"Okay. But be sure to ask him about *all* of Marco's affairs. Ask him about the other woman, besides my mother, he paid off."

Josey had gotten as far as *Dear Mr. Lamar.* She stopped and turned to Della Lee. She felt hollow, and she wanted candy from her closet. When she finished this letter, she would take armfuls out, then close the door on Della Lee and eat and eat and eat until the hollow went away. "That's a little over the top, don't you think?"

"Marco did everything in a big way."

"You're really starting to get on my nerves. Is there anything about my life you haven't insulted yet?" She turned back to the letter. *I apologize for writing out of the blue like this. I hope you're well.*

"I don't know. Let me see your teeth."

"I think I hate you." *I've recently heard an upsetting rumor and only you, as my father's lawyer and trusted confidant, can in-*

validate it. I can't go to my mother with this, you understand. I don't want to upset her.

"Sibling rivalry," Della Lee said. "It happens to the best of us."

Did my father have any other children? Specifically, did he have a child with Greenie Baker?

Chloe couldn't bear the thought of waiting hours to try the stinging-nettle tea. What if this was the thing that was going to make everything all right? She started getting excited about feeling better. As soon as she drank the tea, she would know what to do. She would make a decision she could live with, and she would finally stop hurting. At four o'clock she closed the shop early.

When she left, Hank at the security gate asked what was her hurry. She happily told him she was going home to make tea. He didn't ask her any more questions, just looked at her with sympathy, like losing Jake was making her lose her sanity. And she didn't want to think about how close to the truth that might be.

She dumped her purse and coat on the floor when she got home, and went directly to the kitchen. She ferreted out her tea infuser, then boiled water in a cup in the microwave. When she finally took that first sip, she was surprised to find it bitter. She had imagined it sweeter. She didn't want to put sugar in it for fear that would change its power, so she gulped the rest of it. The warm empty cup still in her hands, she stood still for a moment, hoping the effect would be immediate. It wasn't.

She put the cup down and started to pace. This was

worse than waiting for the results of the at-home pregnancy test she took two years ago. She and Jake always said they were going to wait to have kids, wait until they were married and had enough in savings that they didn't have to be beholden to Jake's parents. She had been scared, but Jake had been so excited. The results had been negative, of course, but she would never forget how buoyant the thought of being a father had made him.

That couldn't be the reason he'd cheated on her, could it? Did he want a child so much he was willing to have one with another woman?

Half an hour later, several things were definitely more clear. She decided to take a long bath, not a shower, later that evening. She decided to have pesto pizza for dinner. She also decided to wait to vacuum until next week.

But nothing was any more clear when it came to Jake.

She stopped pacing, that familiar heaviness settling back in her body, weighing down her limbs. It wasn't working. The tea wasn't going to tell her what to do.

She went to the dining-room table and sat, then put her head down, resting her cheek against the smooth, cool surface. She felt tears come to her eyes. Why had she thought it would be so easy? She squeezed her eyes shut. When she opened them again, she blinked a few times to clear the blurriness, then saw that she was eye-level with the salt and pepper shakers. There, tucked in between them, was the cocktail napkin with Julian's number on it. She'd stuck it there days ago.

She reached for it, then sat up and stared at it.

Everything came back to this. She needed to know who had caused Jake to stray before she could decide if she could forgive him. There would be no moving on until she knew.

She turned when she heard a rustling coming from the kitchen, a small sneaky noise, like mice scurrying around. She got up to see that battle-scarred *Finding Forgiveness* had knocked the paper envelope of stinging nettle off the counter.

She picked up the envelope and put it in a drawer. "Stop that," she said to the book beside the toaster.

When she got back to the table, *Old Love, New Direction* was now lying on top of the napkin with Julian's number on it.

The old bait and switch.

She pulled the napkin out from under the book with an exasperated sigh. She went to the phone and dialed quickly so her books wouldn't have any more say in the matter.

"Hello?" Julian answered. His voice was strangely calming. She sat down, right where she was, in the middle of the floor. He was that good.

"Julian, this is Chloe."

"Chloe sweetheart, I've been waiting to hear from you."

"I'm sorry about Saturday night."

"Don't be. I know how a man gets when he thinks he's lost the love of his life."

"I know you do," she said with sympathy. "Still no word from your girlfriend?"

"No."

"Have you, um, learned anything more about who Jake might have slept with?"

"As a matter of fact, I have. But I'm hurt. Is that the only reason you called?"

"No!" she said immediately, mortified that she'd hurt his feelings. "No, of course not."

"Let's get together tonight. I'll tell you then."

"Why won't you tell me now?"

"Because I'd like to think I can also be a friend to you, someone to commiserate with, not just a source of information about your cheating boyfriend."

That made sense. At least she thought it did. "We can't go to Jiggery's. Jake might be there."

"My favorite weekday haunt is Nite Lite. Meet me there around nine tonight."

Julian hung up before she could say no.

It took a moment before she was sure she could stand, a few minutes more before she could walk. Of course she would go to see Julian tonight to find out. But that's not to say she wanted to go to Nite Lite alone. She knew it was a rough place.

Chloe chewed on her lip for a minute, then she went to her purse. She dug out the card with Josey's number written on it and dialed.

She heard the phone pick up on the other end, then she heard Josey say, "Yes, I know it's my phone, but I've never heard it ring before. And do you really think blocking my way is going to keep me from getting to my candy? What do you mean I've already answered? Oh." She heard Josey put her cell phone to her ear and say, "Hello?"

"Josey?"

"Yes?"

"It's Chloe. Am I interrupting something?"

"No, no," Josey said, laughing, but it sounded forced. "I rarely use this cell phone. I was actually trying to remember how to answer it."

"I was wondering if you would do me a favor."

"Of course I will. What is it?"

She liked that Josey said yes without even knowing what the favor was. That made Chloe feel good. She'd called

Josey first for this very reason. "I know this is a lot to ask, but would you go to a bar with me tonight?"

"A bar," Josey repeated.

"It's a place I've never been to before and I'd feel better if someone went with me."

There was a long pause. "I've never actually been to a bar before," Josey said.

"Then now's the perfect time to experience one first-hand! I wouldn't ask if it wasn't important. Someone there has some information for me that could really help me with my situation with Jake."

"What kind of information?"

Chloe pinched the bridge of her nose. She didn't want to tell Josey. It made her sound trite and desperate. "He knows who Jake slept with," she finally said.

"Chloe," Josey said gently, "is this something you really want to know?"

"It's something I *have* to know. Please come with me."

Josey took a deep breath. "Okay. I'll go."

Nite Lite was located on the winding road leading up to the ski resort. It was set back into the trees, with a large gravel parking lot in front. The sign by the road read: HAMBURGERS! KARAOKE! COLD BEER! Josey figured it had probably been designed to attract the college kids who were on their way up the mountain to ski, but from the looks of things when Josey and Chloe entered, it ended up being a hangout for bearded men in flannel shirts and a couple of rough younger people who wanted to play pool in the back room.

At least there wasn't much of a risk of anyone recognizing her and telling her mother.

They stopped at the door, letting their eyes adjust to the dimness. "I don't see him here yet. Let's get something to drink," Chloe said, going to the bar.

Josey followed, feeling out of sorts and conspicuous. Chloe had given Josey her address, the Firehouse Apartments downtown, and Josey had picked her up after Margaret had gone to bed. Della Lee had made happy squealing noises when she found out Josey was going out with Chloe, but Josey was still so angry about the things she'd said about her father that she'd left without taking any of Della Lee's unsolicited wardrobe advice. It was something she'd regretted when Chloe had opened her apartment door, taken one look at Josey in the same black dress and coat she'd worn earlier that day, and grabbed a bold yellow and red rugby-striped scarf off the coat stand. She'd looped it around Josey's neck and said, "Now, you have color. Perfect!"

Once at the bar, Chloe ordered a lemon drop, so Josey did too. When the drinks arrived, Josey pretended to sip hers. She tried to make conversation, but Chloe was distracted, constantly looking around the bar and saying every ten minutes, "He said he'd be here."

Two hours later, Chloe was flat drunk and Josey was trying to figure out a way to get her to leave. Chloe had refused every attempt. Josey couldn't even stop Chloe from calling Jake and leaving him a slurred message, telling him she was at Nite Lite and having loads of fun without him. But it was far from the truth. Chloe was more miserable than Josey had ever seen her. Despite everything, Josey wished to God she could call Della Lee. She would know what to do. Chloe was in the process of ordering another martini and Josey squeezed her eyes shut. She had a headache and she had to go to the bathroom, but she was too afraid to go alone and Chloe apparently had a bladder the size of Montana.

What would Della Lee do?

Della Lee would take charge. She wouldn't care about being nice.

Just as the bartender was turning away, Josey said, "Cancel that. We're leaving."

"No, Josey, we have to stay," Chloe said. "Just a few more minutes. Pleeease?"

"He's not coming, Chloe."

"He said he would. He said to meet him here and he would tell me who Jake slept with."

"Then he lied. Give her a cup of coffee," she told the bartender. Then she said to Chloe, "I'm going to the restroom. When I get back, we're leaving."

She slid off the bar stool and went to the ladies' room. Ha! Easy as pie. Strawberry pie. Strawberry rhubarb pie with fresh vanilla ice cream.

She decided she would get a pie on the way home and eat it all.

After today, she deserved it.

She walked back out into the dim neon-lit bar a few minutes later, but she only took a few steps before she stopped short.

She turned away quickly, her eyes wide and darting back and forth, trying to get her mind around this. She'd channeled Della Lee and look what happened.

Julian appeared.

She turned back around. Yes, it was definitely him. But what in the hell was he doing here? Julian was sitting with Chloe, surrounding them both in a cloud of rosy-black smoke that only the women in the bar could see. They were leaning in toward each other, smiling, laughing. Chloe was stuck in his smoke, entranced by him. She couldn't get out alone.

Josey rubbed her aching forehead. What would Della Lee do?

When it came to Julian, Della Lee would run.

Run. Okay, Josey could do that.

She just had to get Chloe first.

The bar was dark enough that there was a chance Julian wouldn't recognize her as the woman who'd been in his house. She walked over to them sideways, like she was doing a line-dancing step to the music from the jukebox. Keeping her back to Julian, she angled her way between them. She grabbed Chloe's purse and coat from the bar. "Come on, Chloe. We're leaving."

"No, we don't have to go now," Chloe said jubilantly. "Look, Julian finally made it! Julian, this is Josey."

Josey gaped at Chloe. She'd come here to meet *Julian*?

"It's nice to meet you," Julian said, leaning to the right, trying to see Josey's face. "You look familiar. I thought that the moment I came in and saw you with Chloe. Turn around, pretty. Look at me."

He touched her arm and she stepped away quickly, facing him now.

"She's Josey Cirrini. *Cirrini*. Shh, she's rich," Chloe said.

Josey tried to coax Chloe off the stool. "Come on. Let's go."

Chloe held on to the bar rail with both hands, refusing to budge. "I can't go. I haven't found out her name yet."

"Come on, stand up."

"Leave the kid here," Julian said. "I'll take her home."

"I don't think so." Josey kept tugging at Chloe, but Chloe had suctioned herself to the bar and the harder Josey pulled, the harder Chloe hung on.

"I *know* I've seen you somewhere before," Julian said.

Suddenly, from behind them, Josey heard, "Chloe? Josey? Are you two all right?"

Josey let go of Chloe, which had the immediate effect of Chloe letting go of the bar. They both turned.

"Adam!" Chloe said. "What are you doing here?"

Adam's brows lowered. He did not look pleased. Still, Josey didn't think she'd ever been so happy to see someone. He was wearing a soft brown leather jacket over a turtleneck and a blue scarf the exact color of his eyes. He looked *wonderful*. "You called me, Clo. You left a message on my answering machine."

"I called you?"

"Obviously you intended the message for Jake."

"Oops!" She took Adam's hand and brought him toward her. Josey had to step back to get out of his way. "Adam, I want you to meet Julian."

Adam didn't even acknowledge him. "Let's go, Clo," Adam said, trying to get her off the stool. Chloe immediately grabbed the bar rail again. Josey almost said, *Good luck with that. She's a barnacle.*

"Hold on," Julian suddenly said, and Josey thought he was protesting Adam's trying to take Chloe away from him. But when Josey looked at him, he was looking right back at her. It caused a shock, a painful little tingle, at the base of her neck. "You," he said, pointing a finger at her. "I know who you are. You broke into my house! You took my wallet!"

"Come on, Josey," Adam said. "Help me with Chloe."

"You owe me money, you fat bitch!"

It happened so fast, it was almost a blur. Julian was in the process of standing when Adam turned and punched him across the jaw with absolutely no warning. Julian fell backward and people around them stopped talking and turned to stare.

"Up, Chloe." Adam literally lifted her off the stool and tore her away from the bar. "Josey—with me, now."

Josey stood motionless while Adam half carried, half dragged Chloe away.

"Josey, damn it, with this bum leg I can't handle you both. Come on!"

She forced her feet to move. She ran to the door and held it open as Adam hauled Chloe out.

Chloe was calling, "Julian! Julian! I'm so sorry! Let go of me!"

The night outside was a shocking contrast to being inside Nite Lite. It was cold and quiet and Josey immediately felt like she had cotton in her ears. "Who drove?" Adam demanded as Chloe struggled in his arms.

Josey opened her mouth to try to pop her ears.

"Who drove!"

"I . . . I did."

"Where is your car?"

"Over there."

Adam crunched across the gravel lot toward the car, saying, "Unlock it." She hurried after him and electronically unlocked the doors. He opened the back door and together they got the squirming mass of red hair and glitter into the back seat. "Sit back there with her and give me the keys."

She hesitated and he started to say something. "Okay, okay," she said, handing him the keys and sliding in beside Chloe.

He slammed the door, then trotted around the car and got behind the wheel.

He sped out of the lot, taking the corner easily.

Except for Chloe's progressively vague protests as Josey got her into her coat, the car was uncomfortably quiet. Josey put her arm around Chloe, and soon her head fell on Josey's shoulder.

Adam didn't say anything the entire drive to Chloe's place. He didn't even speak as they carried Chloe up the long interior steps that cut the old firehouse into four apartments. Josey got the keys out of Chloe's purse and opened the door.

She followed his lead to the bedroom. A large bed with a heavy black headboard dominated the red-brick room. This place had a distinctly masculine feel to it. It was hard to believe Chloe lived here. She hadn't put her stamp anywhere. There weren't even bookshelves. How could someone like Chloe live without bookshelves?

As soon as they had Chloe on the bed, Adam rounded on her. "How could you let her get so hammered?" he demanded. "Are you drunk?"

She'd never seen him angry, let alone angry with her. So few people she knew actually got angry. There was indignation, there were snubs, there were insults disguised as compliments, but rarely outright anger. "I didn't have anything to drink," she said. "And I kept trying to get her to leave. I had no idea she was going there to meet Julian."

"You *know* that guy? You didn't really break into his house and steal his wallet, did you?"

She hesitated for a moment, then said, "It wasn't his house and it wasn't his wallet."

"You stole someone else's wallet?" he asked incredulously.

"I didn't steal anything. I got a friend's wallet back."

Adam's jaw worked back and forth. "What's gotten into you lately? Does your mother know you're doing this?"

That did it. "I'm twenty-seven years old! What does my mother have to do with this? But that's how everyone sees me, isn't it? Poor Josey. Fat, unsocial, under her mother's thumb, not living up to her father's name. I'm so tired of worrying about what people think of me, of what they thought of me as a child. And I'm tired of that look," she said, pointing at his face.

"What look?"

"That look of *pity*!"

He actually took a step back, like she'd scared him. If she weren't so mad, if she hadn't had such a lousy day, she would have laughed. "Look," he said, "all I'm saying is that Chloe's vulnerable right now. You should be nudging her back in Jake's direction instead of going with her to dives."

"You know what I think? I think you have no idea what's good for her," Josey groused, and it felt good. She wanted to argue, to fight, to stop this constant feeling of having no control over anything except what went in her mouth. "You just want her to take the path of least resistance because that's safer."

"Damn straight it's safer."

"I've got news for you, Adam. *Safe* is just another word for *scared*. And I'm not going to *nudge* her in any direction. This is her call. Whether or not she and Jake get back together has nothing to do with me, or you, for that matter."

"Jake is living with me right now, I'd say that qualifies as having something to do with me," he said.

"No, it doesn't."

He waved his hand dismissively. "You don't know anything about this."

"I know enough to stay out of it. Like I know you've got a secret. But have I ever asked you about it? No."

She'd surprised him. A couple of seconds ticked by before he said, "What?"

"You're hiding something. You're hiding *from* something. I've known it since the moment I first saw you."

He met her eyes, his head tilting slightly. "You've known a lot since the moment you first saw me."

The room suddenly fell quiet. He had just said he knew. He knew she loved him. Embarrassment felt a lot like eating chili peppers. It burned in the back of your throat and there was nothing you could do to make it go away. You just had to take it, suffer from it, until it eased off. When he spoke again, his tone was softer. "I'll let you get her undressed."

Oh, yeah, like that was better. He was feeling sorry for her again.

As soon as he left the room, Josey sighed and reached down to take off Chloe's boots. She managed to get Chloe out of her coat and sweater, leaving her in the T-shirt she wore underneath. She then took off her watch and earrings. She tucked the blankets around her, then looked around for something else to do. She wasted some time by folding Chloe's coat and sweater and putting them at the bottom of the bed. Then she placed her boots by the closet.

When she knew she couldn't stay any longer, she finally walked to the bedroom door.

She took one last look back and saw that there were three books stacked on the bedside table, near the edge, like they were watching Chloe. Josey hadn't noticed them there before.

She took a deep breath and opened the door. Adam was sitting on the couch, waiting for her.

"Give me my keys," she said, walking up to him. "I'll drive you back to the bar to get your car."

"I'm not letting you go back there." He jiggled her keys in his hand absently as he looked up at her. "I'll get Jake to take me in the morning."

"Then give me my keys and I'll take you home."

He suddenly stood and brushed by her. "I'll drive," he said, walking to the door.

"I told you, I didn't drink anything."

"I'll drive." He opened the door and waited for her.

This night was never going to end. She walked to the door and out into the hallway. She headed for the staircase, hearing him close the apartment door, then the fall of his footsteps as he followed her. They'd left the car unlocked in the small lot beside the old firehouse building, so Josey got in the passenger side and stared straight ahead as he took his time getting behind the wheel.

"This is a . . . nice car," he said when he started the engine.

"What?" she turned to him and said defensively, because he said it the way people remarked on tacky furniture. When you drove a car that would make Liberace proud, it usually helped to have a sense of humor, but tonight she couldn't take it, not from him.

"It's a Cadillac," he said as he pulled out of the lot.

"So?"

"Did your mother pick it out?"

"My mother doesn't drive. This is my car. I bought it."

"You didn't answer my question."

"Yes, she picked it out. She had it specially ordered." She could have sworn she saw him smile. "Stop looking so smug."

"Smug?"

"Yes, like everything you thought of me has fallen back into that nice safe place you had it before."

He seemed to ponder that for the rest of the drive. Soon, he pulled to the curb and stopped behind another parked car.

She knew this neighborhood, unique because the houses on one side were high above the street, each with steep concrete steps from the sidewalk all the way up to the front of the house. The yards were dizzying slopes of grass that must be hell to mow.

Adam's house was a single-story clapboard with a large front window. There wasn't much personality to it, and she was surprised. This was where Adam lived, but this wasn't his home.

"So this is your house," she said.

Adam cut the engine. "You didn't know?"

"Why would I know?" Now that he knew she'd been pining for him, naturally he assumed she must have been stalking him too? She angrily got out and began to walk around the car to get to the driver's side. But by the time she reached the front of the car, Adam had met her halfway. Because of the car parked in front of them, she couldn't walk around him without touching him, and Lord knows how he'd interpret that. So she had to wait for him to move.

Adam stopped in front of her. The glow of the car's headlamps brightened his hair and face as he looked up at his house. He was so beautiful he made her chest hurt. "Looks like Jake's home now," he said. "He's been working late and on weekends ever since this thing with Chloe. Luckily I was the one to get her message first."

"Are you going to tell him?"

"No." He suddenly looked down at her and she had to

fight the urge to step back. His eyes dropped to her neck. "That scarf looks familiar."

She shrugged. "I got it from Chloe. She wanted me to wear it."

"Why would she want you to wear it?" he asked, as if that was the most ridiculous thing he had ever heard.

"She said for color." Adam Boswell, fashion critic? Oh, yes, finding out that she had feelings for him *of course* gave him leave to find all the things wrong with her. How could she still love a man who knew she loved him and was completely appalled by the idea? He was . . .

"This is Jake's scarf," he said, reaching out to touch it. Her body gave a start, and he hesitated. When he seemed sure she wasn't going to bolt, he wrapped his fingers around the scarf and pulled slowly, causing a warm friction against her skin. As soon as he had it pulled off of her, cold air darted into the collar of her coat and she shivered.

Adam watched her hand go to her neck. He unwrapped his own light blue scarf and looped it around her, their hands touching briefly. She could only stare at him. He stared back at her for several impossibly long seconds, his hands holding the ends of the scarf as if holding her to him. Finally he dropped his hands and brushed past her. Up the concrete steps he went, then he disappeared inside.

When Josey got home, she stood on the porch in the dark, holding Adam's scarf. She reluctantly hung it on the mailbox. It was a pity scarf, she decided, and she wanted nothing to do with it.

No, that was a big fat lie.

Not the part about it being a pity scarf, of course, but

the part about wanting nothing to do with it. She wanted *everything* to do with it. She wanted to sleep with it, dance with it, snuggle it like a pet. But that's exactly what Adam thought she'd do, and she wasn't going to give him that satisfaction.

She'd always known he didn't love her. But it was easier to bear when he didn't know she loved him. That way they were even. Now he knew he had all the power. It wasn't fair. She decided she wasn't going to run to the door every day just to see him anymore. She wasn't going to pine for him like a silly girl with a heart as soft as summer fruit.

She silently unlocked the front door, wishing she'd stopped to get that pie after all. She crept into the dark house and clicked the door closed.

When she turned, there was Helena, her eyes wide and excited.

Josey screamed, which made Helena scream. Josey quickly put one hand over Helena's mouth and the other over her own mouth. Then she stood perfectly still to see if they'd woken up her mother.

When no call came from upstairs, Helena pulled Josey's hand away from her mouth and said, "Oldsey! I wait for you!"

"Thank you, Helena. I appreciate that."

"No, I wait to give something! You wait now. Okay?" Helena disappeared into her bedroom, a large room just under the staircase. She rushed back with a small piece of folded cheesecloth. "Here. Sleep this."

Josey took it. Inside the cheesecloth was a small bone, no more than three inches long. "Helena, I really don't need . . . an animal bone?"

"Bad thing still here," Helena whispered.

"What exactly do you think the bad thing is?"

"I don't know. Bad."

"Have you actually seen this bad thing?"

"No."

That, at least, was a relief. Josey only had to keep Della Lee hidden, and Helena from trying to exorcise her, for a few more weeks. "Everything is fine. It's all under control. The bad thing will be gone soon, I promise. I don't need this." She tried to hand the cloth and bone back to her.

Helena got a stubborn look to her. "Take."

"I don't—"

"Take take take take take."

"Okay," Josey said. "Thank you."

"Oldsey a good girl," Helena said, going back to her room, satisfied.

For the time being.

"The sooner I get you out of here, the better. Helena is having a fit," Josey said to Della Lee when she opened the closet door. She thought about not going to the closet at all, just falling into bed and trying to ignore her. But then there was Chloe, and what to do about Julian. Josey actually *needed* Della Lee. Damn it.

Della Lee laughed. She was completely unchanged, like telling Josey she thought Marco Cirrini was her father was just another conversation they'd had. No big deal. "I'm having some fun with her. She chased me around in the dark downstairs last night."

Josey lowered herself to the floor. "She chased you?

Good Lord, she could have called the police. Stop teasing her."

"What do you have in your pocket?" Della Lee suddenly demanded, scooting away from her.

"My pocket?" Josey reached into her dress pocket. "Oh. Helena gave this to me. How did you know?"

"It was sticking out. What is that, a bone?"

Josey shrugged. "I think so."

"Ick. Just keep it away from me." She waited for Josey to put it away before she asked, "So, did you have fun with Chloe?"

"*No*," Josey said vehemently. She fell back onto the floor, like she'd seen Della Lee do so many times. She stared up at the ceiling.

"What happened?"

"Do you know who she's been talking to?" Josey said. "Who she went to the bar to meet?"

"Who?"

She turned her head to look at Della Lee. "Julian."

Della Lee blinked a few times. "My Julian?"

"*Yes*."

"Holy crap! I had a feeling the other day, it just hit me, that Julian had already moved on to someone else. But I never dreamed it would be Chloe! Keep her away from him, Josey. She's no match for him, especially not in her state. How in the hell did she meet him?"

"I don't know!" Josey said, and rubbed her face with her hands.

"You keep an eye on her. You watch her like a hawk."

Josey lifted her hands. "How am I supposed to do that?"

"I don't know. But that man could ruin her life."

"Like he ruined yours?"

"He was just one more destructive tendency." Della Lee shook her head, like she couldn't believe it now, like she was looking back on something she'd done a long, long time ago. "But that's why women are drawn to him, don't you see? He'll ruin her by giving her exactly what she thinks she wants."

9

Snow Candy

Josey had to take her mother to the annual Baptist Women's charity luncheon the next day, Tuesday. But before they were to leave, Josey decided to call Chloe to see how she was doing. She tried her work number first, but didn't get an answer.

"She's not at work," Josey said as she disconnected.

"I still don't think you know how to work that thing," Della Lee said from the closet. Today she was wearing Josey's red scarf as a headband and was trying on all of Josey's shoes.

"I dialed, it rang, no one answered. What exactly do you think I'm doing wrong?"

"It was just an observation. You're so touchy."

"I know how to work a phone," Josey grumbled as she dialed Chloe's cell phone number.

"Hello," Chloe finally answered after several rings. She sounded sick.

Josey sat on the edge of her bed. "Chloe, it's Josey. How are you feeling?"

"I'm so sorry about last night, Josey," Chloe said, and her voice started to tremble. "I never thought I would be the kind of woman to act like this, to fall to pieces, but I . . . I can't seem to help it. I don't know how to move on from it, and it hurts so much. I missed an appointment to see an apartment this morning. Am I going crazy? I feel like I'm going crazy."

Josey hesitated. Della Lee watched her curiously. "I'll be right over," she finally said.

As soon as she hung up, Della Lee said, "You're going to see her?"

Josey picked up her gray coat from the chaise. "Yes."

"Instead of taking your mother to her luncheon?"

"Yes."

"Oh, my baby is growing up."

"You're psychotic," Josey said, leaving the room while dialing another number.

Adam didn't see the scarf draped over the mailbox until he was halfway up the steps. He pulled the buds from his iPod out of his ears.

It had been strange seeing Josey in Jake's scarf last night.

With the way Chloe was acting, Adam wondered if she was trying to push Jake and Josey together. That didn't sit well with him. Jake and Chloe were . . . well . . . Jake and Chloe. But there was Josey wearing Jake's scarf. *Chloe* should wear Jake's scarf. But when he took it, Josey then didn't have a scarf. So of course he gave her his. It was cold. She needed one.

All right, so she didn't want to keep it. Her being in love with him and all, he just thought she would. Hell, it wasn't like she'd given back an engagement ring. But did this mean he wasn't going to see her today? Was she mad at him? He'd been harsh with her last night. But just the thought of Chloe and Josey at Nite Lite, of all places . . . and then that bastard called her fat. That still made him angry.

He took the scarf off the mailbox and put the Cirrinis' mail in. He hesitated and looked at the door.

Josey usually came out before now.

He looked over to the driveway. Her car was there.

He walked slowly to the steps, pulling the Fergusons' mail out of his bag. He stopped and looked back at the door again.

Where was she?

Okay, he could just walk away. Let her avoid him. It would probably make things a lot easier. But then he shook his head and turned back around. He wasn't going to let her do this. He went to the door and raised his hand to knock, not sure what he was going to say. Maybe he would apologize, tell her that he didn't mean to be so hard on her.

Or maybe he would ask her what in the world she thought his secret was.

She'd said it like it was obvious, and he'd gone over and over it in his mind last night. He got the feeling there was a lot Josey knew that she wasn't sharing with him.

He stopped just short of knocking when he heard voices inside.

"I've taken care of everything. I have to do this, Mother. Someone needs me," Josey said.

"Who? Who needs you more than me?" That sounded like her mother.

"A friend."

All of a sudden, the door opened and there was Josey.

She looked tired. But her hair was so curly it could never get limp. And the paler her skin, the more striking her dark eyes seemed. She looked . . .

Okay, he could admit it. She looked beautiful.

When she saw him, she seemed momentarily nonplussed. She actually took a step back and he was afraid she was going to close the door on him, but then her mother called, "Josey!"

She looked over her shoulder, then reluctantly stepped outside and closed the door behind her. "Hi, Adam," she said, looking down to button her long gray coat.

He held out the scarf. "You could have kept this."

Her eyes darted up briefly, embarrassed. "I know."

He reached over and took her mail out of the mailbox. He held it out. "Here's your mail."

But she didn't take that either. "Just leave it in the box, please. I'll get it when I come back."

He put it back in. "Have you talked to Chloe today?"

"I'm going to see her now." She went to the steps and started walking down.

He turned quickly to join her. "Listen, I'm sorry I was so rough on you last night. I was just . . ."

"Angry," she said.

"No, not angry." He stopped her when she reached the

bottom step, putting his hand on her arm. "I could never be angry at you, Josey."

She considered him for a moment, as if to gauge his honesty. She stared at him so long he dropped his hand.

"I've, uh, been thinking about what you said last night," he said. "That I had a secret . . ."

"I also said it was none of my business. I'm sorry." She started to turn away.

"Wait. Why do you think I have a secret?"

"I don't know. Maybe you don't have one. Maybe I was just projecting."

"You have a secret?"

She gave a small laugh and shook her head. "Well, not anymore," she said, and walked to the driveway and the enormous gold Cadillac parked there.

Why hadn't he seen it before? *Three years.* Why hadn't he known she was in love with him? "Are you sure you don't want to keep this scarf?" he called after her.

"No."

"No, you don't want to keep it? Or no, you're not sure?"

She looked over her shoulder at him and smiled slightly. His breath caught.

He felt a strange stirring, something he hadn't felt in a very long time. It felt a little like when a limb falls asleep but then slowly, surely, there's a tingling, an almost uncomfortable sensation . . . of waking up.

After stopping by the store for noodle soup and 7-Up and Milky Way ice cream, Josey knocked on Chloe's door.

When Chloe opened it, she looked miserable. She was wearing a thick terrycloth robe and her hair was all over the place, each tangled curl looking like it should have a wisp of smoke curling off of it. Mascara was smudged under her eyes.

Josey held up the bags and said, "In all my life, I've only ever been sure of one thing. Food makes everything better, at least until it's gone."

Chloe smiled.

And then she cried.

Josey walked in and closed the door behind her. She made a nice pot of stinging-nettle tea, which made the decision to eat the ice cream first much easier for them.

Margaret stood in the sitting room, confused. Here she was, all ready to go, and Josey just came down the stairs and said she had something else to do! It was so unexpected that she couldn't yet build up an acceptable level of anger because of her shock.

A friend, Josey said. She had to help out a friend.

That was clearly a lie. Josey didn't have friends.

What was she doing, then?

Not ten minutes after Josey left, there was a knock at the door.

"Helena," Margaret said, stopping her as she passed the sitting room. "Tell whoever it is that I'm indisposed. Don't say a word about Josey not being here." Josey was supposed to take care of her. Margaret expected it. Everyone expected it.

Shortly, Helena reappeared in the sitting-room doorway. "A man at the door for you."

"I said to tell . . ." Helena probably didn't know what "indisposed" meant. Margaret took a deep breath. "Tell him I'm not feeling well."

"He say he drive you."

"Drive me?"

"Yes, Oldgret."

Margaret got up and followed Helena to the door, leaving her cane behind because there was a chance it was someone she didn't know and she never liked to give a first impression of being feeble. When Helena opened the front door, Margaret felt slightly woozy, strange memories coming to her, memories of the last time he'd stood on her porch like this. For a moment she could even feel how blurry and medicated she'd been, how completely, profoundly unhappy she'd felt. "Rawley Pelham," she said, giving a smart, nervous pull to the hem of her yellow suit jacket, "what on earth are you doing here?"

Rawley turned to Helena. "Please tell Mrs. Cirrini that her daughter called me a few minutes ago and I promised I would take Mrs. Cirrini to her luncheon."

"Josey called you?" she asked, followed immediately by an incredulous, "She made you *promise*?" Pelhams didn't make promises easily, because they knew they couldn't break them. It was astounding that Rawley had not only promised something, but promised to do something for *her*.

He hated her.

"Please tell Mrs. Cirrini yes," he said to Helena.

Helena looked confused and vaguely panicked, obviously wondering why this man wouldn't talk directly to Margaret.

Well, there wasn't really any choice now. If Rawley promised, he had to do it. He would take her to this luncheon whether she liked it or not, or die trying. Livia Lynley-White was going to have a fit. "Helena, get my coat and cane. And tell Josey I want a word with her when I get home."

Rawley walked with her to his cab in the windy noon air. She wondered if the neighborhood was watching. She tried to walk as if she didn't care, but she felt herself leaning toward him, as if he had a gravitational force. She'd made her decision. She lived with it. But staying away from him was easier when she didn't actually have to be near him. He opened the cab door for her, his face without expression. That also made it easier, knowing how much he disliked her. She awkwardly sat and he closed the door.

When he got behind the wheel and pulled out, she couldn't help but wonder over how familiar this was. It felt like soft slippers. Like good wine. She'd fallen into the best part of her past.

She stared at the back of his head. She'd always been attracted to Rawley, from the moment she saw him. Ladies in their circle never drove themselves anywhere. They had chauffeurs, or they called a cab. The first time she saw him—she was in her late twenties at the time—he was helping one of her friends out of his cab at a social function. She'd asked, "Who is *that*?"

All the ladies who were natives of Bald Slope knew Rawley, and they were more than glad to tell her. He was beneath them, but so pretty to look at with his healthy good looks, blue eyes and russet hair. After high school he'd gone into the service. He'd just come back to Bald Slope to work for his father at Pelham Cabs. He met her eyes that day, and it was the start of three years of long looks, three years of her dismissing the chauffeur for the day, then suddenly realizing she had to go somewhere, so of course she had to call a cab. And it was always Rawley who came. She never had to ask for him by name.

It was so innocent at first. He talked with her, laughed

with her. She'd lived for those rides. She was lonely, and he was kind—good-natured and gangly with youth. She knew she should have been more responsible. She was older than Rawley by almost eight years, after all. But she hadn't meant to get so close to him. Not intimate, anyway.

Then it happened.

Rawley had driven Margaret home on the evening of Christmas Eve after the church program. All the servants were gone for the holiday, and the house was as dark as a hole. They'd had a bevy of help back then. Full-time cook, maid, gardener, chauffeur. But not even Marco was home. By that time she'd known about his other women. The first time, she'd been devastated. The second didn't hurt as much. By his tenth affair, she was numb.

She'd looked up at the house that night and felt empty. She hadn't talked to her family in Asheville since she'd left almost ten years ago. Her father was a hard man who'd clung to his old Southern name. His family lost all their money in the market crash, but they never lost their pride. Margaret was his oldest of seven daughters and she took care of her loud, needy sisters after her mother died giving birth to the last one. She cleaned the house from day to night and kept their clothes stitched and fine, because her father wanted to give the illusion to all who knew them that they could afford servants. Even working as hard as she did, her father expected her to keep her appearance impeccable, because he said her beauty was his only thing of value. She thought he meant he valued *her*, and that was the only thing that kept her going. Later, when he brought Marco to dinner, when he forced Margaret to sit next to Marco at the table, then had her younger sisters serve them drinks on the veranda and leave them alone, she understood. All she was to him was an investment. And as soon as all her sisters were out of the baby stage and able to care for themselves, he'd basically sold her to the man who offered the most.

After that, she couldn't wait to get away.

Rawley had opened the door for her and she'd stepped out. She remembered it had been a mild winter. The grass was still green.

"Good night, Mrs. Cirrini," he'd said. "Have a joyous Christmas."

"Good night," was all she'd managed before her voice broke. She tried to hurry away, but Rawley caught her hand. She was wearing her red swing coat with the high funnel collar, a red pillbox hat, and white gloves. She'd looked beautiful, young and stylish. She still had that outfit tucked away in the attic. Later, for years after it ended, she would go up and put it on when Marco wasn't home.

"What's wrong?"

"Nothing. Please let go of my hand. The neighbors will see."

"There's no one around. Tell me what's wrong."

"Nothing. I must be tired, that's all." Then, before she knew it, she was crying. Bawling. She couldn't control it. She couldn't remember the last time she'd cried, and she was appalled at herself for doing so now.

Rawley had taken her into his arms. Oh, it had felt so good, just to be held. He was gentle with her, obviously not wanting to hurt her or scare her, because she was so small and he was so big and inexperienced.

She'd wept for a long time, until at last there were no more tears. She quieted and stilled completely, shocked to find herself in his arms, and then afraid to move because she didn't want him to let go.

"Better?" he'd asked, and she heard his words in his chest, her ear to his heart.

She looked up at him and nodded. They'd stared at each other for a long time.

He slowly lowered his head, slowly enough for her to pull away if she'd wanted to. She should have. She was Marco Cirrini's beautiful ice-queen wife. He was the naive blue-collar son of the man who owned the local cab company. But for all those reasons, and hundreds more, she didn't move.

His lips finally touched hers, and she suddenly felt alive, melting slowly. She never would have known if it weren't for Rawley. She never would have felt her own heart. He'd shown her she actually had one.

And in return, she'd broken his.

She felt a cold gush of air and snapped out of it to see that they'd stopped in front of the newly renovated Downtown Inn, where the luncheon was being held. Rawley was holding the cab door open for her. She looked up at him, the wind blowing his hair, his jacket collar flapping. She felt strangely content, like she felt when she would sometimes dream of him. There would still be Livia Lynley-White to deal with, but she decided to forgive Josey, just this once.

Rawley slowly extended his hand to help her out.

And with a deep breath, she touched him for the first time in forty years.

The next afternoon, mail in hand, Adam walked up the steps to the Cirrinis' porch. It was finally snowing. He'd felt it coming for days. He always could. He loved when it snowed. At least he used to. These days it was more like a memory of happiness. He used to believe good things happened in this kind of weather, but that was before he almost died one snowy day. He deliberately lost touch with the man he used to be. That man was foolish and careless. The man he was today was safe and calm. This was his second chance to live. This was the life he was supposed to lead now.

It didn't always feel like living, though.

But that was the old Adam talking.

He put the mail in the Cirrinis' box and waited for Josey to appear. When she didn't, he frowned and rubbed his forehead. This was ridiculous. So he knew she loved him. He still wanted to see her. He didn't want things to change. Without another thought, he knocked on the door.

A small, pretty woman with caramel-colored skin opened the door. She looked at him curiously.

"Mail?" she asked.

"Oh. Right." He reached over to the mailbox and took out the mail, then he held it up to show her. He felt like an idiot. "Is Josey here?"

"Oldsey?"

"No, Josey."

"It's okay, Helena. I'll take care of this," Josey said, suddenly appearing behind her.

Helena skittered away, leaving Josey there in the doorway, staring at him guardedly. But then her eyes slid past him, and she smiled.

"It's finally snowing!" she said, opening the screen door. "I've been waiting for this for *days*."

She went to the porch railing and stuck her hand out, the rainy snow pooling on her palm. She loved snow. That was strange. He knew she loved snow. He knew that from three years of coming to her door.

"It's so beautiful."

"It's going to be deep. Great for snowmen," he said as he came to stand beside her.

She laughed, as if the thought had never occurred to her. "I've never made a snowman."

"No?"

She shook her head. "It's a neighborhood rule."

He was staring at her now, at her dark shiny curls and her skin so fair it looked like cold fresh cream. "You don't have to avoid me, Josey," he said. "There's no reason for it."

She stared straight ahead, watching the snow. She'd gone very still.

"We're okay. I like what we have," he continued.

"Yes, I'm sure you do."

"What's that supposed to mean?"

"Nothing."

"No, I want to know."

"It means, Adam, that *you* get to be object of someone's affection. I don't." She suddenly waved her hands as if to erase what she'd said from the air. "Oh, God," she said, turning to him. "Forget I said that, please."

He couldn't help but smile.

"Listen, while you're here, I want to talk to you about Chloe," she said, changing the subject in a flash.

He nodded, encouraging her to talk, to interact. Anything to keep her from running away. "Okay."

"The reason Chloe keeps seeing this Julian person is because he's telling her he knows who Jake slept with."

"Damn," Adam said, surprised. "I'll let Jake know."

"No, please don't tell him," she said. "Just see if you can find out who it is, okay? I'm not trying to butt into their relationship. I'm just trying to keep her from seeing Julian again. He's hurt someone else I know. I don't want him to do it again."

She'd never asked him for anything. How could he say no? He handed her the mail. "I'll see what I can do."

"Thanks."

He watched her walk to her door. *You get to be the object of someone's affection. I don't.* "Josey?" he suddenly said.

She turned.

He hesitated. Don't change things. "Have a nice Thanksgiving."

"You too, Adam."

At first the snow was light and mixed with rain like confetti, white and silver, at an anniversary party. It was not enough, Margaret decided, to keep her from her hair appointment that afternoon. Thanksgiving was a day away, and this was the last opportunity to get her hair done before the start of the tedious Christmas social season. Her holiday wardrobe from Wiseman and Farrow had arrived by express courier earlier that week. She used to have Josey drive her into Asheville twice a year for clothes from the old, exclusive shop. But after Margaret broke her hip, Mrs. Farrow's granddaughter came up and took her measurements—she was proud to say she was as trim as she was forty years ago—and the shop sent her clothes twice a year now, at springtime and Christmastime. This year for the holiday they'd sent brilliant reds and tasteful golds and blues the color of her eyes. She would always be the best-dressed woman in Bald Slope.

There were a lot of things about her body she couldn't control—her unpredictable bones, her papery skin—but a nice wardrobe and beautiful hair, *that* she had some power over. Even Livia Lynley-White said she was still a beauty.

Not that she meant it as a compliment.

"I want you to go to the grocery store while I have my hair done," Margaret said as Josey drove her to the salon, after some quibbling that was very unlike Josey. *The snow is going to be deep*, Josey had said. *We don't want to get stuck. Why don't you wait to have your hair done?*

Wait, she'd said. Like it wasn't important.

"Maybe I should stay with you," Josey said, her eyes on the road. "The snow is going to get heavier, and I might not be able to get back to you."

"Don't be silly. Go to the store. I made a list." Margaret snapped open her purse and put the list on the dashboard. "Since Helena has the day off tomorrow, I want pastries for breakfast, a sandwich and apple chips for lunch and a salad for dinner. That should be easy enough for you to prepare."

Josey sighed, just a puff of air, like she was trying to see her breath in the cold. "It's the day before Thanksgiving, and it's snowing. The grocery store will be a madhouse."

Margaret stared at Josey's profile. Something was changing with Josey, and Margaret didn't like it at all. She was spending more time out with her errands. She would not tell Margaret who her *friend* was. She was expressing opinions much more freely. It was almost as if she'd been practicing, like someone had been giving her lessons.

"Josey?" Margaret said.

"Yes, Mother?"

"You *are* going to the grocery store and you *are* going to get everything on my list."

"Of course I am, Mother," Josey said, sounding surprised. "Was there ever any question?"

That was the problem. There was. There suddenly was.

When Margaret entered the salon, she was relieved to see that Annabelle Drake was there. That meant Rawley had already dropped her off and left. Annabelle was a nice enough woman, but she was one of those women who couldn't do anything alone. She never went to the beauty salon without checking to see if four other people she knew were going to be there. She had breakfast with her eldest daughter. She had lunch with her youngest. She had dinner with her middle child, the son. Every single day. She didn't trust herself to do anything alone. This was, Margaret figured, in large part due to her late husband, Don, a successful doctor and all-around louse. He'd told Annabelle that she was incapable so many times that it had sunk into her marrow. Margaret wondered if Rawley found Annabelle's vulnerability attractive.

"Margaret, you have such beautiful hair," Annabelle said when Margaret was seated in the stylist's chair beside her.

"Thank you." Longer hair like hers, almost touching her shoulders, with several shades of blond highlights painted into her gray, was hard to maintain at her age. But she wasn't going to let her hair go steely and get a perm like Annabelle.

"And those shoes are just darling."

"I had them specially made," she said, sticking her foot out so everyone could see. She was beautiful. She was more beautiful than Annabelle. And she had more money.

The salon was busy, the air swimming with plans and rumors and favorite Thanksgiving recipes. It took longer than it usually did for her hairdresser to finish with her hair. Then Margaret had to wait for the manicurist. It was all very inconvenient, and her hip was now aching, but she was generous with her tips anyway. She wanted to be well thought of. And it was always easier to be generous with people you didn't know well. Afterward, she went to the reception area, expecting to see Josey waiting for her.

But Josey wasn't there.

Margaret had just walked up to the receptionist's desk to ask if her daughter had called or been by, when the bell over the door rang. Relieved that Josey was now there, she felt free to be angry with her for not being there when she was supposed to be.

But when she turned, it wasn't Josey she saw.

It was Rawley Pelham.

His jacket and moleskin driving cap were covered in snow and he took a moment to brush them off before he walked farther in. For a moment it was like he was shaking dust off, as if he'd just come out of storage.

"Mrs. Drake will be finished in just a few minutes," the receptionist told Rawley.

"You say that every time," Rawley said with a wink. "I get here later and later each visit, and still I wait."

"Would you like a cup of coffee?"

He took a seat on one of the couches. "That would be nice, thank you."

The receptionist went to get his coffee, leaving Rawley and Margaret to stare at each other. He was in his mid-sixties now, his hair silver. She'd noticed just this past summer, however, that when he stood in the sun, glints of auburn still shone through. The young man she once knew wasn't all gone.

Talk to me, she thought. *Say something*.

When the receptionist came back and handed Rawley a cup of coffee, Margaret finally turned away and headed to the ladies' room, where she intended to hide until Rawley left.

The phone rang as she was walking away. The receptionist said a few words into the receiver, then called, "Wait, Mrs. Cirrini, your daughter is on the phone."

Margaret hastily walked back and took the phone. "Josey? Are you all right? Why aren't you here?"

"I'm just leaving the grocery store," Josey said, sounding tense. "It's going to take a while to get there."

"Why?"

"Because the roads are terrible and there's a ton of traffic. The grocery store was packed."

"I don't understand you, Josey. Are you doing this on purpose?"

"Why would I do this on purpose, Mother?"

Rawley stood and walked to the desk. He set his coffee cup down. "Will you ask Mrs. Cirrini if I could speak to her daughter?" he said to the receptionist, though he was looking at Margaret.

"Mrs. Cirrini . . ." the receptionist started to say.

"Why do you want to speak to my daughter?" Margaret asked him.

He took a few steps to her and gently took the phone away from her. She leaned in slightly, but he didn't quite touch her. *Almost*, though.

"Josey, it's Rawley Pelham. Where are you?" he said into the receiver, watching Margaret the entire time. "I see.

You'll never make it here, not in that car. Go home and be careful. I'm here to pick up Annabelle Drake and it would be no problem at all to drop your mother off at your house. I have chains on my tires." Pause. "You're very welcome. Remember, be careful."

"I can't believe you just did that," Margaret said as he handed the receiver back to the receptionist. "Why are the two of you suddenly in cahoots? Did you ever think to ask me if that was what I wanted?" As soon as she said it, as soon as she saw the look on his face, she knew how hypocritical it sounded, considering what had happened between the two of them.

Rawley turned to Annabelle, who had just appeared at Margaret's side. Margaret smelled her perm before she saw her. "Annabelle, will you help Mrs. Cirrini outside when I pull the cab up to the front door? Josey can't make it here in this snow."

"I don't want you to take me home," Margaret said desperately. *You don't even like me.*

"Don't you agree, Annabelle, that Josey would never make it from the market, to here, and back to the Cirrinis' neighborhood in this weather?"

"He's right, Margaret," Annabelle said, patting her on the arm. "Come with us. You'll be our chaperone. There's a rumor going around about me and Rawley, you know, because we spend so much time together in his cab."

Margaret watched him walk outside and disappear into the heavy veil of snow. "Yes. I know."

It had ended at a summer party Marco had thrown. Marco threw the best parties. Everyone clamored for an invitation. This particular party was island-themed, complete with a tiki bar in the backyard, paper lanterns hung in the trees and waiters who wore white pants and Hawaiian shirts. Each guest was even given a lei. Marco had taken care of everything. He never let Margaret plan their parties. All she had to do was look beautiful.

Livia Lynley-White wore a god-awful muumuu to the party. Her dark hair was just beginning to go white, and her bouffant looked like a dirty cotton ball. She watched Margaret at the party. She always watched her, and that's how she eventually found out. Margaret had been seeing Rawley secretly for over a year now, and she was getting careless. The time she spent with him was never enough, and she had started making mistakes in her desperation to be with him.

It was dusk and Mrs. Langdon Merryweather was ready to leave, so Margaret went inside to call for a cab. The older guests liked to leave early because Marco's parties grew famously rowdy after dark, when Marco brought out his good liquor.

Margaret knew it was Rawley coming to pick up Mrs. Merryweather, so she made an excuse to stay in the house, near the front windows, to watch for him. She wanted him to see her in her outfit, in her sarong and sandals and her tight sleeveless button-down tied at her waist so that a strip of skin at her stomach showed.

She saw him drive by the house. There wasn't anyplace to park in front of the house because of the party, so he had to park down the block. She left and met him halfway, on the sidewalk by the boxwoods in the Franklins' front yard.

His eyes scraped her body and he smiled as she walked toward him.

"Hello, Rawley," she said in the voice she always used when they saw each other in public.

"Hello, Mrs. Cirrini."

"Hot evening, isn't it?"

"It is indeed." She stopped in front of him on the sidewalk. "You look incredible," he whispered, his hands stiff at his sides, as if fighting an irresistible force to lift them, to touch her.

She looked over her shoulder. No one knew he was here yet. They had a few moments, so she pulled him into the Franklins' yard, behind the boxwoods. The Franklins were at the party. No one would see.

They kissed, his big hands going all over her. She loved this about him, how eager he always was, how he let her guide him to all the right places, where it felt the best. He made her eager. She thought about him all the time. Her body ached from his absence and sang when he was near. Sometimes this was all they had time for, a fast, passionate encounter. Sometimes, though, she would hire him to take her to Asheville to shop, but they'd stop halfway there and have a picnic on the Parkway and they'd talk all day. He was a good man, earnest and smart. He could have stayed in the Army, or gone to college, but he came back to help his family with their business. He was their only son. Their joy and pride surrounded him like a halo. When she thought back, she always lingered on that. She'd never known another man like him. His family loved him, and he gave his love so effortlessly. She wanted that. She wanted that to fill her until she was full. But there was never enough time.

He'd had her shirt unbuttoned, his mouth trailing down her neck, when they suddenly heard, "Well, well, well."

They pulled apart and Margaret's hands went to her blouse, fumbling with her buttons.

"I knew it," Livia said, self-righteousness making her

seem ten feet tall, like she could step on them if she wanted to. "I knew if I just waited long enough, I would find out who you really are. Adulterer. *Slut*. You have shamed Marco Cirrini and everything he's done for this town."

Margaret had known she was doing the wrong thing. But she had not then, and still would not, apologize for it. A good person would have regretted having an affair. But she'd never claimed to be a good person. Rawley was, though. And he was better than this.

"Leave, Rawley," Margaret said flatly.

"I'm not leaving you."

"You have no choice."

"No."

She whipped her head around and said, "Rawley, for the love of God, just go."

When Rawley left, Margaret very calmly made a deal with Livia behind the boxwoods. Margaret didn't ask Livia not to tell Marco. She just asked that Livia not say it was Rawley. He was young. He deserved to get on with his life. He didn't deserve the wrath of Marco, and neither did his family. Livia had agreed, because she got the best of both worlds: She got to tell Marco *and* hold something over Margaret.

Marco had been livid, of course. He'd yelled at her, even pushed her against a wall in their bedroom while guests laughed and got drunk outside. It was the first and only time he'd ever hit her. He wanted to know who it was. Livia had been vague. She said she'd seen Margaret with someone, but she couldn't make out who. But Marco couldn't break Margaret, no matter how angry he got. Ice queens didn't break, after all. They melted. And Marco didn't have enough warmth for that.

He left her to go back to his guests, demanding she fix her cut lip and join him. He would never trust her again, he said. He would have her followed. He would always know what she was doing. He would not be made to look bad.

And he *would* find out who she had been with.

Then he would ruin him.

Rawley came to the door late that night, banging on it. He was going to declare his love for her and he didn't care who knew it. He was going to take on the great Marco Cirrini. Thank God Marco was already passed out upstairs after hard sex she'd taken Valium to get through. She could remember fragments of what came next. She remembered telling Rawley that she didn't love him, that she didn't know how to love. She remembered the feel of the ice forming inside again. She told him she was older. She was married. She'd taken advantage of him. He needed to move on.

She remembered him begging. She remembered trying not to cry, desperate for him to just go away. She'd found how to give love from somewhere deep inside her, a place she never knew existed. She'd been mad at Rawley for making her capable of feeling this way. If he hadn't shown her how, she wouldn't be hurting so much.

And finally, she remembered watching him walk away. The words *please don't leave* stuck in her throat.

And to this day, Rawley had never said another word directly to her.

10

Mellowcreme Pumpkins

She wanted to do this, Chloe told herself. She made another cup of stinging-nettle tea that afternoon, hoping to feel like the decision was the right one. But the only decisions the tea made easier were whether or not to cook a turkey this year (she decided against) and whether or not she should wear a hat if she went out (she decided for). Whether or not she should actually go out with Julian that night was still as murky as the Green Cove River.

What to cook and what to wear were not what she

needed help with. Maybe Nova hadn't given her a high enough dose of the stuff.

Chloe poured the rest of the tea into the sink and watched it swirl down the drain. She was depressed about tomorrow being Thanksgiving. She wouldn't be going to Jake's parents' house this year, and she'd always enjoyed that. She loved seeing what Faith came up with every year, how she would decorate, what her signature libation would be. This was, in fact, going to be Chloe's first Thanksgiving alone. Friends and acquaintances had been calling and leaving messages all day, wishing her a happy holiday. She didn't want to talk to them, didn't want to field their sympathetic offers for her to join in their family celebrations. In fact, the only person she wanted to talk to was Josey, who had called earlier to check up on her. She'd tried calling Josey back, but got her voice mail. That's when Chloe got it in her head to call Julian. She hadn't contacted him since the incident at Nite Lite. She should at least apologize, wish him a happy Thanksgiving.

And, of course, maybe he would finally give her the name of the woman Jake had slept with.

Yesterday when Josey came over with food, Chloe told her that she was through trying to find out who the other woman was. She even said she was definitely not going to see Julian again. And at the time she meant it, because Josey was there and that made Chloe feel better. But what seemed like a good idea then felt like a horrible one now. She didn't have a good rein on her emotions, and her own unpredictability scared her.

Nothing else was working. If she just found out who it was, then everything would get better.

Julian had answered right away, as if he'd been expecting her.

"Hi, Julian, this is Chloe. I'm so sorry about Monday."

"You have some crazy friends," he said, even his censure a seduction, the way it made her feel sorry for him, want to be with him. "My jaw still hurts."

"Why does your jaw hurt?" she asked.

"The big blond guy hit me."

"Adam hit you?" She remembered Adam being there, and Josey had told her it was because Chloe had done some drunk-dialing and called him. But Adam, good-natured Adam, had *hit* him?

"You don't remember?"

"No."

"You were pretty hammered," he said, and that seemed to make him feel better. "All is forgiven, sweetheart. Why don't you come over to my place this afternoon? We can spend the holiday together. I'll tell you all about this other woman. I'll even show you where she lives."

But once again, he wouldn't tell Chloe her name over the phone. It was a way to get her to come to him, and she wanted to believe it was because he didn't want to be alone. He was probably depressed about the holiday too. And what better way for two broken hearts to spend a holiday than spying on one of the people responsible for their heartbreak? Right?

Later, when Chloe walked outside, the snow was coming down heavier than it had a few hours ago, when she closed her shop at noon. She was surprised to see how much of it was on the sidewalk and street. It was a wet, heavy snow and it already reached her ankles. When she got to her VW Beetle in the parking lot beside the building, she sighed. Cars had come and gone in the lot, pushing snow up against her tires. She tried kicking it out of the way, then she bent and pushed it away with her gloved hands. As she was digging in the snow, she noticed something strange. There, at her back tire, under the snow, was a book. She brushed more snow away and picked it up.

Madame Bovary.

She rolled her eyes and threw the book into a snowbank. Books thought she was going to cheat on Jake. That was rich.

Traffic was mad, the heaviest snow falling just as people were getting off from work early for the holiday and skiers were on the road to the slopes to take advantage of the first big snowfall. The secondary roads were quieter, so Chloe cut through Summertime Road. She had to take the highway to get to the address Julian had given her, but there was a wreck and traffic got backed up on the ramp. That's when her little car got stuck. Some people behind her helped her push her Beetle to the shoulder, and she was offered the warm sanctuary of many cars waiting on the ramp, but she declined.

The tea hadn't made her decision easier, and the snow had taken away the choice altogether.

She felt strangely relieved.

Now all she wanted to do was go home.

It took Chloe nearly an hour and a half to walk back to Summertime Road. She was shivering with cold and the snow on the ground was so high now she was forced to adopt a high step that made her thigh muscles burn. Her cheeks were like holly berries, her pink down coat was nearly white with snow, and her favorite Ugg boots were thoroughly wet. She finally let herself stop for a breather when she reached the yellow house that had captured her imagination since the day it had gone on the market.

She stood there and stared at it, stared at it so long that her footprints were covered with snow and it looked like she'd grown there, right out of the sidewalk.

She was startled when the door to the house suddenly flew open and a bald man ran outside to the tiny porch. He was wearing oven mitts and carrying a turkey pan, the turkey inside charred and smoky. He threw the turkey, pan and all, into the snow, where it made a smoke-filled hole.

A short woman in her sixties, wearing overalls and bright purple leather high-tops, stood at the door, shaking her head. "I told you I smelled something burning," she said to the man.

"I followed the directions!" he insisted.

"You put it on broil! I told you we shouldn't have cooked."

Almost simultaneously, they turned, both becoming aware of the person watching them from the sidewalk.

"Hello!" the man called, waving an oven mitt at her. "Are you all right?"

She snapped out of it. "Oh, yes. I'm sorry. I didn't mean to stare."

"You look like you've been out here awhile," the man said. "I thought you were a snowman."

"My car got stuck on the highway. I was walking back home. Sorry about your turkey," she said, and started to trudge toward downtown. Her legs had grown stiff standing there. It hurt to move them.

"You've walked all the way from the highway?" the woman said. "George, help her in here."

George immediately walked down the front steps and into the snow, even though he was wearing Birkenstocks and black socks. "No, I'm fine." She waved to get him to go back. "It's just another couple of blocks."

"You'll get frostbite," the woman called. "And look how heavy the snow is now. George actually looks like he has hair."

By the time he reached her, George's bald pate had a fine layer of snow on it. She was too tired and cold to argue, so she let him lead her inside.

"I'm Zelda Cramdon and this is my husband, George," Zelda said when she closed the door behind them and they all stood in the small foyer.

"I know," Chloe said, trying to smile, but her face was frozen. "I've met you at your open houses."

"You know, you do look familiar, now that I see you up close," Zelda said, taking off Chloe's wet crocheted cap, then helping her out of her coat. "I remember your red hair."

George took off his Birkenstocks and peeled off his socks. "What's your name?"

"C-Chloe Finley," she said, trying to get her boots off herself, but Zelda had to help her.

"Come with me, Chloe, and I'll get you some dry clothes," Zelda said, leading her down the hallway. "George, for God's sake, open a window. The smoke is so thick in here you could eat it."

"Ungrateful woman. You should applaud my budding culinary endeavors," George said, walking barefoot to the kitchen.

"I'll applaud when you cook something edible."

"Am I interrupting your Thanksgiving preparations?" Chloe asked.

"No, no. Our daughter, her husband and the grandkids

were coming in, but they got as far as Asheville and the snow stopped them," Zelda said, showing Chloe into one of the bedrooms that had obviously been made up for her incoming family. There were small touches like a water pitcher and glasses on the nightstand, and a jar of soft peppermints and a stack of folded towels on the bureau. Zelda took one of the towels and handed it to Chloe. "I thought there was no sense in cooking, since it was just going to be the two of us, and I put my feet up to read and watch the snow. Sounds nice, huh? Well, that's when George decided to cook his first Thanksgiving dinner ever—hence the black bird in the yard. We're going to miss our daughter entirely this year. They probably won't be able to get out of Asheville until the day after tomorrow, and that's when they have to leave to go back home." Zelda went through the drawers and brought out a pair of socks, pink sweatpants and a Yale sweatshirt. This, Chloe guessed, had been their daughter's room.

"I'm sorry your family can't be here," Chloe said as Zelda put the clothes on the bed.

Zelda shrugged, though Chloe could tell it really did bother her. "They're staying in a hotel with an indoor pool. The grandkids are in heaven." Zelda focused on Chloe with her sharp bird eyes. "Can I share something with you?"

"Of course," Chloe said, rubbing the towel vigorously over her hair.

"Our daughter bought us a house last year, near her home in Orlando. She bought it and put it in our names and said, 'When you're ready, come down and live close to your grandkids.' When George and I visited and saw what a lovely house it was, how wonderful the weather was, we thought it was a great idea. We were going to do it. We're retired, and these snows take a toll on us. So we put this house on the market, but we priced it so high that we knew no one would be interested. We thought, if it doesn't sell in a year, it's a sign. We would stay. We weren't really ready to leave, you see. Now a year has gone by and we've missed the birth of another grandchild, and now Thanksgiving. We need to be closer to them. George and I decided just this afternoon that we have to move. We're lowering the price on the house."

Chloe stopped drying her hair at that startling news. She forced herself to say something, not to just stare at Zelda. "That must have been a hard decision to make."

"It was. But we made it, then we said we would wait for a sign that it was the right decision. That's when the smoke alarm went off. Then we opened the door, and there you were." Zelda turned to the door. "I'll leave you to change. Just drape your wet clothes over the radiator."

When Zelda left, Chloe peeled off her clothes. Her skin was icy. She felt shivery inside, too, but she wasn't so sure that had to do with the cold.

They were lowering the price on this house. Her house.

After she'd put on the dry clothes, she left the room. She found George and Zelda speaking in serious tones in the kitchen, which looked like a grocery store had exploded in it. There were packages half open and vegetables half cut all over the countertops. Flour coated the floor. Pots and pans were everywhere.

They stopped talking when she entered. "I'm going to try to salvage what's left in here," Zelda said. "George, show her around."

George led her out of the kitchen. "You said you've been to our open houses. Do you go to a lot of others?"

"No, just this one. Just this house."

"Do you have a favorite room?" George asked.

"Yes."

"So quickly she answers. Which one?"

"The library," she said softly.

George smiled. "My wife's favorite too. Lead the way."

There was a fire in the fireplace and it made the dark wood of the ceiling-high built-in bookcases glow. There wasn't an inch of wall space that didn't have a shelf occupied by books. The room felt so complete, so warm. She'd dreamed of this room for weeks after she saw it at their first open house.

George sat in the window seat by the bay window and crossed his legs, resting one ankle on the opposite knee. He was now wearing bunny slippers. "What would you do with this room, if it was yours?"

"Nothing," Chloe said as she walked around. "It's perfect as it is. I have books. Hundreds of boxes of them. They would all go here."

"You're a reader, hmm?"

She stopped, her back to him. She smoothed her hand over the spines of a row of books. "I have a . . . special relationship with books."

"Books can be possessive, can't they? You're walking around in a bookstore and a certain one will jump out at you, like it had moved there on its own, just to get your attention. Sometimes what's inside will change your life, but sometimes you don't even have to read it. Sometimes it's a comfort just to have a book around. Many of these books haven't even had their spines cracked. 'Why do you buy books you don't even read?' our daughter asks us. That's like asking someone who lives alone why they bought a cat. For company, of course. Here, come here. I want to show you something." He stood and led her to the hallway and opened the coat closet.

It was packed, absolutely crammed, with books. "Look at this. Howard, our realtor, told us that we had to move all the stacks of books out of the bedrooms and hallway in order to stage the house. He said clutter distracted potential buyers. He called books *clutter*."

Zelda came out of the kitchen, the warm scent of charred Thanksgiving trailing behind her. She handed Chloe a cup of coffee. "George, Howard said not to deliberately show people that."

"We've got ourselves a reader, Zelda."

"Really," Zelda said, looking at Chloe thoughtfully. "Well, you didn't manage to ruin everything in the kitchen, George. Dinner will be ready in a little while. We can talk books, Chloe. How would you like that?"

"I'd like that very much."

"When I first heard your name, I knew it sounded familiar," Zelda said. "I finally remember why. I remember there being a Finley farm off the highway."

"Yes! That was where I grew up."

"Whatever happened to it?"

"My great-grandparents raised me. When they got sick, I had to sell it to pay their medical bills."

"That must have been hard for you."

"Giving up a house you love is always hard."

"That," Zelda said, "was the perfect answer."

Josey had turned off all the lamps in her bedroom so she could stand at her window and watch the snow fall in the darkness, but Della Lee wanted the light on in the closet so she could see to cut photos from Josey's travel magazines. She was going to make a collage. It was her new thing. Josey had given up trying to make sense of Della Lee, but she figured it really didn't matter now. As soon as Mr. Lamar's letter came, she would be leaving anyway.

It wasn't as comforting a thought as she wanted it to be, mostly because when Della Lee left, Josey wouldn't even have Adam anymore. He said he didn't want things to change, but they already had. She could feel it.

Well, at least with no more distractions, Josey would be able to focus solely on her mother again, and that would make Margaret happy. Margaret had come in after Rawley had walked her to the door in the snow, and had gone directly to her bedroom. She hadn't said a word to Josey, and she'd only talked to Helena once, to tell her she would take her dinner in her room.

Josey could feel her censure like a slap. She didn't like displeasing her mother, but at the same time she didn't understand how Margaret could blame her for the weather. She wondered how long it would take to live this down. She could imagine, for years to come, every time it snowed, Margaret would bring up the time Josey had left her at the salon with no way home.

Good times, good times.

"You have a message on your cell phone from Chloe," Della Lee said from the closet.

Josey turned to her, sitting in a pool of light in the otherwise dark room. "How do you know that?"

Della Lee shrugged as she carefully cut out a photo of the Eiffel Tower with the scissors she'd filched from Josey's desk drawer.

Josey sighed. "I'd be mad about you using my cell, except I never get messages and I never would have checked." Josey went to her purse and got her phone. She walked over to the closet, to the light, in order to see the buttons to retrieve the message. "Who did you call?"

"No one."

"Was it Julian?"

"I didn't call anyone."

"Fine. Don't tell me." Josey retrieved the message and listened as Chloe told her that she was fine, not to worry about her, and that she'd call Josey on Thanksgiving. She didn't sound as bad as yesterday, and Josey was glad. Maybe Chloe was over the rough part now.

Josey put her phone back in her purse. Now, to take care of *her* rough part. "Della Lee," she said, turning to her, "I think we need to talk about what you're going to do when Mr. Lamar's letter arrives. You don't have much time, so you need to start planning. I'd like to think that going through all my travel magazines is a good sign. Do you want to travel?"

Della Lee pointed to the stack of magazines she'd brought out of the secret closet and set beside her. "Obviously not as much as you do."

"You're going to have to leave. You promised."

Della Lee made a happy sound when she found a photo of the Arc de Triomphe. She began to cut it out. Apparently Paris was going to be an important part of her collage. Josey had always dreamed of going to Paris. "I've got to get you settled, then I'll go."

"But I am settled," Josey insisted. "So we're back to figuring out where you're going when you leave."

"It's all planned," Della Lee said.

This was news to Josey. "It is?"

"Of course. I knew where I was going the minute I left my house."

The minute she left her house. The minute she left behind her childhood with a troubled mother. The minute she left behind her criminal record. The minute she left behind Julian. She left her *entire life*. How did she do that? Josey had only dreamed of that kind of gumption. "Then where are you going? Tell me all about it."

"I told you, north."

"But where north?"

"I don't have to tell you everything," Della Lee said. "And, really, it's none of your business anyway."

Typical Della Lee. "Why does that line not work on you?"

Della Lee just smiled.

For three years now, Adam had been going to Jake's parents' house for Thanksgiving, which they always celebrated on Wednesday night instead of the traditional Thursday. This was the first year, however, that he'd gone as Jake's date.

"I still think you should have bought me a corsage," Adam joked as they walked up the steps to the door.

Jake shook his head. "I can't take you anywhere."

"This just feels strange without Chloe."

"Everything feels strange without Chloe."

They stopped on the porch and brushed snow off their coats, then stomped off what little was on their shoes. It was still snowing, yet there was no snow on the driveway or the walkways leading to the Yardleys' large home. Adam had always thought this place was inhabited by magically perfect people. Snow didn't fall on their concrete. Weeds never grew in their yard. The house never needed painting. And there was always shade when you needed it in the summer, though there were no trees around.

Adam thought it was a fascinating place to visit, cool and otherworldly. But then again, he wasn't related to anyone inside. Jake hated everything about it.

"I'm dreading this," Jake said, going to the door and pushing the doorbell.

A maid opened the door and they were shown inside. Faith Yardley had outdone herself with the decorations, and apparently at the last minute. There were crystals that looked like snowflakes hanging on strings falling from the ceiling. The cornucopias and the leaf arrangements on the mantels and tabletops had been lightly sprayed with artificial snow. Rims of glasses were dipped in sugar and Jake told him the punch this year was called snow soup.

"How did your mother manage to do all of this in such a short period of time?" Adam asked as the maid took their coats.

"A lot of caffeine and paying the help triple-overtime. When I talked to her this morning, she was so excited. She's been doing this for twenty years, and this is the first time there's been snow for her Thanksgiving party."

They walked into the grand living room with the large fireplace. Despite the snow, the Yardleys' dinner party still had a good turnout. There were about thirty people there this year, a large enough number to get lost in, which Adam could do with a little more ease than Jake, the host's son, whom everyone wanted to say hello to.

Faith was the first to greet them. She was beautiful in a red off-the-shoulder dress. "My baby," she said, hugging Jake. "I'm so sorry Chloe couldn't be here."

"I am too, Mom." He gave her the box of candy he brought her every Thanksgiving. She took the box like it was the best gift she'd ever received.

"And Adam, I'm glad to see you again." Adam handed her the bouquet of flowers he always brought for the hostess, and she gave him a hug. She smelled like sugar cookies. "I watched you walk in, and I do believe your limp is worse this evening. Normally I can't tell you have a bad leg at all."

"It's the snow and the cold, Faith. It just stiffens up a little."

"Then stand by the fire. I'll have a waiter bring you a drink. If you'll excuse me." She started to turn but then stopped and smiled at Jake. She actually pinched his cheek. "You're my beautiful boy. I love you so much."

"I like your mom," Adam said as they watched her walk away.

"She's a saint."

"Jake," his father called.

"And that's the reason why," Jake murmured.

Kyle Yardley approached them, smiling and saying hello to guests he passed along the way, kissing women on the cheek, clapping men on the back. He and Jake looked so much alike it sometimes caused people to look twice when they were together. "Jake, I just got a very interesting call from Howard Zim," Kyle said when he stopped in front of them. He held out his hand to Adam. "Good to see you, Adam."

Adam shook his hand. "Kyle."

"Who is Howard Zim?" Jake asked.

"He's a realtor. I play racquetball with him. I told him about your troubles with Chloe."

Jake was instantly riled. "Why in the hell did you—"

"Just listen to me. He knows about your troubles with Chloe, which is why he thought I might like to know that the Cramdons on Summertime Road called him not an hour ago to say that they were ready to lower their price on the house, and they wanted to give first dibs to someone—a charming young woman named Chloe Finley."

The shock of this obviously had Jake reeling. He couldn't seem to say anything.

"This is your fault for telling her in the first place. You should have listened to me. But now you have to focus on stopping her from making this terrible mistake. You should consider buying the house out from under her."

Jake's face was tight, growing red. Before he totally lost it, Jake turned and left the room.

Adam caught up with him in the foyer, getting his coat from the maid. "Jake, you're not really going to buy it, are you? Anyone who knows Chloe knows she's always loved that house."

Jake jerked his coat on and walked out.

Adam nodded to the maid and she handed him his coat too.

When Adam got outside, Jake was on the porch, staring into the snow-covered yard. "He told me to give her space, to let her realize how much she needs me. What a load of crap! He doesn't know Chloe. I know Chloe. She quit college to care for her great-grandparents. She had to sell the house that had been in her family for generations, and she got a damn good price for it, all on her own. She was just twenty. She moved into the storeroom of her shop and didn't complain because her great-grandparents were being taken care of and that's what mattered most to her. She's as strong as hell, Adam. But she was devastated when her great-grandparents died. They left her alone. I knew she hated to be left alone. And I left her alone." Jake slapped one of the porch pillars. "I've lost her, haven't I?"

"No, you haven't. Don't go there."

Jake grew silent. After a while, he said, stunned, "I can't believe she's buying a house."

Adam thought of what Josey had told him earlier that day. It wasn't something he would normally ask Jake. He thought if Jake didn't want to tell him, that was fine. But for Josey, he asked, "Who was she, Jake? Who was the woman you slept with?"

Jake shook his head. "No one."

"Chloe wants to know. Why not tell her? It might help," he said, carefully avoiding the Julian issue.

"I can't."

"Why not?"

"Because I can't."

"Don't you think Chloe is more important than keeping this a secret? What's the point?" Adam said, stuffing his hands in his coat pockets.

"For the love of God, Adam, you know Chloe is the most important thing in my life. But it's not my life I'm worried about."

"I'm not following."

"I've messed everything up." Jake suddenly barged down the front steps. "I'm a fucking idiot," he said, furiously kicking snow onto the walkway. It was as if he couldn't take it anymore, as if he didn't want anyone believing that the Yardleys were so perfect that snow never fell on their concrete. When the snow melted quickly, he made snowballs and threw them at the house. One hit the pillar Adam was standing beside, and he got pelted with icy pellets.

"Hey!" Adam said.

"Sorry."

Adam walked down the steps. "I may have a bad leg but I still have great aim," he said, packing a firm snowball and hurling it at Jake.

Ten minutes of this and their suits, coats and wingtips were soaked. This is why Faith sent Jake and Adam home with their dinner in paper bags, but with no dessert.

For they had been very bad boys.

When they got to Adam's house, they ate in front of the television, which they both agreed was a much better way to spend the evening. But they both admitted they missed the pumpkin pie. Jake went to bed early after trying to call Chloe several times and not getting an answer.

Adam stayed up. He could still hear the snow ticking, like small bird pecks, against the large front window, but it was slacking off. He'd wanted to stay out in it longer that evening, but between his aching leg and Jake's mother, he couldn't.

He turned off the lights and opened the blinds in the living room. One of his neighbors across the street already had his Christmas lights up. Off in the distance he could see Bald Slope Mountain. He could even make out, faintly, the edge of the lights from the slopes on the other side.

He wondered if Josey skied at all. She loved the snow, yet she had never made a snowman. He'd been thinking about her all day. It was easy to resent people who forced you to see things in a different way. And that's exactly what Josey was doing, by telling Chloe that she loved him, by stepping outside of the confines of what people expected of her. He supposed he did resent it at first, because her changing meant everyone around her had to change. It meant *he* had to change, even if it was just his way of thinking. But when he finally gave in to it that evening, staring out at Bald Slope Mountain, he found it was surprisingly easy. He wanted things to stay the same between them, but he knew now they couldn't and he was almost . . . excited about it.

He grabbed his coat and went to the door.

Josey suddenly opened her eyes. It was unusually quiet. So quiet, in fact, that the sound of something hitting the side of the house had drawn her out of her sleep. She waited to hear it again, but there was nothing. "Della Lee?" she whispered.

"Yes?" Della Lee called from the closet.

"Did you hear that?"

"It sounded like it came from your window."

Josey sat up. Her stomach felt jumpy, but she wasn't hungry. And something else wasn't right. It was too dark. "Is the power out?"

"It went out about an hour ago. I was downstairs when it happened. Helena was chasing me from room to room in the dark. She finally had me trapped in the kitchen, but when she tried to turn on the lights, they wouldn't come on. Saved my ass. You should have heard her curse."

"I asked you not to tease her."

"It gives her something to do. She's lonely."

She was startled again by the sound, like a wet slap against the side of the house. "What *is* that?" Josey threw the covers off and went to her window. Had a tree fallen? The wind wasn't blowing.

She opened her window and stuck her head out. It had stopped snowing. The world outside looked like it was coated in a thick layer of white cake frosting, like it would stick to the roof of your mouth.

"Josey," someone called in the quiet night.

She looked down to see a figure standing in the yard. His head was tilted back as he looked up at her. He was grinning, his entire face illuminated by the moonlight. "*Adam?*"

"Your mailman?" Della Lee asked from the closet, sounding equally surprised.

"Come down," he called, like in a fairy tale. "Let's make a snowman."

The air was cold on her face. The floor was hard beneath her feet. She could smell the peppermint on the windowsill. Inside her own skin, her heart was drumming against her chest and she could feel the blood surging through her veins. She had all this as proof that she was, indeed, awake, that all this was real.

But she still couldn't believe it.

"Josey?" Adam said again.

"What are you doing here?"

"I told you. Let's make a snowman."

"Are you insane?"

He knelt and scooped up a handful of snow, then he packed it between his hands. "Come down or I'll throw a snowball at you."

"You wouldn't dare."

His grin turned cunning. "Are you sure about that?" He tossed the snowball from hand to hand. "Which one is your mother's window?"

"You *wouldn't*."

He lifted his snowball threateningly.

"Okay, all right. I'll be right down. Just don't throw anything." Josey quickly ducked back inside and closed the window. She just stood there for a moment.

"Well, this is interesting," Della Lee said. "What does he want?"

"To make a snowman. To make a snowman at . . ." She automatically looked at her digital clock, then remembered the power was out. "I don't even know what time it is."

Josey was wearing pajamas, so she fumbled around in the darkness until she found her snow boots and a sweater. Then she put on her long black coat and grabbed a wool cap and gloves on her way out.

"Have fun. Use condoms!" Della Lee called after her.

As soon as Josey reached the downstairs landing, Helena stepped out of her room. She was holding an industrial-sized flashlight, which she'd bought along with Mace and a personal emergency alarm after Wade Beasley had been arrested for murdering his housekeeper earlier in the year. Spells and superstitions were all well and good, but even Helena saw that a good defense sometimes involved a ten-pound flashlight too.

"It's just me," Josey said, shielding her eyes from the light. "I'm going outside for a minute."

Helena lowered the flashlight. "The mail here."

"I know."

"Oldsey like mail."

"Yes," Josey said. "I do."

Helena smiled and shut her bedroom door.

Josey went to the front door, then stepped outside onto the porch. Adam was waiting there for her. Waiting for *her*. This made no sense. She closed the door behind her and crossed her arms over her chest. "Are you drunk?"

"No."

She looked out to the street. There were no tire tracks in the snow. It was like he'd dropped from the moon. "How did you get here?"

"I drove. I have four-wheel. But I had to park at the bottom of the hill and walk the rest of the way."

"And you couldn't make a snowman in your neighborhood because?"

"Because you weren't there."

Words left her.

"You told me today you've never made a snowman. I want to teach you."

"Oh." He was feeling sorry for her again. "Well, I'm sorry you had to come all this way, but we can't do this here," she said, taking a step back to the door.

"Why not?"

"Because it's against neighborhood rules."

"Who's going to know it was us?" He turned. "Come on."

"What about your leg?" she asked. He was struggling a little with it as he walked down the steps.

"To hell with my leg." He got to the bottom step and looked up at her. He was wearing a yellow Thinsulate jacket, black gloves and a black beret, the kind with a toggle in the back. She'd loved this man for three years, but she knew so little about him. She'd been too afraid to ask him about his injury, to ask him anything personal, because then he might suspect how she felt. But now that he knew how she felt about him, what was the harm in asking?

"How did you hurt it?"

He nodded to the yard. "Come make a snowman with me and I'll tell you."

"I don't want to know that badly."

"Yes, you do." He held his hand out to her.

So what if this made her pitiful? So what if her desire to be with him overruled her pride? This was Adam holding his hand out to her. Of course she was going to take it. Just for tonight. Because when would it ever happen again?

Snowman 101 included instructions on first finding the perfect place to build, preferably as close to the street as possible so everyone could see your creation. Then there was the art of packing a firm snowball, putting it in the snow, and then rolling it around the yard in a wide circle, letting it pick up snow and grow. This, he said, you did three times. The bottom was the biggest ball, the middle was medium, and the top was the smallest.

Adam made it look easy. She kept trying, but her snowballs all fell apart when she tried to roll them.

"You're pressing too hard," Adam said.

"I am not. I just want a small snowman."

When he laughed at her, she picked up her pitiful snowman ball and threw it at him.

He straightened slowly. "The young apprentice has provoked the master."

Josey started to run, to take cover behind the stringy forsythia bushes, but his snowball hit her in the back. She made an indignant sound and stopped. This was war.

He had better aim than her, but that didn't matter once she got close enough to pelt him. She hit her target several times, once even in the face, she was proud to say. Unfortunately, she was close enough now for him to grab her by the arm, then drop a handful of snow down the front of her sweater. She shrieked, slipped, then suddenly fell back into the snow, taking him with her. He was halfway on top of her, his hands in the snow on either side of her shoulders. She clutched one hand to her wet sweater and put the other hand over her mouth to muffle her laughter. It was a wonder they hadn't woken up the whole neighborhood by now.

She threw her head back and laughed so hard her eyes filled with tears and she had to squeeze them shut. Tears popped out and fell down her temples, warm against her cold skin. God, when had she had a better time? Letting go felt so good. When she was finally able to catch her breath, she opened her eyes and saw that Adam was staring down at her with the most serious look on his face. She moved her hand away from her mouth, her laughter dying. His eyes went to her lips and lingered there a moment.

Then he suddenly rolled off of her and got to his feet.

"I hurt my leg skiing on Bald Slope Mountain," he said, extending a hand to her.

She sat up, dazed. *What just happened here?* She looked up at him, then took his hand. He pulled her to her feet. "It must have been a bad fall."

"It was. No more skiing for me. No more skiing, no more sailing, no more cliff diving, no more mountain climbing. No more travel."

It all sounded so wonderful, so exotic. "You used to do all those things?"

"Yes." He turned and walked to his snowman-in-progress.

She quickly followed. "Why don't you anymore? Are you not able?"

"I don't know. I haven't tried." He shrugged. "It was time to settle down."

"Did you like traveling?"

"I loved it. Here, help me lift this middle ball onto the bottom one."

She walked over to him and together they lifted the big snowball. "So you haven't left Bald Slope at all since your accident."

"Maybe sometime in the future I'll go see my brother in Chicago. See some old friends there. I'm not ready yet." He started making the last ball.

"I didn't know you lived in Chicago."

He smiled as he rolled the ball around, making it bigger. "We think we know each other, but we really don't, do we? I was a lawyer in Chicago. Before the accident."

Her brows rose. Adam was a lawyer? This was like *candy*. "Did the accident make you give up the law?"

"No. I gave it up because I hated it." When he got the head of the snowman the right size, he picked it up and walked back to the body. His limp was getting worse the longer he was out there.

"Why didn't you give it up before the accident?"

"I don't know," he said, setting the head on top with a plop. "I guess almost dying makes you reevaluate things."

She couldn't speak for a moment. "You almost died?" she finally said softly.

"It was the first time I was ever hurt. Broken femur. Broken back. Internal injuries. Lost my spleen." He said it mechanically, hiding the emotion.

She watched as he went to the forsythia bushes and snapped off two bare branches. She looked at him carefully in the moonlight, and it was like a door had finally opened and she could see inside. "You're afraid to leave, aren't you?" she said. "It happened and you're afraid it's going to happen again if you do . . . anything." He'd stopped moving for a moment, not looking at her. "That's your secret."

"I'm staying still. There's nothing wrong with that," he finally said. He stuck the forsythia branches into the sides of the middle ball, then stepped back and reviewed his work.

Josey felt strange, like there was a shifting in the universe somewhere. She suddenly felt like there wasn't more going out of her than there was coming in anymore. She followed the light shining on him through the snow-laden trees, across the sky and to the moon. She stared at it as if seeing it for the first time. The wonder, the mystery, the cool white brightness of it.

It took her breath away.

Chloe rolled over onto her side on the bed in the Cramdons' guest room and looked through the window at the same moon at the same time, and felt exactly the same shift.

She stuck her arm under the pillow to snuggle it to her. But then she paused. There was something under there.

She sat up and brought out a book.

The Complete Homeowner's Guide.

She put her head back on the pillow, staring at the book. Finally, a book that didn't have anything to do with her love life. It felt like a reward. She brought it to her, wrapping her arms around it, and looked back out into the cold, silent night.

Then she closed her eyes and went to sleep.

11

Candy Hearts

Margaret barreled into Josey's bedroom Thanksgiving morning. "There's a snowman in our front yard!" she said, as if locusts weren't far behind.

Josey sat up in bed, sleep-tousled and stiff from the snow. She looked over to her closet to make sure the door was closed.

Margaret walked to Josey's window. "Look!"

Josey got out of bed and joined her mother at the window. The neighborhood was pristine, the snow evenly coating everything . . . except their front yard. It was a mess, the snow pockmarked by footprints and in great uneven mounds, then there was the gelatinous snowman, which looked like it had been sprayed from a can of Reddi-wip.

With Adam's blue scarf wrapped around its neck.

Josey pinched her lips together to keep from smiling.

He must have done that after she'd gone back inside.

"Do you know anything about this?" Margaret asked suspiciously.

"I've never made a snowman before. That one looks like it was made by someone who knew what he was doing."

"Who would do such a thing to us? Call our lawn man," Margaret said as she walked away. "Tell him to come over and smooth our snow."

Josey had no idea what to say to that. Smooth our snow?

Margaret stopped in the doorway suddenly when a chirping sound came from somewhere inside the room. Josey felt a jab of dread and slid her eyes to her purse.

"What is that?" Margaret asked, looking around, probably expecting locusts. "What is that sound?"

Josey went to her purse. "It's, um, the cell phone ringing."

"You gave out the number? To whom?"

"Her name is Chloe Finley and she's my friend," Josey said, bringing out the phone. She knew Margaret would have found out sooner or later, she was just hoping for later. At least until yesterday's left-at-the-salon incident had blown over.

Margaret's face grew tight "*Finley*? *That's* who you've been seeing? Who told you about her?"

"What are you talking about? Told me what?"

"Nothing." Margaret turned with her cane and left quickly.

Josey answered the phone, watching her mother leave. "Hello?"

"Happy Thanksgiving!" Chloe said, sounding better than she had in all the time Josey had known her. "Josey, you're never going to believe this. I'm going to buy a house! I'm going to buy the house on Summertime Road!"

Josey rubbed her eyes with one hand. "What? Really? How?"

"I met the owners yesterday. Actually, I had to spend the night here because of the snow. Long story. Anyway, they had just decided to lower the price on the house. And they agreed to sell it to me!"

Josey dropped her hand and laughed. "Oh, Chloe, that's fabulous!"

"I have so much to do. My mind is spinning."

"If you need any help, I'm here for you."

"Thank you. But I can do this on my own. I have great credit and I've been putting money into savings for a long time, and now I won't have to pay for that storage rental anymore!"

"Good for you, Chloe. Good for you."

"I'll talk to you soon."

"Congratulations," Josey said as Chloe hung up.

"What was that all about?" Della Lee called.

Josey went to the closet and opened the door. "Chloe is buying a house."

Della Lee was wearing the sweater and snow boots Josey had worn outside last night. "It's nice that you offered to help her."

"I like her," Josey said, taking a dress off its hanger. "And take off my clothes."

"You two stick together, okay?"

"Why? What do you mean?"

Della Lee shrugged. "Nothing."

Josey sighed and turned away. Again with the nothing.

Two days later, on Saturday, Chloe called again and wanted to give Josey a tour of the house on Summertime Road. Josey agreed to meet her there that afternoon, glad to get out of the house. Margaret was emitting a low, constant level of vexation, making the air around her hum and crackle. And Josey had avoided Adam both Friday and Saturday when he'd been by with the mail, which seemed to make the days even longer.

At one point on Friday she'd been in her room, reading on her bed, when she felt him getting closer. She got up and went to her window. Margaret had gotten so worked up over the snowman that she had insisted their yard man leave his Thanksgiving dinner and come over Thursday to knock it down. Adam stopped in front of the house and smiled and shook his head when he saw that it was gone. Then he headed up the walk to the house.

Instead of going to see him, she went back to her bed.

"What's wrong?" Della Lee asked from the closet.

Josey stuffed another pillow behind her head and picked up the book, one of the romances Chloe had loaned her. "Nothing."

"Why did you go to your window?"

"No reason."

"Your mailman is here, isn't he? Why aren't you going

to see him? I thought you two had a good time in the snow the other night. Is there something you're not telling me? Did he do something to you? I'll kick his ass!" Josey saw a shoe come flying out of her closet.

She got up and retrieved the shoe Della Lee had thrown, amused that Della Lee would get so mad on her behalf. She brought the shoe back to the closet. "He didn't do anything to me."

"Then why aren't you going to see him?"

Josey set the shoe down. "I don't feel like finding out which Adam is out there today—the one who likes things the way they are, or the one who came to my window to make a snowman."

Della Lee suddenly smiled. She had a pretty smile, with her slightly crooked front teeth. "You're tipping the balance of power. You're making him curious, curious enough to come to you. Good call."

Josey rolled her eyes and went back to her bed. "That's not what I'm doing."

"Maybe not on purpose. But it's something I would do. I think I'm wearing off on you. I think I'm in your head."

Needless to say, Josey was more than ready Saturday to get away for a little while. Snowplows had cleared the roads and there was a lot of traffic as Josey headed out to see Chloe's new house. Vacationers from the ski resort and holiday shoppers from all around had descended on downtown businesses. The Christmas season was officially under way, transforming Bald Slope into a snowy picture-postcard paradise.

It was Marco Cirrini's dream come true, every winter.

The Cramdons were happy to let Chloe show Josey around. They were very fond of Chloe. And, judging by the amount of books they owned, it was clear Chloe had found her lost tribe. Chloe loved everything about each room. She told Josey about what pieces of her great-grandparents' furniture would go where, sometimes stopping herself when she mentioned something she remembered belonged to Jake. Josey understood that it was Jake Chloe wanted to be showing this to, not her. She hoped Adam had gotten some information from Jake about the other woman. He hadn't said anything about it the other night in the snow. She would have to talk to him soon about it.

The last stop was the kitchen, where George and Zelda were having coffee. Zelda poured cups for Josey and Chloe.

"I can tell why you're friends," Zelda said. She had sharp, intelligent eyes, like she knew more than she would say. "The two of you even look alike."

Josey and Chloe looked at each other, surprised. Josey was so used to her mother being offended when compared to Josey that she was startled when Chloe laughed and said, "Oh my gosh, it's true! We even have the same color eyes. And all this wild curly hair."

Something suddenly occurred to Josey.

No, it couldn't be.

Damn it, Della Lee, Josey thought.

Chloe was chatting with the Cramdons and they said something about the backyard.

"Oh, the backyard!" Chloe said. "Josey, I want to show you the backyard."

Cups of coffee in hand, they went outside to the screened-in porch. The snow-covered backyard was large, large enough for a swimming pool, Chloe said, if she wanted one. But the Cramdons had gardened for years and the soil was good, so she might try her hand at that first.

"Did you know your father?" Josey suddenly blurted out.

Chloe raised her eyebrows at the sudden change of subject. "No, actually. I have no idea who he is. His name isn't even on my birth certificate. My mom got pregnant with me when she was eighteen. Three days after I was born, she left town. I was raised by my great-grandparents."

"Have you ever tried to find out who he is?"

"No," Chloe said. "When I was young, I lived on fantasies of who he was. My favorite was that he was European royalty. I had a rock-star fantasy for a while too. He was from another planet in one daydream. But I realized long ago that if I really knew who he was, I'd only be disappointed. In my mind he's sorry he never got to know me. Not knowing me is one of his biggest regrets. Secretly, over the years, he's been watching out for me. And when my mom ran away, she ran to him. They're happy together. I don't want to know any differently." Chloe suddenly smiled, realizing she'd gone dreamy. "Why do you ask?"

"I was just thinking of my dad."

"He was a great man."

Josey nodded absently.

"Girls," George said, sticking his head out the back door, "who's up for leftover pie?"

"You wanted me to ask Mr. Lamar about the other woman my father paid off. You think it's Chloe's mother, don't you?" Josey demanded when she finally got home late that afternoon and went straight upstairs to Della Lee in the closet. She was slightly out of breath, not from the dash to her room, but from the panic of how fast Della Lee's influence was growing in her life. "You think Chloe is another one of his daughters. The first day you were here, you mentioned her by name. You kept sending me to her for sandwiches you never ate."

"Well, that took you long enough. What are you, blind?" Della Lee said, looking up from her collage. Today her blond hair was tied back into a ponytail with a pair of tights Josey had taken from her house. "But Chloe doesn't know. Her mother took off with the money Marco gave her. It's all in my mother's notebooks. She documented their entire affair."

Della Lee had grown up with this. She'd been told this all her life, so of course she believed it. But the depth and detail, her complete confidence in something so wholly improbable, was getting under Josey's skin. She was getting *in her head,* just like Della Lee said. "Della Lee, don't take this the wrong way, but I think you might need professional help. I can help you. I can pay. Think about this—you're wearing a pair of pantyhose in your hair. Is that normal?"

Della Lee snorted. "Oh, don't give me that. You're starting to doubt yourself. You see how all three of us have his eyes. You see how Chloe's hair is as crazy-curly as yours. You're starting to believe me, aren't you?"

"No, I'm not," Josey said firmly.

"You're saying you haven't even considered the *possibility* that your father *might* have had other children?"

"My father was a great man."

"That's what everyone says. I wonder how many people who actually knew him believe that."

"I believe it."

"Do you? Do you really? Do you really believe that the man you knew was all there was to him? You don't think there was something else?"

That reminded her of Adam. Not that she thought Adam and her father were anything alike, but what she'd found out about Adam, what she never even suspected . . . could her father have had secrets too? Josey hesitated before saying, "You think my mother paid off your mother, that my mother knew about you. Do you think she knew about Chloe too? I mean in your fantasy. Not that I'm saying it's real."

"I'm sure Margaret knew about all of Marco's affairs."

Could that be why her mother had such a reaction to Chloe's name?

No, she thought as she walked away, she wasn't going to go there.

Mr. Lamar's letter was going to settle everything anyway.

"So you don't want to go?" Adam asked the Sunday after Thanksgiving, waving the invitation as if that might make it more enticing.

Jake was sitting on the couch in Adam's living room, flipping through the television channels with the remote. "While going to the retirement party for your postal supervisor sounds like loads of fun, a bunch of us at work will be staying late Monday night. We're ordering takeout."

"You're a lousy date anyway." Adam tossed the invitation on the coffee table and sat beside Jake. It wasn't like anyone expected him to bring someone to these functions. He'd known about it for weeks. He'd also known Jake wouldn't want to go. So why was he staring at the invitation instead of watching the television?

Because of Josey.

She was still avoiding him. He knew he had told her he

liked the way things were, but that was before Wednesday night. She had somehow reached into him and seen exactly what he was trying to hide. He wasn't here because he wanted to settle down. He missed his old life. He missed it so much that sometimes his body would shudder, as if fighting with his mind to put him in motion again. He'd felt it Wednesday night, that pull, when he was looking down into Josey's face. It would have been so easy to kiss her. But he'd backed away instead. Was that the reason she wouldn't come to her door now? Was she disappointed in him?

"I think I'll ask Josey Cirrini to the party," he suddenly said.

Jake muted the television and turned to him.

"I like her."

Jake just stared at him, uncomprehending, as if Adam had suddenly started speaking Swahili.

Adam shook his head and got up and walked to the kitchen. After a moment, he heard Jake get up and follow him. Adam opened the fridge and handed Jake a beer, then took one for himself.

Jake was quiet as he opened his bottle and took a long drink. "Okay," he finally said, "now that the shock has worn off . . . *What?*"

"She's nice."

"Well, yes, I guess she is. She sent me a card my first week at the DA's office, saying congratulations on my new job. And she was the first person to send my mother flowers in the hospital when she had her hysterectomy. But you know what my mother said? 'I can't believe *she* sent me flowers.' Yes, my nice little mother said that. Apparently, when Josey was a little girl, she kicked my mother in the shin when my mother saw her eating candy in the grocery store and my mother told her she should probably pay for it first. She left a scar."

Adam opened his bottle. "Have you ever noticed her hair?"

"Her hair?"

"She has great hair."

"I guess so."

"And amazing skin. And that figure . . ."

"Figure?" Jake repeated. "Come on, Adam."

Adam was disappointed. Jake was usually more generous than this. "What did she do to you? Out with it."

Jake tried to look innocent. "What do you mean?"

"She apparently did something to everyone in this town. What did she do to you?"

Jake shuffled his feet for a while. "She stole my piece of chocolate cake," he finally mumbled.

Adam laughed. "So naturally you're scarred for life."

"Well, I love chocolate cake."

Adam had done stupid things as a kid. Most people did. But when he left for college, he never looked back. His parents were gone, so he didn't have any reason to keep in touch with anyone from his hometown in California. He couldn't imagine what it was like for Josey to be constantly reminded, and judged, by something she did when she was so young. The dynamic of her relationship with this town was fascinating.

Adam suddenly set his beer down and grabbed the phone book. He left the kitchen, Jake watching him curiously. When he got to his room he sat on the edge of his bed and looked up her number. He couldn't believe how nervous he actually was. It felt like being at the starting gate at a downhill competition. He used to feed on this feeling. And, God help him, he still liked it. He couldn't forget it.

He dialed and their maid answered. "Cirrini house."

He cleared his throat. "Could I speak with Josey, please?"

"Oldsey?"

"No, Josey."

"I get. Who speak?"

"This is Adam Boswell."

"Ahhhh, the mail," she said, sounding pleased. "Hold. I get."

He hunched over and stared at the floor, taking deep breaths, his heart pumping heavily. A few minutes later, Josey came on the line. "Hello?"

His head jerked up. "Hi, Josey, it's Adam."

Pause. "Hi, Adam."

"I haven't seen you in a couple of days. Are you okay?"

"Oh, yes. I'm fine," she said awkwardly. "Thanks for calling."

"Wait," he said. "Josey, you're backing off and I don't know why. I'm hoping it's not because you've changed your mind."

"About what?"

"About me."

Silence. "It's not my mind that needs changing."

That made him smile. "Listen, I'm thirty-four and I haven't done this in a long time, so forgive me my teenage-boyness."

"What are you talking about?" she asked.

"I'm asking you out on a date."

Silence again.

"It's a retirement party on Monday night. It's short notice and not very exciting. Feel free to say no."

"Of course I'll go out on a date with you," she said simply. *Of course.* Like how could he have thought otherwise? Okay, so he didn't expect her to squeal. He just thought this might be met with a little more enthusiasm. Maybe she was in shock.

"Okay then."

"Okay," she said.

"I'll pick you up on Monday at seven o'clock."

"Oh, no."

"You already have something planned?"

"No, it's not that. I meant, don't pick me up here. I can meet you somewhere."

His heart rate had picked up again at the jolt of a near miss, like he could have fallen. "I want to pick you up."

"I can't let you do that. You'll be berated by my mother and possibly have a curse put on you by the maid."

"My favorite things," he said.

"Seriously, I can meet you somewhere."

"Seriously, I want to pick you up," he insisted.

"For a date," she said, as if to verify, to make sure she didn't have it wrong.

"Yep."

He was smiling when he took the phone book back to the kitchen. God, he felt good. He'd made it to the bottom of the hill. A hell of a ride.

"Look, I'm sorry I said that about Josey's figure," Jake said from the living room. "I was out of line."

"Yes, you were." Adam picked up his beer from the kitchen counter and joined Jake on the couch.

"Chloe is going to be over the moon about this. She's always wanted you to date more."

Adam knew Jake had been trying to call Chloe all weekend, to find out more about her buying the house. "You still haven't been able to get in touch with her?"

"No. She's not answering the phone," Jake said, staring at the television. "I'm happy about you and Josey too."

"Thanks."

Jake waited a couple of beats before he said, "I could really go for some chocolate cake."

Jake approached Chloe's shop the next day, Monday, her first day back at work after the holiday. After not being able to reach her by phone, he'd stopped just short of going to the apartment to see her.

She was buying a house.

She was slowly, surely, moving away from him, and he didn't know how to stop her.

It was just after lunch, a slow time for her, and she was sitting at one of the café tables reading a book titled *The Complete Homeowner's Guide*. Her hair was braided into one long plait down her back. She always wore it like that when they would go skiing or hiking. And sometimes she would stand in front of the bathroom mirror and sigh in the mornings, lifting her arms to braid it because she couldn't do anything else with it. He remembered how her breasts moved under her shirt when she braided it, how he would come up behind her at the sink and kiss her neck, cupping her breasts. Once they'd even made love that way, her arms lifted and in her hair, his hands on her breasts, watching each other in the mirror.

Chloe took a deep breath, like there was something in the air she had picked up on. She looked up and saw him walking toward her. She immediately stood and hurried around to the other side of the counter. He counted his blessings that she didn't hide in the storeroom this time.

He stopped a few feet from the counter when he saw she was backing into a corner. "You don't have to stand back."

She pointed to the coffeemaker. "The water."

That surprised him, that she would still have the ability to sense his feelings, and that his feelings still had the ability to cause a passionate physical response in her. "Still?"

"It didn't stop the moment you said you cheated on me. This might be a little easier if it did."

He took a moment to appreciate how precise that shot was. It wasn't a low blow, and it didn't go over his head. It hurt right where it was supposed to. "I tried calling you over the holiday."

"I know." She didn't seem to know what to do with her hands. She tried clasping them in front of her, then crossing her arms over her chest. Finally she stuffed them into her jeans pockets. "I've been a little busy."

"You were missed at my parents' Thanksgiving dinner."

"I missed going," she said. "How was it?"

"I really don't know. Adam and I got sent home early for getting into a snowball fight."

Chloe smiled slightly.

"Did you hear Adam and Josey Cirrini were going out?"

"Josey called me today and told me. I'm happy for them."

"I knew you would be. So, I heard you were buying the house on Summertime Road," he said, knowing the segue was wrong, and the casual tone didn't feel right either. Well, hell, none of this felt right. He had no idea what he was doing. He just wanted to be near her. It was getting harder and harder to stay away. This past month had been excruciating without her. He would lie awake in Adam's guest room and think about her. Every moment without conversation or distraction was filled with her. He had to let Chloe deal with this on her own terms. He knew that. What could he do, after all, when being sorry wasn't enough? But it went against his very nature not to *fix* this.

She paused, searching his face for something. "I was at the right place at the right time."

"I know how much you love it. I'm happy it's going to be yours." He wanted to ask why, why did she do it without him? He wanted to share the joy of it with her. Who better than Jake knew what buying that house meant to her?

"Thank you," she said.

"What's going to happen, Chloe? Are you moving out?"

"Once I close on the house, I will. But if you want to come back to the apartment, I can find somewhere else to stay."

"No," he said immediately. There was no way he was going to push her even farther away. "Stay there. It's as much your place as it is mine."

She shook her head. "No, it's not."

That surprised him. Did she buy the house because the apartment was an issue with her? "Chloe, I've never made you feel like it wasn't."

"I know that."

"Tell me what to do," he said. "Tell me how to make this right, Chloe. I don't want to lose you, but I don't know how to make you stay."

"What is her name?" she asked softly.

He lowered his head. This was an impossible situation. Was he going to tell her? Could he? "I tell you, and you'll forgive me?" He looked up and met her eyes. "Is that what you're saying?"

She didn't answer.

Jake walked around the counter toward her. She backed farther into the corner and put her hand out. "Don't, Jake."

He walked all the way up to her hand and pressed her palm against his chest under his suit jacket. "I tell you, and everything will be okay. Is that what you're saying?" He never thought he would compromise the Beasley case like this. But he never thought he could hurt like this either. He never thought he would be a man who cheated. When she tried to take her hand away, he grabbed it and held it there. Her elbow bent, just slightly, her arm relaxing. It was like she was trying to let him closer, trying to let him in. Their bodies inched toward each other. He could feel his skin grow warm. Chloe's eyes began to dilate.

"Jake, I . . ."

But what she was going to say was lost, interrupted by a voice booming through the rotunda. "Jake!"

Jake turned his head to see his father walking briskly toward the shop.

Kyle Yardley reached the counter and said, "I need a word with you."

The spell broken, Chloe again tried to tug her hand out of his. Jake turned away from his father and met Chloe's eyes, trying to reestablish the connection. "Go away, Dad."

"I told you to stay away from her," Kyle said.

Jake felt his skin grow tight with anger. He couldn't believe his father just said that in front of Chloe.

Chloe looked confused and slightly alarmed. She tugged harder at his hand.

"This isn't the time," Jake said, still looking at Chloe, trying to get her to see him, to feel him, to know that everything was going to be all right. He was so close.

"You're going to ruin everything. Chloe, I'm sorry," Kyle said.

Chloe looked at Kyle over Jake's shoulder. She knew something was going on. "Sorry for what?"

"Dad, get the hell out of here."

"Come with me," Kyle said.

Jake knew his father well enough to know that he wasn't going to leave. He let go of Chloe's hand and cupped her face. "We're not through, okay?"

Her expression was flat now, and he could only guess what was going through her mind.

"Jake!" Kyle said when Jake took too long.

Jake reluctantly left her. When he passed by the coffeemaker, he heard the water boiling inside, which gave him a small but precious bit of comfort.

He crossed the rotunda, his father on his heels. When they got outside, the air was apple-cool, moist and crisp from the snow last week. Jake rounded on Kyle. "Stay out of this."

"How can I stay out of it when you're messing everything up?" Kyle said. "You don't know what you're doing. I told you to stay away from her. I told you to let her come to you. And I thought we agreed you would buy that house out from under her. If you had only told me you'd chickened out, I would've been able to do it. But no. I called this morning and they're not accepting any other offers. Now she's moving out on you."

Jake stared at his father. It might not make him much of

a Yardley, but Jake had never understood how anyone could withhold approval. If someone did something good, what was the harm in acknowledging it? Kyle was certainly fast enough with his comments when Jake screwed up.

"I've done more things right than I have wrong," Jake said. "But you're never going to see it that way, are you? Chloe sees it. In fact, she's the only person in my life who does. I'm making my choice right now, and I have more faith in her forgiveness than I do in yours. Excuse me."

Jake left him standing there and went back inside. But when he got back to her shop, Chloe had gone into the storeroom and closed the door.

12

Mr. Goodbar

Monday night Josey looked in the mirror over her dresser and tugged at her lucky red cardigan. She wore it with a gray wool skirt she rarely went out in because it had subtle red embroidery along the hem and her mother didn't like it. She didn't have a turtleneck that matched, so she was actually wearing one of Della Lee's, a Lycra one that was too small, but if she kept her cardigan buttoned, hopefully Adam wouldn't be able to tell.

Her hair was down, her curls tamed. And she was

wearing makeup, thanks to Della Lee's tutelage. Josey finally turned away from the mirror and picked up her coat. When she put it on, her fingers were clumsy with the buttons. She grew impatient with herself and dropped her hands in frustration.

She walked to her window for the fortieth time. She felt a catch of panic that made her lose her breath. There was an SUV there that wasn't there before. "Oh, God. He's here."

Della Lee looked up. She was still working on her collage. She'd taken all the images she'd cut from the travel magazines and was using a glue stick to paste them on the flat surface of the lid from her private box. She'd started with the individual letters she'd cut out that spelled BON VOYAGE. "I don't understand you, Josey. Shouldn't you be a little happier? I thought this was what you wanted."

Josey turned to her. Della Lee had, inexplicably, several pencils in her hair today. "This is what I want," Josey said. "I just wish I knew what *he* wanted."

"Because asking you on a date is so unclear?"

"That's just it. Why did he ask me? Is this just a friend thing? Maybe he only needed a date for this specific function, and any woman would do. Maybe it's just a pity date. He did make a point of asking about my feelings for him before he asked me out, like he was making sure I knew he was doing me a favor." She suddenly wanted to go in her closet. She wanted Mallomars and Jelly Nougats and creme-filled cookies. Her eyes went to the wall at the back of the closet.

"Oh, no. No, no, no," Della Lee said when she saw the look on Josey's face. She set aside the collage and put her arms out wide. "Nothing is real in here. Your life is outside. It's waiting for you."

Josey closed her eyes There was only one thing she wanted more than Mallomars and Jelly Nougats and creme-filled cookies.

Adam.

She picked up her purse, then hesitated at the door. "You'll be here when I get back, won't you?"

"I'm not going anywhere yet," Della Lee said. "For God's sake, smile. This isn't an execution."

Josey walked downstairs and into the sitting room. Helena was sewing crosses into the hem of a new dress, and Margaret was reading a true-confession magazine, which she kept hidden from company under her chair cushion. The television was on in the corner, the volume low.

Margaret lifted her head, took off her reading glasses, and stared. "What is this?"

Josey straightened her shoulders. "Mother, I know this is going to come as a surprise, but someone is about to come to the door. I have a date tonight. I won't be gone long, and Helena will be here for you. Everything will be fine."

Helena didn't look up from her sewing, but she smiled.

"You're wearing that sweater again," Margaret said, as if she hadn't heard a word Josey said. "You told me you threw it away."

"I know."

"And are you wearing *makeup*?" Margaret asked.

"Yes."

"I've always told you, with your coloring, makeup only makes you look cheap."

"Mother, did you miss the part about me saying I had a date?" There was a knock at the door and Josey felt lightheaded. "There he is. I warned him, but he wants to meet you anyway. Please be nice."

"You warned who? What did you say about me?"

Josey walked to the front door and opened it. He looked wonderful in a cream-colored sweater and leather jacket. He was smiling. But for how long? She took him by the arm before he could say anything. "I apologize in advance," she said as she pulled him in.

"Why? You're shaking." He walked in and was immediately distracted. "Wow. I've never seen the inside of this place. It's gorgeous."

She led him to the sitting room. She started to take her hand off his arm, but he put his hand over hers and kept it there. She could have cried. "Adam, this is Helena. And this is my mother, Margaret Cirrini."

"We've met a few times before," Adam said affably. "But it's nice to be formally introduced to you both."

Margaret's brows rose. "You're the mailman."

"Yes."

"I can't believe it," she said, laughing. Her bad mood, now over a week old, seemed to disappear. "Oh, Josey, Josey, Josey."

Adam looked at Josey curiously. Josey just shook her head and took comfort in his hand on hers. *Hold on,* she wanted to say. *Don't let go.*

"I apologize for my daughter," Margaret said to Adam, her laughter fading to a chuckle. "She's not very schooled in these matters. I've always known she liked the mail, but it never occurred to me it was the *mailman* she liked. Josey honey, he doesn't come to the door every day just for you. It's his job. He does it for everyone." She stood and walked over to them without her cane. She didn't like to use her cane in front of visitors. "This is certainly awkward. If you'd like to leave now, young man, you may. There is no obligation."

"Actually, for years now I *have* come to the door just for her. Good evening, Mrs. Cirrini." Still holding Josey's hand on his arm, he turned and led her out. When they reached the porch, he said, "Can I take it you weren't kidding about your maid putting curses on people either?"

Before Josey could respond, Helena herself opened the door and stepped out.

"Oldsey," she said, thrusting her hand out to give Josey something. Josey hesitated, not wanting to take her hand off Adam's arm. But Helena made a jerking motion with her hand. She wanted Josey to hold out her palm. Josey glanced at Adam, then reluctantly took her hand off of him. Helena immediately put a quarter and three small painted stones in Josey's palm. "Keep you safe."

Josey wouldn't be surprised at that moment if Adam decided to turn tail and run. "Thank you, Helena."

Helena turned to Adam and wagged her finger. "Oldsey love mail. Be good," she said, then turned around and went back in the house.

Everything was quiet for a moment. Josey stared at her palm. Adam stared at the front door.

"Should I be scared?" Adam finally asked.

"Only three orange stones," she said, lifting her hand. "You got off easy."

He cupped her palm and lifted it to better see them. He was touching her a lot. Did that mean something? "What exactly does three stones mean?"

"That she cares."

He laughed and folded her fingers over the stones. "Then I like her. Come on." He led her to his SUV, then he helped her in. Minutes of awkward silence passed while he drove. She kept looking over to him, wanting to memorize everything, at the same time wondering when would be the right time to ask him why he was doing this. Maybe she should wait until the evening was over. Maybe she would know herself by then. Finally Adam cleared his throat and said, "So tell me about your mother."

Josey shifted uncomfortably. "What do you want to know?"

"Is she always like that?"

"I tried to warn you."

"She's quite a bit older than you."

"She had me when she was forty-seven. My father was sixty-nine."

He gave a low whistle. "You were either a surprise, or a very long time coming."

"I'm still trying to figure that out."

"Me too," he said thoughtfully. "I got a little distracted back there. Did I mention you look beautiful tonight? I've always liked that sweater on you."

She turned to him. "You recognize this sweater?"

He nodded. "You were wearing it the first day I met you."

Well, if she'd had any doubt before, it quickly disappeared. This sweater really *was* magic. "Just don't ask me to take it off."

"Excuse me?"

"Oh, no, wait, I didn't mean it like that," she said quickly. "I just meant that the turtleneck under this sweater is too tight. It's a little obscene."

He cut his eyes at her and smiled. "Now I'm intrigued."

Josey turned her head away. "I can't believe I said that. That was one of the things I was not going to say."

"You had a list?" he asked. "It just so happens I like obscene women."

"You look very nice tonight too," she said, trying to change the subject.

"I'll take off my sweater if you want me to," Adam offered. "It's not obscene, but I have some really interesting scars."

"Well, I think this is going well so far, don't you?" Josey sighed.

But Adam laughed and said, "In case I forget to tell you at the end of the night, I had a great time."

The retirement party was held in the VFW hall. There were paper streamers and garlands and tables piled high with fried food and desserts with frosting. Mostly, though, there was laughter. The hall echoed with it.

It was serendipity that Adam had found this job. He'd only been in Bald Slope a few months, still going to the gym as part of his rehab, when he had a chance encounter with his mailman. It turned out the man was retiring soon and his sub was taking over his route, which meant they were looking for more subs at the post office. Adam figured all the walking would give him the exercise he needed, so he took the test. Later he bid on his own route and became full-time.

It didn't take long to learn that the downtown branch of the Bald Slope post office was known among the employees as Ski Bum Central. Over half of the carriers had come to Bald Slope just for the slopes and stayed. And half of those had some injury because of it. They all laughed about it and shrugged it off. Got back on the slopes again. They knew about Adam's injuries, and he was sure they wondered why he was still there, since he didn't ski anymore. They didn't ask him, though. They all seemed to sense how guarded he was about what had happened to him.

He and Josey drew a lot of interest when they walked in. He figured that would happen. What he didn't count on, however, was the fact that they had no sooner made it to the punch bowl when Josey was descended upon and taken away by some women at the party. One of the women was Sabrina, a clerk, who prided herself on knowing everything about everyone at the post office. And Adam was her last, and toughest, nut to crack. Josey gave him a questioning look over her shoulder, as if to say, *Is this normal? Is this supposed to happen?* He smiled and was about to go after her, when Sabrina said something to her and Josey suddenly laughed.

It stopped him short.

He didn't think he'd ever heard Josey laugh, not like that, unrestrained, unselfconscious. It was as clear and pure as water. He spent the rest of the evening watching her from across the hall. She surprised him by socializing with his coworkers better than he did. She was having a wonderful time. Without him.

Sure, he hadn't dated in a while, but he was pretty sure the purpose was to spend time *together*. So what was he doing all the way over here?

As things were winding down, Adam finally walked across the hall to where she was sitting with Sabrina and a few other women. "Are you ready to go, Josey?"

Sabrina nudged her with her elbow, like they'd been talking about him.

They walked outside after they'd said their goodbyes. The stars were out, pinholes in dark fabric. They lingered at his SUV.

"Want to get some coffee, maybe walk through the park?" Adam asked.

She was flushed from the heat of the hall, still smiling from being around all those people. She didn't get to do this often, he realized. She didn't get to be herself, with people who didn't know her. She was meant to be a social creature. He held his breath, waiting for her to answer, waiting to hear she actually wanted to spend time alone with him. "I'd love to," she said.

"Good." He opened the passenger-side door for her. She got in, brushing him with the scent of peppermint.

They got coffee at Dang! That's Good, the bookstore café downtown. The bookstore, the newly renovated Downtown Inn, and a curving line of other shops surrounded the courthouse and the large open park. All the shops were decorated for Christmas, with twinkling white lights and foil and tinsel. Even the bare trees in the park had lights in them. The downtown library, one street over, rose up behind the buildings, its dramatic arches almost white in the moonlight. It looked like a frosted confection, like God could break off a piece and eat it.

"Look at that," he said, pointing to the library as they walked slowly through the park, cups in hand.

"Beautiful, isn't it?" she said. "It's been forever since I've been in there. I had a tutor named Holly who convinced my mother to let us go to the library to study several days a week. We would spend all day on the Internet there, just goofing around. I loved that. She was the only tutor I had who wasn't afraid of my mother. She was just here for the ski season, though." She stared at the library's arches while she spoke, but then she turned to him with a smile. "I was home-schooled."

"I know. Your neighbor Mrs. Ferguson told me."

She tucked her chin into the collar of her coat. "I get the feeling you've heard a lot about me."

He leaned in closer to her, nudging her playfully. "That's because you're the daughter of the late, great Marco Cirrini."

She lifted her chin out of her coat. "But who are you, Adam Boswell? Even your coworkers don't know much about you. I think they wanted me to give them some sort of inside information. But I didn't have anything to tell. Or anything I thought you'd want me to tell."

"I'll tell you anything you want to know, Josey," he said. "Just ask."

She hesitated. "Listen, if tonight was just about needing a date for a function, I understand. This doesn't have to be anything serious. That night in the snow, thank you for sharing what you did. But you don't have to tell me anything else."

"So *that's* what this is all about," he said, and he could have laughed at how relieved he was. "Josey, I didn't just need a date for a function. I wanted a date with you. *You*. Just ask."

She hesitated. "I think I've lost my train of thought."

"Okay, so I'll tell you." He told her about growing up in California and about his competitive skiing days when he was a teenager. He told her about how he ended up here after hearing about Bald Slope's steep runs. How he hadn't talked to the friends he'd gone skiing with since the accident. How he got the job at the post office. He told her about his brother

Brett, that they had different fathers. He told her about his relationship with his brother, that he called every week telling him to come back to Chicago.

"But you don't have any plans to leave," Josey said.

"You've brought that up before. Why? Do you want to leave?" he asked, just joking. He was completely blindsided by her answer.

"I want to leave so badly I can't stand it sometimes," she said vehemently. "Too many people, particularly the people in my mother's social circle, see me the way I was as a child. There are too many stories floating around. Ones I'm sure you've heard."

Adam stopped under the light of an old-fashioned streetlamp and threw away their coffee cups. "What would you do if you left?" he said, staring down at her, something almost like panic in his chest.

"I'd go everywhere, see everything I could."

"What about your mother?"

"Sometimes it seems like I'm just waiting for her to say she's finally forgiven me for all the things I did, waiting for her to say, *You can go now. Go live your life.*"

"You don't need anyone's permission, Josey. You could do it. I can see you doing it. You have the rest of your life in front of you, wide open. I can't even explain how that makes me feel. It makes my chest hurt. I want to take some of what you have and eat it. I want to feel that way again."

"Do you?" she asked. "Do you really?"

The moon spun a spiderweb of light around her hair. He took a step toward her. "Yes, I do." He bent slowly, stopping several times along the way to gauge her reaction.

"Adam?" she whispered when he was close enough to feel her breath.

He pulled back slightly.

"Don't do this unless you mean it. Don't do it because I want it, or because you feel sorry for me, or anything like that."

"Oh, I mean it, Josey."

"Right. Okay then," she said seriously. Then she seemed to steel herself, becoming very still.

That amused him. He had to turn his face away to compose himself. "Don't make me smile," he said. "I can't kiss you if I'm smiling."

"Sorry."

He turned his face back and slowly, slowly touched his lips to hers. He wasn't prepared for what he felt. His panic and tension suddenly dissipated and he was filled with *her*—open, expressive, hopeful Josey. His hands went to her arms, as if afraid she might disappear, at the same time he angled his head and pressed harder. Did she understand the question? She had the answer. Yes.

His kiss went deeper. He raised her hands and put them around his neck, then he wound his own arms around her, inside her coat, and pulled her to him. To this place. The right place. Right here.

His hands teased the hem of her sweater. She sucked in her breath when his cold hands touched the bare skin of her back under the stretchy-tight turtleneck.

He broke the kiss, his lips still close to hers. "Too cold?" he asked.

"No."

He watched her closely as his hands moved to the front, still under her sweater at her waist. Her stomach muscles trembled with the advance of his chilled fingers.

He suddenly kissed her again, hard and fast and deep,

taking one hand off her stomach to hold the back of her head, to hold her to him. She made a sound somewhere deep in her throat, a moan, an acquiescence, trembling with need and uncertainty.

Fast, he found himself thinking. *Faster. Faster.*

Suddenly, he stopped and stepped back. It was all coming back to him, how to do this, the sheer exhilaration of *everything*. But he'd always gone too fast. That was his trademark. His downfall. He took an impossibly deep breath, then whooshed it out.

"I . . . I should take you home." He ran a hand through his hair. "I don't want your maid to put a curse on me."

"Promise me you're going to mean this again," she said softly.

He laughed. "I'm going to mean this every chance I get from now on." He put an arm around her waist, his fingers tight, like he was hanging from a cliff by them, as if he might fall. She made him feel like he could do this. It was all at once gratifying and terrifying.

Together they started walking again.

"Tell me again," Della Lee said into the darkness late that evening, just as Josey was falling asleep.

"He kissed me," Josey said into her pillow.

"No. Say it like you said it before."

Josey smiled. "It was the best first kiss in the history of first kisses. It was as sweet as sugar. And it was warm, as warm as pie. The whole world opened up and I fell inside. I didn't know where I was, but I didn't care. I didn't care because the only person who mattered was there with me."

There was a long silence. Josey had almost dozed off

again when Della Lee said, "I think heaven will be like a first kiss."

"I hope so," Josey murmured.

"Me too."

The December meeting of the ladies' club was the following Thursday afternoon, and Margaret half expected Josey not to take her. She'd even worked up a fair amount of indignation, ready to be left at home, forgotten. Or worse, ready to have Rawley come pick her up to be his and Annabelle's chaperone. Josey was too busy talking on the phone with the mailman and that Finley girl to care about anything else. And she was unusually tired in the mornings, as if she'd been staying up late. Margaret was suddenly suspicious. What was she doing at night?

But exactly on time, Josey walked into the sitting room and asked if Margaret was ready to go.

Josey was a different person than she was even a month ago. She reminded Margaret so much now of Marco's cousins from Italy. They'd shown up in Bald Slope without warning once, early in Marco and Margaret's marriage. They were magical women, with their long curly hair, large breasts and movements like dancers. Their bracelets sounded like wind chimes when they walked. Margaret had been fascinated by them. Marco had ushered them out within hours of their arrival and taken them to Asheville for their stay. He was ashamed of them, of their earthiness and sensuality, of their provincial ways. No one from Italy ever visited again.

"Well, I'm surprised to see you here," Margaret said.

"Why?" Josey asked, putting on her gloves.

"I thought you might have more important things to do."

"No, Mother."

Margaret eyed her critically. That was her only weapon. "Where did you get that scarf?"

Josey touched it briefly. "I bought it from Nova Berry."

"I told you, you look horrible in red."

"I think it looks good on me."

"Did your mailman tell you that?"

"As a matter of fact, he did."

She suddenly realized it was *jealousy* she was feeling. She was jealous that there was a man in her daughter's life who made her happy, who complimented her, who told her she looked good in red. Horrified, Margaret walked past Josey without another word and headed for the car.

When Josey parked in front of Mrs. Herzog's home, where the meeting was held every month, Rawley was already there, helping Annabelle Drake out of his cab. There was a cab in front of him, and another driver was helping another lady out. Between the old society ladies in town and the skiers, Pelham Cabs did a brisk business, operating three cabs and two vans. When Annabelle saw Margaret, she waited for her on the sidewalk and they walked up to the front door together. Josey followed.

"I knew it had gotten too much for him, all those rumors about us," Annabelle said. "Rawley said to me in the cab today, out of the blue, 'It was nice having Margaret ride with us, wasn't it?' I think it would make him feel better if someone rode with me all the time, so everyone would stop talking about us having an affair. Why don't we ride together more often, Margaret?"

Margaret looked over her shoulder. Rawley was watching them walk away.

The meeting was late to begin because everyone was talking about the latest news: a body had been discovered in the Green Cove River that morning. Margaret had heard all about it from Helena at breakfast. Helena was now in a frenzy, hanging pouches filled with God knows what in doorways and jumping at every sound. The Beasley murder case was still fresh in everyone's mind, and the ladies at the meeting were saying, *Was it murder? Again? Are we not safe in our own homes? Things like this aren't supposed to happen in Bald Slope.* But Margaret tuned out the gossip. Skittishness was better left to those who were unsure of their own lives and decisions. She was not going to be one of those people. She went to the window and looked out. Rawley was standing there at his cab. She couldn't believe he would say something like that to Annabelle. He had to have known it would get back to Margaret. Since the meeting didn't look like it would be starting any time soon, she turned and walked to the door. Josey got up and followed her.

"Is something wrong, Mother?" Josey asked.

Margaret opened the door. "I forgot something in the car."

"I'll get it."

"No, I will. Go sit down."

"But your coat . . ."

"This will just take a minute," Margaret snapped as she stepped outside.

No matter the weather, Rawley always leaned against his cab and watched the house, watched it as if expecting this very thing to happen, for Margaret to walk out to him. He straightened as she approached.

"Annabelle told me what you said. You will have to find someone else to ride with you so no one thinks you're having an affair," she said bitterly when she reached him. "It won't be me. I never flaunted anything in front of you. In fact, I went out of my way to *avoid* doing that to you. Why, after all these years, are you doing it to me? I will have nothing to do with this. Nothing at all, do you hear me?"

Rawley's brows lowered, but he didn't speak.

Of course he didn't.

"Marco would have ruined you," she said, even though she knew the explanation was too late. "As long as he didn't know who you were, the identity of the man I was with that night, you were safe. You could move on and have a good life with someone who didn't value money and status over the love of a good man. But when Marco died, and you still hadn't married, I thought things might change between the two of us. It was just a tiny thought. I was wrong, obviously. I understand why you still hate me, why you never speak to me. I have always accepted that what happened was my fault. But that doesn't mean you can put me in the middle of your affair with Annabelle. I may deserve it, but I don't think my heart could take it."

She turned and walked back into the house, clinging to the last of her dignity. She would *not* be jealous of her own daughter. She would *not* be jealous of Annabelle. She made her decisions and she lived with them. That was that.

When the meeting was over, Rawley was still there, waiting for Annabelle, but his eyes zeroed in on Margaret and followed her intently, almost angrily, as she and Josey walked to their car.

When they arrived home, Helena met them at the door, closing it quickly and locking it behind them after they entered. She took Margaret's coat and purse, telling them to be careful of the small orange stones she'd placed on the floor at the thresholds.

Josey hurried to her room. Margaret just sighed and walked to the sitting room to wait for Helena to bring her the glass of water and pain pill she always took after a day out. She stiffly sat in her favorite chair.

There was a knock at the door and Margaret almost groaned. She was in no mood for company. Shortly, Helena walked into the sitting room. She didn't have Margaret's water and pill yet.

"Who was—" Margaret started to say, but stopped when Rawley Pelham walked into the room behind Helena.

"If you'll excuse us," he said to Helena, "Mrs. Cirrini and I need to talk in private."

Helena looked at him suspiciously, her eyes darting to the orange stones on the floor. She must have figured, if he could pass the threshold, he couldn't be that bad.

He shut the sitting-room door behind her and turned to Margaret with an ominous look.

"Now," he said, speaking to her directly for the first time in forty years, "it's time to get a few things straight."

Margaret sat up straighter, her body at attention. *He was speaking to her*. He was no longer a malleable youth. He was a commanding man now. She had both loved and resented the changes in him over the years, how his confidence had grown, how well he'd done without her.

"First, I'm not having an affair with Annabelle Drake. But even if I was, it is none of your, or anyone else's, business. Second, I had no idea that you protected my identity from your husband. All these years I thought he knew. Third, you know very well that the reason I don't speak to you is because you made me promise never to speak to you again in public."

Margaret jerked as surprise entered her body. It traveled through her nervous system, setting every hair on end. "Excuse me?"

"You don't remember?" he asked incredulously. "We stood there on that porch. I was ready to fight your husband, especially after I saw your lip. But all you wanted was for me to go away. You were so miserable that night. I would have done anything to make you feel better. You made me promise to never speak to you in public, that no one could ever hear me speak to you again."

She shook her head in sharp, jerky movements. "That's not possible. I knew I had taken a lot of pills that evening, but I can't believe I would make you do such a thing," she said. "I was always careful about promises around you."

"Not careful enough."

Everyone knew Pelhams didn't make promises easily, because they were incapable of breaking that promise, once made. It simply was not possible for a Pelham to go back on his word. And it wasn't good old-fashioned taught honesty, either. It was in their genes, like their blue eyes and their russet hair.

"And of course the only—" His voice suddenly gave out, but his lips continued to move, as if he hadn't realized he'd lost his vocal ability. She didn't understand what had happened until she saw that they weren't alone anymore. Helena had entered the room quietly, a glass of water in one hand, Margaret's pill in the other. Rawley's lips stopped moving and they both watched as Helena put the water and pill on the table beside Margaret, then walked out of the room again.

Rawley's voice immediately returned. "The only time I saw you after that was in public, so how could I say to you how much I missed you, how much I wanted you? How could I say when your husband died that I had never stopped dreaming of you? You never approached me. You were always so firm in your decisions."

She reached for the water to take a sip. Rawley watched her, his eyes taking in every movement, every splash of water, every quiver of her lips. She shakily set the water back down.

"Do you remember, under the tree in the woods behind the old theater?"

Her hand went to her heart, just a fluttery movement, as if to brush away a bit of lint, or worry her brooch. "Of course I remember that place."

"We were making love one day and you looked up at me with those beautiful blue eyes. I said, 'I love you, Margaret. I will love you forever.' And you said, 'Promise?' "

"Oh, God," she whispered. How could she have done such a thing?

His gaze was steady. "You've always known what you wanted, and I've always admired that. I never really wanted anything as I was growing up. I could never make up my mind. School, Army, home. But then I met you. Every day since then, my life has been about wanting. Wanting you, Margaret. It's been my choice, and I've reveled in the beauty of it. *My choice*. Promising to love you has been the easiest promise I've ever made."

She had to look away. This was too much. When she heard the scrape of the doorknob turning, her head shot up.

Who would be more wrong, God, for giving her this

second chance when she clearly didn't deserve it, or her, for refusing to take it?

"Wait, Rawley," she said.

He paused in the doorway, his back to her.

She took a deep breath and said what she should have said forty years ago. "Please don't leave."

13

Life Savers

Chloe had just gotten in from work late that afternoon when there was a knock at the apartment door. She put down her coat and answered it. To her complete surprise, Jake's mother was standing there, looking perfectly pressed and nervous.

"Faith! What are you doing here?"

Jake's mother smiled and held up a basket. "I brought you a gift."

"Your Christmas goodies." Every year Faith filled beautiful willow baskets with a variety of gourmet holiday treats for all her friends. Her cook started going over recipes months in advance and made samples the day after Thanksgiving for Faith to taste and approve.

"I know you always liked tasting the samples with me. I hope you like what I decided on this year."

"Your taste is always exquisite. Thank you. Come in." Chloe took the basket and stepped back. She closed the door behind Faith, then walked over to the coffee table and set the basket on it. "Can I get you something?"

"Oh, no. I'm fine." Faith toyed with the clasp of her handbag. "I heard you're buying the house on Summertime Road."

That was why she was here? Was she wondering when Chloe was going to move out of Jake's apartment? Was she here to ask her to leave? It seemed so unlike Faith, but after that incident at her shop when she heard Kyle tell Jake to stay away from her, she didn't know what to think. Was Jake's family encouraging a breakup? The very thought of it made even her skin hurt. She loved Jake's family. "Yes, I am."

"Tell me when you move in. I'll bring you a housewarming basket."

"Okay," Chloe said, confused.

Faith, still by the door, looked around the apartment. The silence grew uncomfortable. "I'm glad you're doing it," Faith suddenly said.

"Excuse me?"

"I'm glad you're buying the house. It's important to have something of your own. You have a good head on your shoulders. I've always liked that about you." Faith walked up to her by the couch, her expression anxious. "Do you blame me for what Jake did?"

"Blame you?" Chloe said, taken aback. "Of course not."

Faith sat down on the edge of the couch and folded her hands in her lap. "I didn't want him to turn into his father."

"He hasn't," Chloe said.

"At least he told you, right?" Faith said, looking up at her. She was a pretty, delicate woman, as anxious as a bird. "You didn't find out from someone else. And he acted like he was sorry, didn't he? Please tell me he did."

"Yes. I think he's very sorry."

"Good. That's good." Faith took a deep breath. "I love him so, Chloe. I fought Kyle over sending him to boarding school, but in the end I let him go, even though it broke my heart, because at least it meant Kyle wouldn't be a daily influence on him. Maybe it was a good decision, after all. Still, if I had just been closer to him, maybe he would understand that it isn't right to treat a woman this way."

Chloe really didn't want to do this, but she sat down and said anyway, "Faith, Jake is a good man with a healthy respect for women. You did a good job with him. And he loves you too."

Faith smiled and looked down at her hands. "I put you in the position of defending him when I know that's the last thing you want to do, and yet you still try to make me feel better. Thank you for that. I really just wanted to come by to give you some Christmas treats and say hello. I've missed you."

"I've missed you too."

"I should be going," Faith said, standing. "Remember, tell me when you move. Invite me over."

"I will." Chloe followed her to the door, more confused than ever.

Chloe opened the door for her and Faith walked out.

But she'd only taken two steps when she stopped and said, "Oh my."

Chloe looked out to see Julian leaning against the wall directly opposite her door. Faith stared at him, as all women did, before turning to walk down the staircase. She cast a few glances back as she did so, almost tripping. Julian watched her go, easily, lazily. When Faith had disappeared, he turned his eyes on Chloe.

He didn't move, just smiled at her. His long hair was down and seemed to float around him. She could feel his pull from here.

"Julian," she said, "what are you doing here?"

"I haven't heard from you in a while. I wanted to see if you were all right." His words surrounded her like perfume. It felt so soothing after her awkward encounter with Jake's mother.

"I'm sorry. I've been busy."

"Back with your boyfriend?" he asked, but he already knew the answer.

"No."

"Are you going to invite me into your place?"

She looked back into the apartment and thought about it. It didn't feel right, Julian in Jake's apartment. "It's not my place."

"You don't live here?" he asked, surprised. "I was told you did."

"I just meant it belongs to Jake. I'm buying a house, though," she said.

He tilted his head, interested. "Really? I'd love to see it. I might be looking for a place of my own soon too. Maybe you can help me out."

"How?"

"How many bedrooms does the house you're buying have?"

She hesitated. "Three. Why?"

"Just wondering," he said gently. "Are you ready to find out who Jake slept with?"

Her lips parted and she felt a ping of unadulterated excitement. "Is that why you're here?"

"Of course, sweetheart. I've been sitting on all this information. It's not doing me any good. Come on." Julian pushed himself away from the wall and walked down the stairs.

"Where are you going?" she called after him.

"To your car. Don't you want to see where she lives?"

She didn't seek out this information, the information came to her. That was important. That was a distinction. That meant she was supposed to know.

Didn't it?

She stood there for a moment. Which would be worse, spending the rest of her life knowing who it was, or spending the rest of her life not knowing?

"I'm coming," she said, grabbing her coat and purse.

When they got in her Beetle, Julian said, "Are you ready for this?"

"As ready as I'll ever be."

"All right. Go left at the end of the street. Head east toward the Catholic church on All Saints Boulevard."

It was going to take some time to get there, so Chloe turned on the radio, eighties music. On the half hour there was a news break, and they listened while at a red light.

"Police now confirm that it was a jogger who discovered the body in the Green Cove River this morning. They're still not releasing any more information, just that it's the body of a woman and it appears to have been in the water for several weeks."

"That's terrible," Chloe said, and her first thought was of going to Jake to see if he'd heard anything more about it at his office. People were still jumpy after the Beasley murder case, and this was sure to have tongues wagging. But then she realized she couldn't do that anymore, she couldn't go to him.

She turned off the radio.

Once she reached All Saints Boulevard, Julian said, "Turn on Saint Joseph's Lane. It's number twelve."

She was feeling woozy when she got there, so she pulled over and parked opposite the house. It was a beautiful colonial-style home behind an iron security gate.

"This place looks familiar," she said, which she didn't understand. She'd never been on this street before.

"This is where Eve Beasley lives."

She jerked her head around to face him. "*Beasley*?"

"You have no idea what I had to do to find this out. I feel so dirty," he said, grinning.

"Jake slept with *Eve Beasley*?" Chloe said, completely bowled over.

"You know her?"

"You don't?"

He shrugged. "I've never heard of her."

The Beasleys were fairly new residents in Bald Slope. They'd bought a vacation home and spent about three or four months out of the year there. Wade was a fifty-five-year-old retired stockbroker, and Eve was his beautiful forty-five-year-old wife. No one knew much about them, and it would've always been that way, had Wade Beasley not murdered their housekeeper, an illegal immigrant, and dumped her body off a trail near the state park.

There was only circumstantial evidence tying Wade to the murder, and halfway through the trial Jake was prosecuting, it had looked like the jury was going to acquit. But then Eve Beasley, who had stood by her husband from the beginning, suddenly filed for divorce and agreed to testify against him. She was the only one who knew her husband had sexually harassed their housekeeper. She'd seen it. She was the only one who knew, who had experienced, his violence first-hand. She'd been away visiting her sister when the murder occurred. When she came back and found the housekeeper gone, she'd asked her husband what happened. Wade had said, "She couldn't take it. She wasn't as tough as you."

That turned the jury around quickly.

Jake had worked closely with her. He used to talk about her, how he felt sorry for her and how sweet she was. He felt for her because most people treated her like a pariah. Everyone blamed her for not speaking up sooner. But Wade Beasley had abused her for years. She was terrified of him. Chloe knew that Jake made her feel safe. Jake was the one who had ultimately convinced her to testify.

Then, when the case was over, when everyone was celebrating, *they'd slept together*.

Chloe knew now. She understood why he couldn't tell her. If this got out, there was the possibility of a mistrial. People might think Jake had seduced Eve Beasley into testifying. Wade Beasley might go free because of this. And if he did, who knows how many other lives might be in danger?

"Ah, look," Julian said. "I'd hoped we would be here for this. She leaves for church every day about this time."

Chloe ducked as the gate opened and Eve Beasley pulled out, driving an Audi. She peered out the window as Eve passed. Eve was an elegant-looking woman, her hair prematurely silver, but her face was unlined and her skin was absolutely luminescent. No one knew why she was staying in Bald Slope. Most thought she would have left long ago. Was she staying for Jake?

"Jake and an older woman," Julian said as he watched her car disappear. "Not much of a scandal, but people make do, I suppose."

It was obvious Julian hadn't followed the trial. It was obvious he didn't know what was at stake. This was the second time in the space of an hour that she was put in the position of having to protect Jake, to defend him. And she didn't want to. "Jake is called the wonderboy at work. I'm sure everyone had a good Mrs. Robinson laugh," she said, to keep Julian on the wrong track. She still wanted to be angry with Jake, but she found the hurt was fading. There was a hole left where the hurt once was. It was deep and empty and numb.

"Now you know," Julian said, watching her carefully. "Here, sweetheart. Let me drive." Julian got out and walked around the car to the driver's side. Chloe obediently scooted to the passenger seat. She wasn't sure she could drive anyway. *Now what?* she kept asking herself. *Now what?* She'd spent all this time thinking that once she knew who Jake had slept with, everything would be clear.

Instead of driving back to the apartment, Julian took her to his house.

She was just going to drop him off and go home. She wanted to call Josey. "I need some time to take this all in," she said.

"Sweetheart, the last thing you need to do is think." He got out, taking her keys with him. "Come inside."

She would be lying if she said she wasn't curious about where this strange, beautiful man lived. So she followed him to the door of the yellow bungalow. When they stepped inside, Julian immediately picked up some piles of clothing from the living-room floor and threw them into a bedroom. He straightened the couch cushions and looked embarrassed, which, despite everything, Chloe found endearing. He probably knew that.

"I guess you still haven't heard from your girlfriend," she said.

"No. And I'm not much of a housekeeper. Sorry."

Chloe looked around. There were feminine touches everywhere, baskets on the wall with artificial roses in them, a white wicker rocking chair with pink pillows. "This still looks like her place."

"It is, actually. She owns the house."

"It's like living in Jake's apartment."

"Exactly. I know what you're going through."

She nodded. He made her believe it.

He took her by the hand and sat her on the couch. "Let's get drunk."

Josey felt small gusts of wind brush by her the entire time she was downstairs that evening. Once, sitting in the kitchen with Helena while eating dinner, she even got up to see if the kitchen windows were fully closed.

Helena kept rubbing her crucifix and mumbling under her breath.

Margaret and Rawley took dinner together in the sitting room, behind closed doors. It was well into the evening when Margaret finally walked him out, speaking to him softly. Josey and Helena came out of the kitchen to watch her.

Margaret smiled slightly, but didn't offer any explanation. She simply walked up to her room.

"What do you think that was all about?" Josey asked Helena.

"Oldgret like cab."

"Hmm," Josey said thoughtfully as she walked to the staircase. It felt like she was stepping into small swirls of frantic, nervous air. She stopped. "Helena, is there a draft in here?"

Helena glared at the ceiling and said, "No."

Josey shrugged and finally retreated to her room. She went to her closet and opened the door, then she took a startled step back. Della Lee was standing there. She'd never seen Della Lee stand in her closet before. The first thought that struck her was that Della Lee was shorter than she was. She hadn't known that. Her second thought was, *Something's wrong.*

"What took you so long to get up here?" Della Lee demanded. She was nervous. Scared, almost. Tension was undulating from the closet like heat.

"I ate dinner. Then I waited to see if Rawley Pelham would come out of the sitting room alive."

"Check your messages," Della Lee said.

"What?"

"Check your cell-phone messages!"

Josey went to her purse on the lounge chair. She pulled out the cell phone. There was one message. She retrieved it and put the phone to her ear, staring at Della Lee in the closet while she listened.

"Hi, Josey, it's Chloe." Pause. "I really wish I could talk to you. Um, I'm at Julian's house right now. I know I told you I wasn't going to see him again. I didn't mean to lie. Out of the blue, he came to see me today. He took me to see the woman Jake slept with. I'm not sure why I thought it would make me feel better. It made me feel worse, because I know now why he wouldn't tell me and it really was for a good reason." Another pause. "I saw Jake earlier this week. I don't think I told you. He found out I was buying the house. I wanted to tell him that I wanted him there with me, but then his father came up to us, and I got a bad feeling that he was telling Jake to move on. I miss him, Josey. I'm not supposed to, because he hurt me. But I do." Chloe took a deep breath. "Anyway, I'm here with Julian. He's in the next room pouring drinks. He's not all bad, you know. I know you think he is, but he's not. I . . . kind of like him. Not in the way I like Jake, but he doesn't have to be Jake. I'll talk to you tomorrow."

Josey slowly lowered the phone.

"Go," Della Lee said frantically.

"Come with me."

"*Go!*"

Josey turned and ran out of the room.

She got in her car and raced down the street, forgetting to turn on her headlights until she was at the bottom of the hill and a car coming in the opposite direction flashed its high beams to tell her she was driving dark.

She made it to Della Lee's house in under fifteen minutes. Chloe's car was there and Josey pulled to a stop behind the Beetle at the curb. The lights were on in the living room and music was pounding from the house. She could almost see the house throb with the force of each bass note. It was a wonder the neighbors hadn't called the cops. Josey got out and ran up the walkway, then up the stairs, shivering in her light sweater and skirt because she hadn't stopped to grab a coat when she left the house.

She went to the living-room windows and looked in, trying to make out images through the thin curtains. There was no movement inside.

She went to the door and opened the screen. The door was locked, so she knocked. When that didn't get a response, she began pounding on the door and calling out Chloe's name until her fist hurt and her voice turned raspy.

Chloe was a grown woman. If this was anyone else but Julian, Josey wouldn't be doing this. But if Della Lee and all her rough ways couldn't handle Julian, Chloe didn't have a chance. She had no idea what she was getting herself into. Not every man was like Jake. Not every man was sorry when he hurt a woman.

She went back down the steps and picked her way around the house, scratching her legs on the thorns of a dead rosebush and falling once in the darkness. She managed to find the back door off the kitchen, but it was locked too.

The only thing besides her keys that Josey had taken with her was the cell phone she still had clutched in her hand when she ran out. She went back to her car and got in, her teeth chattering. She fished the phone out from under the seat where it had fallen, and she fumbled with the buttons. She called 911.

"This is Marcie Jackson and my neighbor won't turn down his music," she said, exaggerating her accent. "It's so loud that it's shaking my windows and it woke up the baby. The whole neighborhood is complaining. He's a nuisance."

She gave the address and they promised to send someone out. Josey hung up and stared at the house. She leaned forward when she suddenly caught some movement coming from inside. A shadow moved by the curtains.

Josey got out of the car again. She was at the bottom of

the porch steps when she heard the tumble of the deadbolt, and then the door flung open. The music from inside rushed out like smoke, louder than ever.

Chloe appeared, her shirt half off and her lipstick smeared. She was carrying her coat and purse. Her words were muted by the music. It sounded something like "I thought I could."

Josey started up the steps.

Chloe was just pushing open the screen door when Julian came up behind her and put his arms around her in an embrace, causing her to drop her coat and purse. "Come on, baby," he said, talking loudly over the music. He sounded drunk. "Don't make me do it like this. It'll be good. I can make everything okay. I'm magic that way. You'll see."

"Let me go, please," Chloe said weakly, like she didn't understand what was happening, like she needed a good, deep breath of air. Julian turned and pushed her into the living room. He tried to close the door, but Chloe's purse and coat prevented him from doing so. He knelt to move them out of the way, and when he looked up, Josey was there.

"I'll be a fucking monkey's uncle," he said, slowly straightening. "The thief returns." He was wearing boots and unbuttoned jeans, but nothing else. The smooth tan skin of his bare chest almost crackled with electricity.

Josey opened the screen door and called into the house, "Chloe? Chloe, come on."

"Josey? Is that you?" Chloe came running up to the door. Julian blocked her way, his hands gripping the door casing, regarding Josey with a leer.

"Let her go," Josey said.

Chloe started pulling at Julian's arms from behind. "Julian, please. I told you I was sorry. I just can't do this."

"I had three hundred dollars in that wallet," he said to Josey, his voice a seductive hiss. "How about the money in exchange for Chloe? Will you give me more if she's unfucked?" He tried to close the door in Josey's face, but Chloe's coat and purse were still there.

Josey caught the door and pushed against it as hard as she could. He pushed back for a few seconds, then he quickly stepped away, sending Josey flying into the house.

Julian kicked Chloe's things out of the doorway and started to close the door. Josey took Chloe's hand and was about to run to the bedroom at the end of the hall. She prayed the door had a lock, and that they could get to it before Julian got to them. The police would surely be here soon.

But then Julian's long hair suddenly flew behind him, off his shoulders, like a sharp wind had blown through the door. He staggered back toward the kitchen at the other end of the living room.

"What the fuck?" he said, when the wind blew at him again, sending him falling through the swinging kitchen door.

Josey saw the clear path and darted for the front door with Chloe. She had no idea what was going on until she heard Julian say, "Della Lee, is that you?" Josey grabbed Chloe's coat and purse and ran out just as they heard one crash, then another, like dishes being thrown, broken. "Get away from me, bitch!" Julian yelled.

How on earth did Della Lee get here? She must have come in through the back door.

She rushed Chloe to the Cadillac and got her into the passenger seat. She saw the police cruiser at the four-way stop down the street. Thank God. She ran to the other side of the car and got in, pulling away from the curb as the cruiser turned down the street. She didn't want Chloe to have to explain what she was doing there. In her rearview mirror, she saw the cruiser come to a stop in front of Della Lee's house. Two patrolmen got out.

She parked at the end of the road and watched as they walked up the steps and banged on the screen door.

Chloe was shakily adjusting her clothing. She tugged on her coat and sat shivering in the seat.

"Are you all right?" Josey asked her.

Chloe nodded and pulled her knees to her chest.

Josey caught some movement and looked back at the house. Julian had shot out of the door. One of the patrolmen caught him by the arm and Julian struggled against him, swinging his fist and catching the patrolman across the jaw. The other patrolman tackled Julian on the porch and together they cuffed him.

"Chloe, stay here. I'll be right back." Josey left the car running and the heater on high, then got out. Neighbors had come out of their homes, and a few were on the sidewalk in front of Della Lee's house. Josey walked up behind them.

Julian was yelling, "Get her out of my house! She's crazy! The woman is crazy!"

One of the patrolmen entered the house, and a few seconds later the loud music that was holding the neighborhood hostage stopped. The patrolman came back out shaking his head.

"She's in there! I swear to God, *someone* is in there! She threw plates at me!"

Josey backed away from the crowd, then jogged back to the car. Della Lee had left. Josey didn't want to imagine how she got there, or how she was going to get back. The words *grand theft auto* crossed her mind.

Chloe was leaning her head against the passenger-side

window when Josey got in. "I'm going to take you home now, okay?"

Chloe nodded.

Chloe stared out of the passenger-side window. Every muscle in her body was tight, and her stomach was churning. If she didn't move, if she kept her teeth clenched, maybe she wouldn't get sick. She bolted out of the car and raced ahead of Josey right after Josey parked in the lot beside the old firehouse. She knew Josey was following her, so she left the apartment door open and ran to the bathroom. She went to her knees in front of the commode and started to retch.

She stayed there on the cool tile floor for about ten minutes, her eyes closed, images of the evening swimming through her head. Desperation. Despite everything, this evening was still about desperation. She'd been desperate with Jake. She was desperate without him.

When would it ever stop?

Suddenly she knew she wasn't alone anymore. She'd left the bathroom door open, so she assumed it was Josey. She shakily made her way to her feet and turned to the door, but no one was there.

Her eyes went to the floor and there, in the doorway, was a stack of books. The book on the bottom was *Finding Forgiveness,* the old warhorse. Even though books hated the bathroom, *Finding Forgiveness* was halfway across the threshold, as if carrying the other books toward her.

"You're going to get wet," she said as she walked to the sink. She turned on the faucet and splashed her face, then washed her mouth out. She dried her face and pulled her hair back into a ponytail. When she turned to leave, the books were still there, a little farther in, tiny droplets of water from the sink on the tile all around them.

She picked them up—*Finding Forgiveness; Old Love, New Direction; A Girl's Guide to Keeping Her Guy; Madame Bovary;* and *The Complete Homeowner's Guide.* She carried them into the bedroom and set them on the nightstand. She stared at the stack, the syllabus of her life for the past month, a map of what she'd been through. Then she couldn't look anymore and turned away.

After changing into sweats, she walked back into the living room. Josey was pacing, but stopped when Chloe appeared. "Are you okay?"

She was grateful for Josey, for her friendship. It had come at the best, the worst and the most unexpected time in her life. "I don't know. I don't know anything anymore. How did you know where Julian lived?"

Josey hesitated. "It's a long story. Did he hurt you?"

"No." Chloe went to the couch and sat, tucking her legs under her and grabbing a pillow to hug. "But I knew what he wanted. I've known that all along."

Josey came to sit beside her.

"I thought I could do it," Chloe said. "It wouldn't have been cheating. Jake and I aren't together. We're so not together I'm buying a house by myself. But I couldn't do it. I love Jake too much. Why didn't Jake love me enough not to do it?"

"It wasn't because I didn't love you enough, Clo," Jake said from the doorway. Josey and Chloe both turned, startled. Jake was standing there, his hair disheveled, his coat buttoned wrong. Adam was to his right, behind him in the hallway. "I love you more than my own life."

Chloe looked at Josey.

"I called Adam while you were in the bathroom," Josey said as she stood. "I'm sorry. I didn't know what else to do. But I didn't ask him to come over, I swear."

Jake entered the room and Adam followed, reaching around Jake to take Josey's hand. "Come on," Adam said. "Let's go."

"No," Josey said, trying to shake him off.

"It's okay, Josey," Chloe said.

"I can stay."

"No." This needed to be done. "It's okay. Really."

Chloe watched Adam lead Josey toward the door. She could tell Josey was not happy with him. As soon as the door closed, Jake knelt in front of the couch where she was sitting and said, "Chloe, look at me."

She met his eyes. Those magnetic light green eyes.

"It was Eve Beasley," he said.

"I know."

Jake looked poleaxed. "You do? Who told you?"

"It doesn't matter."

"I didn't mean for it to happen. Neither did she. We instantly regretted it, and we haven't seen each other since. I don't blame it on the case. *I* am to blame. I know that. And if I could take it back, I would. I'm so sorry." He tried to take her hands, but she hid them behind the pillow she was holding. "I miss you, Chloe."

"What about your family? Your father said to stay away from me, and your mother brought me a parting gift." She jerked her chin toward the Christmas basket on the coffee table.

"My dad wanted me to stay away from you until you were ready. He didn't want me to push you. He wants you in our family. My mom brought the basket because she wants to be in your life, whether or not it's through me. It's their insane way of saying they love you." Jake shook his head. "We're parts of a crazy whole, Chloe. But we don't make sense without you. *I* don't make sense."

There was a clapping sound and a book that was sitting on the arm of the couch fell to the floor beside them. *Finding Forgiveness.* Chloe pinched her lips together, tears coming to her eyes as she stared at the book.

Paper, string and glue.

Separately, they were just objects waiting for a purpose. Together, they were parts of a whole. Something significant, something solid.

They were a lot like relationships that way.

"Let's start over, Clo," Jake said, and she lifted her eyes to meet his. "Let me call you up and ask you on a date. I'll knock on the door to your house. I'll have flowers. I'll be nervous. I'll wait until the third date to kiss you, though I'll think about it every second until I do. Then that night you finally let me stay over, I'll whisper promises, promises I'll always keep. I'll promise I will never, ever hurt you. I'll promise to die before I do."

The first time, they didn't have time for a conventional courtship. It had been very hot very fast. Could they really start over, and then do it the traditional way?

"Never do this to me again, Jake." She tried to say it harshly, but her voice shook.

"I won't."

She lifted her chin. "I have books."

"I know."

"A lot of books. And they're going to be around from now on. You have to accept that."

"I've never had a problem with your books, Clo. They're who you are."

Jake slowly leaned in. The closer he came, the stronger the draw, like food when you're hungry, or a bed when you're tired. He moved the pillow away and wrapped his arms around her. She found herself nuzzling him, hiding her face in his neck. She would always be desperate about him. Even now, breathing the scent of his skin, she could feel it. But she wasn't as disoriented as she used to be. She didn't feel that panic. She felt a strange sort of grounding, like she knew she wasn't going to lose her way anymore.

She turned her head on Jake's shoulder to look at *Finding Forgiveness* again.

But it was gone.

Josey kept looking back at the apartment door as Adam led her down the stairs. "She'll be fine. You know they need to do this, or you wouldn't have called," Adam said.

"I called because I was worried that Chloe was sick," Josey said, nervous that Chloe might be angry with her. "I didn't ask you to bring Jake over."

"You didn't have to ask. It was obvious that's what needed to be done."

Josey pulled her hand out of his and jerked open the door at the bottom of the stairs. "I told you, I told you from the beginning of all this, that it wasn't our place to get in the middle of their relationship."

"Yes, you said that," Adam said calmly, following her out onto the cold sidewalk. She could see that he'd parked on the street. Her car was looming large around the corner in the parking lot. "And, as I recall, I didn't agree. Bringing them together tonight is good for them."

"How do you know? You have no idea what she went through tonight."

"Then why don't you tell me?"

She'd walked right into that one. "Chloe just had a bad night, that's all."

"In other words, you're not going to tell me."

Josey rubbed her arms, trying to close herself off from the cold. "It's not my secret to share."

Adam frowned. "Where is your coat?"

"At home. I left in a hurry."

He shrugged out of his yellow Thinsulate jacket. "Here," he said, holding it out for her. She slipped into it. "They're going to be fine. I promise. Do you want to go somewhere? Get something to eat, maybe?" He stared at her, his hands resting on her shoulders. She *almost* reached up to touch her mouth, even though she knew she hadn't eaten in hours. Old habits die hard. "Or we could go to my house," he said with a significance she couldn't ignore. "Jake and I just had a pizza delivered when you called. It might not be cold yet."

She felt her chest catch, setting off a wild array of racing shivers. This past week they'd upped the notch of intimacy every time they met. Short, desperate surges in the dark of her porch or his SUV after she'd sneaked out. No one could see. No one would know. It was a secret, like most everything else in her life. It was easier that way, easier to work around her fear instead of facing it, easier not to tell her mother. Now he was asking her to put it out in the open, and despite everything, despite wanting it more than she wanted her next breath, she hesitated. "I don't know."

He dropped his hands. "Are you mad at me?"

"No."

"But you're going to use this as an excuse not to come home with me."

She turned away from him and looked up at the brick firehouse. It was outlined in small white Christmas lights, making it look like gingerbread. "That's not fair."

"It is what it is. You're scared."

"So are you."

"But I asked anyway."

Josey closed her eyes. "What do you want me to say, Adam?"

"I want you to say yes."

"What are we really changing here? Nothing. We're still stuck in our same patterns. We're still stuck here. If I stay with you tonight, it will be all over town by tomorrow."

He looked genuinely confused. "So?"

"You really don't understand, do you? I still hide. I still sneak out of my mother's house because I don't want her disapproval. I still worry about what people here think of me."

"Then let's leave," he said quietly.

She gaped at him. "You're not serious."

"I'm completely serious. I've met your mother, so I understand why you do it. But making you hide isn't fair to you, and it's not fair to me. Neither of us wants to be here. Let's go."

"You would leave?" she asked incredulously. "Really?"

"I would leave." He took a deep breath. "But only with you."

She couldn't believe what she did next.

She left, all right.

And ran home.

Helena met Josey at the door. "Oldsey, bad thing leave tonight!" she said excitedly. "Leave when you leave! But it come back. It here now."

At least Della Lee had gotten home safely. "I know," Josey said tiredly. "It won't be long before she leaves for good, I promise. Good night."

"Wait. Oldgret want to see you." Helena made an apologetic face and pointed toward the light coming from the sitting room. "She wait up."

Oh, hell. She squeezed her eyes shut for a moment. She'd just been worried about getting caught, and then suddenly she was. Her life was one big self-fulfilling prophecy.

"Oldsey?"

She opened her eyes and tried to smile. "It's okay. Thanks, Helena." Then she did the death march to the sitting room.

Margaret was in her nightgown, sitting in her favorite chair. She looked up and set aside her magazine. "Where have you been?" she demanded. "And whose jacket is that?"

Josey looked down. She'd forgotten she had it on. There was no use denying who it belonged to. "It's Adam's."

"I won't have you acting this way, do you hear me? I had enough of you embarrassing me when you were a child. Imagine my surprise when I got up to tell you something, only to find you gone. For days now I've suspected you've been sneaking out after I've taken my sleeping pill. Well, I didn't take one tonight. You're not a silly teenager, Josey. I won't have you acting like this."

"I'm sorry, Mother."

That was what she wanted, Josey thought. She wanted Josey cowed. She wasn't even trying to disguise it with false concern or backhanded compliments anymore. She stood up and said, less harshly, "I wanted to tell you to pick up pork tenderloins at the grocery store tomorrow. I left instructions with Helena on how to prepare them. Rawley Pelham will be dining with me tomorrow, and I remember he likes them. He's my guest and I would prefer if you would stay in your room when I'm with him. Also, I won't be needing you to drive me to my eye appointment tomorrow. I'll be taking a cab for the foreseeable future."

Josey watched her mother walk toward the door with her cane. She couldn't believe what she'd just heard. "What am I supposed to do, then?"

"You're supposed to behave. Don't see that Finley girl or the mailman. And don't sneak out again. What would the neighbors think if they saw you? And what if I had needed you tonight?"

"You just said you *didn't* need me, Mother!" Josey laughed, but with an edge, very close to crying. She'd just run away from the man she loved because she couldn't let go of the faraway hope that, if she stayed long enough, one day Margaret would love her, accept her, *forgive her*. "When is it ever going to be enough? When are you ever going to forgive me? Why did you even have me? Was it really just to keep his money?"

Margaret set her jaw and walked past Josey. "I'm going to bed now."

Josey followed her and stood at the base of the steps as her mother walked up. "Was he really that bad?"

Margaret didn't answer until she reached the top of the

steps. Then she stopped, her back to Josey. "Yes, he was," she finally said as she disappeared down the hallway. "And you look just like him."

Josey stared at the place her mother had been. It had taken her twenty-seven years to finally figure this out. Margaret wasn't going to be happy as long as Josey was there, but she would never tell her to leave. And Josey wasn't going to be happy until she left, but she wanted her mother to tell her to go.

This wasn't about forgiveness. It never had been.

This was about two women punishing themselves for no good reason.

And it was time for it to end.

Twenty minutes later, Josey said, "Can I come in?"

Adam hesitated in his doorway, then stood back. "Of course."

She walked into the living room of his house. It was sparse, temporary. Secondhand furniture for the most part, an unusual blue couch with purple cushions, a 1970s-era orange reading chair, and some scarred end tables. The large leather recliner and flat-screen TV above the fireplace stood out. Those were deliberate purchases for comfort.

"I think I'm scared of your furniture," she said, trying to smile but it made her lips tremble, so she stopped.

"I was living day by day here at first, not sure what I should do, just that I wanted to be still. I bought a bed, the recliner and the television. All I thought I needed. Then, every once in a while, someone at work would say they were getting rid of something, and I asked if I could have it. This is what happens when bad furniture happens to good people. I do actually have some great furniture, but it's all stored in my brother's basement in Chicago."

She turned her back on him to look around some more. The television was on and she pretended to watch it. He came up behind her and took off her jacket. His jacket. She jumped a little and turned to face him. They stared at each other for a moment.

"Why are you here, Josey?"

She took a deep breath. She'd thought of things she would say to him on the drive over here, elegant things about fear and love and pithy things about both running to him and running away. But what she ended up saying was, simply, "You go, I go."

He dropped the jacket and in one step he was in front of her, his hands on her face, kissing her. There was no lead-up. It was all at once frantic, hands everywhere. Still kissing, he backed her to the couch then pushed her down to the cushions, angling his body over hers. His kiss was deeper this way, hungry, like she was candy. He *feasted* on her. His hands went to the sides of her sweater and slowly brought it up. Her muscles quivered and her skin prickled. He broke their kiss to pull the sweater over her head. Her nipples tightened as he looked down at her, breathing heavily.

He hovered above her, his curly blond hair falling across his forehead.

"What?" she asked in response to his stare.

"I was afraid I'd pushed you away for good tonight. It was all about speed with me. I've always gone too fast."

"But that's exactly what I need, Adam."

"You go, I go," he whispered as he undid the buttons on his shirt and shrugged out of it. There was a thick white scar on the left side of his chest, just under his rib cage.

She nodded and reached out to touch his scar. He kissed her again, urgently, their skin-on-skin friction electric. His hands went up to cup her breasts through her bra. She thought she was going to faint. But no, she couldn't faint. Then she would miss this.

She didn't realize that she had squeezed her eyes shut and was taking deep breaths through her nose until Adam broke their kiss and looked down at her. "Josey?"

"I'm here," she said, putting her hands in his hair and bringing his head back down. "I'm here."

She was distantly aware that the eleven o'clock news had just come on, and the lead story was the body that had been found in the Green Cove River that morning. Not breaking their kiss, Adam stretched one hand above her and reached for the remote control on the end table.

The news anchor started the broadcast by saying, "We are now able to confirm identification of the body as that of thirty-seven-year-old Della Lee Baker of Bald Slope."

Josey suddenly sat up, so fast she knocked heads with Adam. "Wait. Stop," she said, putting her hand on his and lowering it so he couldn't use the remote. She turned to the television.

"Baker's abandoned car was found in a grassy area this afternoon near the Green Cove Bridge, where officials also discovered what appears to be a suicide note. Baker had a long criminal record that included assault, solicitation, DWI convictions and shoplifting." They showed an arrest photo of Della Lee. She was smiling, like she wanted it to be a pretty picture of her. "In breaking news, we've also learned that her live-in boyfriend, Julian Wallace, also of Bald Slope, was arrested tonight on unrelated charges—assaulting an officer who was responding to a disturbing-the-peace call at the home the couple shared. Wallace confirmed to police that Baker has been missing for weeks, which supports the coroner's initial findings that the body appears to have been in the water for an extended period. At this time, officials do not suspect foul play. We'll have more on our morning broadcast, including an interview with the jogger who found the body."

"Josey, what's wrong?" Adam said, threading his hands in her hair, trying to get her to look at him. But her eyes were fixed on the screen. "You look like you've seen a ghost."

That made her turn to him. Suddenly her chest hurt. She couldn't breathe. She quickly stood, disengaging herself from him in a tangle of arms and legs, pinches and pulls. She grabbed her sweater from the floor. "I've got to go home."

"What?" he said, clearly thrown by her abrupt change in mood. "Wait, Josey . . ."

But she was already out the door.

Josey shot into her house and ran up the stairs in the dark, not even giving Helena time to pop her head out of her room. When she got to her bedroom, she threw open the closet door.

"Thank God," she said, going to her knees in front of Della Lee, who was in her familiar sitting position on the sleeping bag. She was wearing the clothes that she had on the first day Josey saw her—cropped white T-shirt, blue jeans and only one shoe. Her hair was heavy and flat again. "Helena said you'd come home, but I had to make sure. You'll never believe what they're saying about you on the news!"

Della Lee just stared at her. She didn't seem curious at all.

"There was a body found in the Green Cove River. Your car was found near the bridge, so they think it's you!"

She still didn't say anything.

Josey's heart was pounding. She felt strange, like she was halfway between the real world and a dream. "You know what's funny? There was a moment there, when they said your name, that I thought about how I never see you eat anything, how you never let me touch you, how you move around without anyone seeing you at night and—you're going to love this—I thought, what if it's Della Lee's ghost in my closet?"

Della Lee remained quiet. She didn't even blink.

Cold prickles rose on Josey's skin. Blood rushed to her head. "Isn't that funny?"

"It's time for me to leave, Josey," Della Lee said.

Josey laughed, a tad hysterically. "What are you talking about? Mr. Lamar's letter hasn't even come."

"Josey . . ."

"And we both know what it will say, right? You'll wait until the letter comes and we'll laugh over how you tried to convince me—"

"Josey!" Della Lee said loudly.

Josey finally stopped.

"You made the right decision tonight. I could feel it. You don't need me any longer."

"I know I said I wanted you to go, but I didn't mean it. I want you with me, Della Lee. I really do!"

"You just needed a little push, that's all."

"Della Lee," Josey said, her voice watery and thick. She sounded like she was drowning. "I don't understand."

"I didn't know how to change," Della Lee said, and as she spoke, smudges of mascara slowly appeared under her eyes like bruises, trails of it snaking down her cheeks again, just like that first day Josey found her in the closet. "I didn't know how to be around decent people, or how to live without stealing or lying. Destructive behavior was a comfort to me. A cold comfort, because I didn't think genuine happiness was possible. So I gave up. I was standing on the bridge and my last clear thought was of you. It was strange, because I hadn't thought of you in years. Then suddenly I was here, in your closet, and it became clear to me what I had to do. Maybe by helping you, I might mean something. *That* makes me genuinely happy." She smiled. "You're going to be okay now, Josey."

They stared at each other for a long time. Slowly, Josey lifted her hand and reached out to Della Lee, to finally touch her.

"Oldsey?"

Josey jerked her head around to find Helena standing at the end of her bed. Josey stood and quickly motioned her forward. "Helena, come here. This has to end. I want you to meet Della Lee."

She took Helena's hand, but when they looked in the closet, Della Lee was gone.

"Della Lee?" Josey stuck her head in and searched the dark corners. Della Lee's bags and the box were still there, but not Della Lee. She pushed back her clothes, then slid back the secret door. She wasn't in the candy closet, hiding behind the bags of marshmallows or between the towers of cola. "Della Lee!" She turned around, her eyes searching the room. She went to her knees and looked under the bed.

She got up and was heading out of the room when Helena said softly, "She no here."

Josey turned to her, shaking her head. "No, she's here. I know she is."

"She no here."

"How do you know?"

"The air." She took a deep breath. "Clean."

"You knew she was here," Josey said desperately. "You saw her. Right? She was real."

"See? No. Feel." Helena reached up and touched the crucifix on her necklace. "Feel Oldsey's ghost."

Josey barely made it the two steps to her bed. She sat down, so dizzy she had to put her head between her knees. Helena came to sit beside her. After a moment, Josey sat back up. "I don't want to believe it," she said, tears coming to her eyes.

Helena put an arm around her and tucked Josey's head to her shoulder. She was small but strong, and she felt like gristle. "There, there, Oldsey. Dead not dead. Dead only different. Oldsey be okay." She started rocking Josey back and forth, then she said in a soft, singsongy voice, over and over, "Old-sey be o-kay. Old-sey be o-kay."

After a while she stopped singing and just rocked her.

"Helena?" Josey finally said. "My name isn't Oldsey."

Helena lifted Josey's face so she could look her in the eye. "I know, Josey. And my name *Marlena*."

Josey paused, looking at her strangely. "Your name isn't Helena?"

"No."

Josey laughed without meaning to, laughed through her tears, laughed at the thought of knowing this woman for the better part of a year and calling her by the wrong name the entire time. And instead of actually correcting Josey and Margaret, Marlena purposely called them by the wrong names too. A joke, like so many other things, that only Marlena understood.

Marlena smiled as she used her thumbs to wipe away Josey's tears.

Suddenly there was a knock at the front door and Marlena stood and went to the window. She gave Josey an enigmatic look and left the room without another word.

As soon as she was gone, Josey slipped off the side of the bed and sat on the floor, bringing her knees to her chest. She finally looked into the closet and saw Della Lee's collage sitting there on the sleeping bag where Della Lee had been. She crawled over to it. Della Lee had cut out every photo from Josey's favorite marked pages. Next to the BON VOYAGE at the top, Della Lee had cut out five more letters and put JOSEY.

She suddenly heard heavy footsteps in the hallway. "Josey?" Adam called. "Josey, where are you?"

She craned her head over the side of the bed. He stopped in her bedroom doorway. He looked worried, tense. When he spotted her, he walked around the bed.

"Josey, what's wrong?" He knelt in front of her, putting his warm hands on her knees. The warmth seeped through her skirt and threaded through her skin. "Why did you run away? Why are you crying? Talk to me."

She looked up at him. "The woman on the news tonight, the woman in the river, I knew her."

He lowered himself to the floor beside her, his stiff leg not giving way easily. "Oh, honey," he said, putting his arm around her. "I'm so sorry."

"Adam?"

"Yes?"

"She was my sister."

14

Now and Later

Dear Josey,

I loved the postcard from Sweden. But you have to stop asking me to join you. How many times do I have to tell you, I am not traveling with you on your honeymoon, you crazy woman.

Everything is fine here. You can stop pretending that your visit next month is just the whim of you two world travelers. I found the ring. Jake honestly thought he could hide it behind my books in the library. The minute I walked into the room, I knew which book it was behind. Oh, Josey, it's so beautiful. I stood there and bawled like a baby when I found it. Then I heard Jake coming and put the ring back and ran to the kitchen, where I started chopping an onion to explain my tears. I ended up making this huge onion soufflé, which we've had for the past three nights for dinner. Did I mention I hate onion soufflé?

I saw your mother yesterday. What is up with her and this cabdriver? I see them all the time. Yesterday she was in the back of his cab, which had stopped at a red light downtown. She was talking nonstop. I didn't see her let up once. And the cabdriver was smiling and nodding, but not saying a word. He was watching her in the rearview mirror. The light turned green and he didn't even know, he was so busy watching her.

Last week I went to the cemetery like you asked and put flowers on Della Lee Baker's grave. It's been a year and people are still talking about it. One day you're going to have to tell me why you paid for her funeral.

I had a weird dream about her the other night. I dreamed you and Della Lee and I were walking down a busy street somewhere, but the road was gold, like in The Wizard of Oz. *Our arms were linked and we were laughing. People were looking at us like we were movie stars. We were going somewhere, somewhere wonderful, but I didn't know where. Why am I dreaming about a dead woman I didn't even know? Is that creepy?*

I guess I'll go now.

No, not yet.

I've been thinking about this for a while . . . and I want to tell you something, something I've never told anyone.

God, my hands are shaking.

Okay, you know about me and books, that I have so many, that they're always around. The thing is, books just appear to me. Out of nowhere. I haven't bought a book since I was twelve. I'll walk into a room, and there's a book that wants me to read it. They follow me sometimes too. I don't mean they walk after me. I mean, a book I'll leave at home will show up at work, in my car, on the table at a restaurant. I'm always worried people are going to find out and think I'm crazy. But I thought, I don't know, that you'd understand.

It's midnight and I've had too much wine and Jake is asleep. I'm going to send this now and regret it. Just remember, if you sic the men in white jackets on me, you don't get to be my matron of honor.

Love,

C.

Adam came up behind Josey and kissed her neck. Josey closed Chloe's e-mail.

"Chloe knows about the surprise engagement party," she said, staring out at the sea as Adam moved her hair away for better access.

"Jake was never good at keeping secrets," he said into her skin and it made her shiver.

Josey closed her eyes. The things this man could do to her. She was still amazed. Her eyes flew back open when her laptop almost fell off her knees to the balcony floor. "If you keep this up, we're not going to leave the room. Again. I want to see the ship in the daytime at least once."

"Josey, get in my bed," he whispered in her ear.

"That stopped working when you said it in the dining room last night, in front of that elderly couple at our table."

"In my defense, I didn't know they were there. And it did work."

"Okay, yes, it worked but . . ."

He laughed and straightened, his hands still on her shoulders. "Write Chloe back. I'll take a shower and show you the ship in the daytime. But I don't know what the big deal is. It looks the same as it does at night, only brighter."

"Brighter?" she said eagerly, looking up at him. "*Really*? I can't wait! Brighter. Wow."

He looped one of her curls around his finger and gave her hair an affectionate tug. "Tell Chloe I said hello," he said, then walked back into the stateroom.

Something caught Josey's eye, and she turned. Della Lee had suddenly appeared by the railing at the corner of the balcony. She was gazing out at the water.

Della Lee turned her head and looked at Josey. She nodded in the direction Adam had gone and winked.

Josey smiled and quickly moved her laptop aside. She got up and went to the railing beside Della Lee, just to be near her. She missed having her around. She missed talking to her. Della Lee rarely spoke these days. In fact, the last time Josey remembered her saying anything was in Las Vegas. Chloe and Jake had flown in with Adam's brother to attend Adam and Josey's wedding ceremony. Josey had met Adam's brother Brett once before, when they went to Chicago. That's when she found out Adam owned a house on the North Shore that he rented out. *This can be home base,* Adam had told her, *when we decide we need it.* Chloe had just walked down the short aisle ahead of Josey. Josey was about to follow, to walk to Adam at the front of the small chapel, when suddenly she saw Della Lee standing there to her left.

"Congratulations, kid," she'd said.

Sometimes months would go by without Josey seeing her. But just when Josey would start to worry that she'd gone away for good, Della Lee would always return.

They stood like that for a while, both staring out at the sea. Josey didn't know how much time had passed before Della Lee turned to Josey, her brows raised, as if she knew what Josey was thinking.

It was time.

"Stay here," Josey said. "Don't go yet, okay?"

Della Lee nodded.

Josey went into the stateroom. She could hear the shower water running and Adam was singing Elvis Presley's "A Little Less Conversation." She went to her luggage and dug out her passport wallet. Tucked into a pocket inside was a folded envelope. It was the letter from Samuel Lamar. She took it with her wherever she went, convinced there would be a right time to finally open it and learn the truth.

She walked back out to the balcony and stood by Della Lee at the railing again. She stared at the plain white envelope, at her name written in a hesitant, elderly scrawl. The wind made the paper flutter in her hands. Della Lee watched her curiously.

Josey toyed with the edge of the envelope flap. The glue was weak, so the flap wasn't secured tightly. It would be easy to open.

Taking a deep breath, Josey tore the envelope in half, then in fourths, then eighths. She tossed the pieces into the wind, where they turned into paper birds that floated through the air, finally landing peacefully on the water.

Della Lee laughed, but no sound came out.

Josey smiled at her, then turned back to the water, satisfied that she'd made the right decision.

When she turned back again, Della Lee was gone.

She would never get used to that.

She went back to her seat and picked up her laptop.

Dear Chloe,

We're slowly crossing the ocean toward you as I type. How do you know our coming back to Bald Slope for a visit isn't just a whim? Adam and I are all about whim. (I have to say that, you know. I promised Jake. But I can't wait to see the ring!)

I don't understand what's going on between Mother and Rawley. When I call, Marlena says she's happy. She says that Rawley actually spends the night there sometimes, too, though no one is supposed to know. Maybe I'll finally talk to Mother this visit. Or maybe, like last time, she'll refuse to see me and I'll just talk to her through the personal secretary I hired for her. I know this has less to do with me personally and more to do with memories she won't share, memories of my father. But there's nothing I can do about it.

Thank you for taking the flowers. Della Lee was a special person. I'll tell you about her someday. I promise. In fact, there's a lot I need to tell you.

And about the books, I don't think you're crazy. Not at all.

Josey looked up to the place Della Lee had stood.

In fact, I understand completely.
Love,
J.

About the Author

Sarah Addison Allen was born and raised in Asheville, North Carolina, where she is currently at work on her next novel, which Bantam will publish in 2009.